CONFOUNDING THE EARL

Courting a Curious Lady, Book 2

Lexi Post

Dragonblade Publishing, Inc. is an imprint of Kathryn Le Veque Novels, Inc.
P.O. Box 23
Moreno Valley, CA 92556
ceo@dragonbladepublishing.com

Produced in the United States of America

First Edition September 2024
Trade Paperback Edition

ARE YOU SIGNED UP FOR DRAGONBLADE'S BLOG?

You'll get the latest news and information on exclusive giveaways, exclusive excerpts, coming releases, sales, free books, cover reveals and more.

Check out our complete list of authors, too!

No spam, no junk. That's a promise!

Sign Up Here

www.dragonbladepublishing.com

Dearest Reader;

Thank you for your support of a small press. At Dragonblade Publishing, we strive to bring you the highest quality Historical Romance from some of the best authors in the business. Without your support, there is no 'us', so we sincerely hope you adore these stories and find some new favorite authors along the way.

Happy Reading!

CEO, Dragonblade Publishing

Additional Dragonblade books by Author Lexi Post

Courting a Curious Lady Series
Uncovering the Lord (Book 1)
Confounding the Earl (Book 2)

Marrying a Mabry Series
Stealing the Duke (Book 1)
Painting the Earl (Book 2)
Revealing the Viscount (Book 3)

Acknowledgments

For my wonderful husband who happily listens to my rambles and is always happy to help me get back on track.

For my sister Paige, who thoroughly enjoyed this story and chuckled in all the right places. Your help in bringing Dory and Felton to life was invaluable.

Thank you to my wonderful critique partner Marie Patrick for reading through all Dory's soliloquies and asking me to "add more" when my mind would race faster than my fingers could type. I couldn't, and wouldn't do this without you.

A special thank you to my Lexi's Legends, and especially Bette Read for coming up with wonderful names for Dory's suitors. I always know where to turn when my brain grows tired.

And thank *you*, for spending the time with these lovely characters to enjoy this story. I only write because of you.

Author's Note

The Courting a Curious Lady series was inspired by two of my three favorite books of all time, Louisa May Alcott's novels, *Little Men* and *Jo's Boys*, published in 1871 and 1886 respectively. These were the next two books after *Little Women*, and I fell in love with Jo's school for boys. In Alcott's novels, there were a dozen boys as well as a few girls, all of whom go through the trials and tribulations of growing into adults. In *Stealing the Duke*, Lady Joanna sets up a school for ladies of the peerage modeled after Oxford and Cambridge. It's called The Belinda School for Curious Ladies.

Confounding the Earl is specifically inspired by Adolphus or "Dolly" in Alcott's books. While Dolly has a terrible stutter, Lady Dorothea Ainsley of Preston, or "Dory" as her friends call her, actually talks on and on, always losing her audience. Adolphus eventually gets over his stutter and attends Harvard, but becomes a bit of a dandy, far too focused on how he appears to others. Dory is similar in that she is well aware her rambling conversation, which leaves others perplexed, and she wishes, more than anything, that she could control herself to better fit in. While Adolphus has Jo to guide him, Dory's mother is the opposite of helpful, so it is no wonder that the dour Lord Harewood's suggestion is quickly taken. But like Adolphus in Alcott's book, there is a price to pay for fitting in, and for Dory, it may very well be her heart.

CHAPTER ONE

London
July 1817

"I PREDICT THEY will marry by the coming year." Felton Ambrose, the Earl of Harewood, looked to his good friend Andrew Crauford, the Earl of Sommerset, and gave a quick nod to punctuate his statement.

Sommerset, dressed in shades of brown to accentuate his blond hair, presenting a far opposite image from Felton's own austere black, seemed to ponder his prediction. "Should I enter that into the book at White's then?" His friend's eyes crinkled with amusement.

He sniffed. "Hardly. I already did."

"Of course you did." Sommerset chuckled. "I do not understand why anyone takes your bets. You're always right."

He shrugged, even as he perused the room, observing the *ton* in its element. "There's a fool born every day." Returning his attention to his companions, he found Lady Sommerset giving him an impish smile.

His friend's wife, dressed in a lilac gown that complemented her eyes and blonde ringlets, waved toward the opposite side of the room. "Tell me, Lord Harewood. Did you predict the marriage of my cousin Teddy to Lady Elsbeth of Astor?"

He moved his gaze to find Lord Theodore Mabry and his new wife on the edge of the dance floor having a quiet conversation that included many smiles and not a few tender looks. At their obvious love for each other, he felt the familiar pang of love lost in his chest. He ignored it and returned his attention to Lady Sommerset. "As the two were not in London but overseas, I did not think it prudent to suggest an outcome. My predictions, if you will, come from observation."

The lady rolled her violet eyes at him. "And here I thought it was some divine spirit that whispered in your ear."

Her husband shook his head. "Of course not. Harewood makes his bets based on instinct."

Though Felton frowned at them both, he was well aware they teased. "You do me an injustice by assuming my clarity of perception is anything but a skill well-honed."

Lady Sommerset laughed, drawing not a few looks from those nearby. "Truly? But that is so very boring. I'm going to continue to believe it is a faerie who lands on your shoulder and makes outrageous suggestions."

"Amelia." Sommerset's tone held kind reprimand.

She gave her husband a secret smile. "I only meant to say that Lord Harewood's predictions are often surprising."

That he had predicted Sommerset and Lady Ameila Mabry would suit each other well when no one else had seen it did stroke his ego. But if any were to know the true reason he had expected the match, they could well claim he had cheated.

He had spent his youth as a neighbor of the four Mabry ladies and knew them all well. Sommerset had become a good friend during their days at Eaton. Therefore, some might say he had an unfair advantage—foreknowledge, so to speak—that no one else had, but that had simply been him capitalizing on a fortuitous situation. But if any were to discover he'd *suggested* Lady Amelia to Sommerset, they would most definitely call him out. However, he need not defend himself on that account, either, as it was not as if the marriage had been a sure bet.

"Please, my dear," Sommerset inclined his head. "Do not feed his egoism. He is barely sufferable as it is."

"I simply stated fact, but I do see what you mean." Lady Sommerset turned from her husband to him as if to be sure he was not insulted.

"I assure you both that your words have little effect upon me."

Sommerset chuckled. "As I suspected." He held his arm out to his wife. "Come. I believe we are boring poor Harewood. Let us take a walk in the gardens that he might remain here in his own logical and quite complicated thoughts."

The lady smiled tenderly at her husband and took his arm. "We shall see you at dinner, my lord."

As the two left, he watched them meander through the guests toward the open garden doors. He couldn't deny he was quite pleased with himself for suggesting the match. As the youngest Mabry sister, Lady Amelia had been the last to wed, though her oldest sister recently married again. Having all three wedded had halted his mother's many hints at him marrying a Mabry lady. He'd already loved one of them, even if she'd never debuted, so he knew none of the others could live up to her perfection.

Fortunately, since his father was hale and hardy, all talk of finding a wife and having heirs had drifted away on the ether, much like Lady Belinda Mabry had drifted away from her mortal coils. At the thought of Belinda, melancholy instantly settled in, but he'd lived with the feeling for so many years, he knew exactly what to do—move and find a distraction. Out of habit, he began to amble around the outskirts of the ballroom, preferring to observe others and discover something many might miss. Though he claimed his predictions were due to observation only, they were far more complicated. A strong understanding of the history of each family of the *ton* and their many values and characteristics also played into his calculations.

He stopped for a moment next to a Grecian column decorated in greenery that was already starting to wilt in the heat of the ballroom. Sommerset's younger brother, Christopher Crauford, the Viscount of Tamworth, caught his attention near the exit of the room. The man's light brown hair was a bit too long, which made him easy to recognize. If he wasn't mistaken, Tamworth was inching toward the doorway, no doubt planning to leave before dinner. A small part of him envied the younger man's joy in life. He couldn't remember being so free to indulge in life's small pleasures. Then again, Tamworth was a second son, while he was the only son of a marquess and had been born the Earl of Harewood. His responsibilities were many. Finally, Tamworth slipped out as he'd expected, and he resumed his observations.

Immediately, his attention was caught by a group of ladies not far from him. He recognized them as students of the Belinda School for Curious Ladies. Though the school had never been officially announced, it was well known that it had quietly opened last winter to its first class of students. That in and of itself was of little consequence, but what set the older ladies' tongues wagging was the fact that those running the school touted it as the Oxford and Cambridge for ladies of the peerage, a description many, including himself, disliked immensely.

But his reasons were far more substantial than any society lady's. He resented that the scandalous school had been named after the only woman he'd ever loved. It besmirched her name in a myriad of ways. Belinda, though intelligent, had been kind, caring, as sweet as a trifle, and as warm as a Christmas kitten. She was most happy when helping someone else, whether it was her sisters with a problem, the local vicar with the poor, or a maid with a torn sleeve. She wasn't interested in the pursuit of knowledge for the sake of knowledge that would be of no use in the life of a wife.

At the start of the season, there had been much talk—and not much of it positive—about the school. So much so that he'd almost made a bet that it would close within the year, but the talk had disappeared as soon as the next piece of gossip made the rounds. It wasn't until just a few weeks ago that it had surfaced again when Lady Elsbeth Rawley had married Lord Theodore Mabry. No one had expected any of the women in attendance at that school to marry. He'd breathed a relieved sigh at the news as Belinda had wanted nothing more than for people to be happy.

But earlier in the week, he'd been at White's and happened upon a conversation between four men who disparaged the school as well as Lord Mabry. The assumption was that the lord was desperate for an English-born wife since he was a widower with a Spanish daughter and he needed heirs for the vast holdings he would one day inherit. The last had been said in envy, of course, but it still rankled. As much as Felton wished the Duke and Duchess of Northwick would change the name of the school, he acknowledged that was a lost cause since the duchess had named it so to honor her younger sister. Did she not understand that it did everything but her intended goal?

He tapped his fingers upon the column as he leaned against it to study the women of the school. There had to be a way to make them a valuable commodity as opposed to leftover slops to be thrown to the dogs. Granted, he exaggerated, but the concept still held. It seemed an impossible task, but if he could accomplish such a miracle, it could be his way of honoring Belinda and all that she had been. He rarely aided others except Sommerset, so it would be a monumental task on many levels. He doubted anyone else had a reason to take on such an impossible quest. The question, though, was how to do it.

He studied the ladies in question. There were four present at the ball, though he'd been informed by Lady Sommerset that her older sister was sponsoring a Mademoiselle Lissette to attend the winter term. She was not present. That would make his task easier. All of them were pleasant to look at, so that was not a drawback. The issue was their studies and most likely their conversation. There had been grumblings among the four gentlemen he'd overheard about the subject of science, about which the women were knowledgeable and for which they had little use. He had no doubt that like himself, the gentlemen had not spent their entire time at Oxford in their assigned studies. What they'd done at Cambridge he couldn't say.

Making a match for one of the ladies obviously wouldn't help stop the gossip about the school as Lady Elsbeth, the first one to attend the school, was now married and that had not solved the problem. He pondered the issue. What if one of them were to become very popular, maybe even have multiple men vying for her attentions? But how?

He could start a rumor that one was royalty. But all four had well-known ancestry. He could attend to one of them himself and spread her praise. Men did like competition. But that could end in his own character being dragged down, which was an appalling thought. Women were far better at this sort of work than he was, but he refused to ask Lady Sommerset to aid in his quest. If he was to accomplish this herculean task for Belinda, he wanted to do so alone.

The four ladies moved closer as two others joined them. That the classmates were not shunned by their peers was very interesting. Nor did they sit on chairs against the wall meekly awaiting their fates, though he was quite sure the diminutive Lady Sophie Howard would be far more comfortable doing exactly that. Having only spoken to her once, he'd noticed immediately that she was painfully shy. The woman who stood next to her was quite the opposite. Lady Eleanor Compton, the daughter of Countess Dulac, could hold people's attention with her conversation, but her bright-red hair caused many to immediately discount her.

Moving his gaze past the Lady Eleanor, it landed on Lady Dorothea Ansley, whose hair was of a more muted tone of auburn. Actually, it was rather more like mahogany, but as with her fellow classmates, she tended to converse a bit too much. He hadn't had a reason to speak with her beyond an introduction, but he had observed her over the season. She seemed more prone to soliloquy than conversation. Last, standing next to her was Lady Georgina Bridgeman of Edgerton. She was a wisp of a thing whom he'd seen more often near the food and libations than conversing. But again, he had not had reason to interact with her, either. The only reason he knew them at all was due to Lady Sommerset.

He continued his observation just as his sister Rose and two other ladies, joined the group. He strained to hear the conversation, but the music and voices around him overrode any chance of success. So he settled for watching their interactions. The dynamics were puzzling. The new ladies, including his sister, interacted with each of the classmates. It wasn't until the music stopped and his sister was asked to dance that he subtly moved closer to make sure the man in question was worthy of her.

"Lord Harewood, I didn't know you would be here this evening. What a pleasant surprise."

He turned to find Belinda's mother on the arm of her husband. "Lady Wakefield, it is always a pleasure to be in your presence."

She gave him a warm smile, causing wrinkles to appear around her blue eyes, so much like Belinda's. "But not such a pleasure as to be in the presence of all these lovely ladies?"

He looked blankly at her, not sure to what she referred.

"She means the column. It appears to have captured your complete attention." Lord Wakefield nodded to a column against the wall that he had inadvertently moved to in trying to see who his sister would dance with.

"Ah, not at all. I was simply fulfilling my brotherly duty." He gestured toward the dance floor where his sister was standing opposite Mr. Wheatly, a man barely out of Eaton.

Lady Wakefield sighed. "Your sister is truly a sweet woman. I'm so pleased that she has a partner." The woman leaned in as if to impart some great wisdom. "Though the gentleman in question is far too young for her."

"I agree." He didn't elaborate, as the topic was spent. "Will you be staying after the end of the season?" Though the Wakefield estate bordered his parents', he rarely visited. He asked only to make polite conversation and to have the information in case it was required.

"Most certainly. Since all our daughters are married now, we are in no hurry to return to Bedford."

He clenched his jaw to keep from correcting the woman about having *all* her daughters married. Belinda would never be married nor grace the halls of Thornwood Park again.

"Oh, there's the Countess Dulac. Excuse us, Lord Harewood. I have yet to greet my good friend."

"Of course." He gave the older woman a nod and the couple moved through the crowd toward the corner of the room.

Free to return once again to his new project, he was surprised to see the only lady left from the school was Lady Dorothea. He slowly made his way closer, as her back was turned to him while she spoke to the other women he recognized as his sister's companions. He'd met Lady Dorothea briefly at Lord Mabry's wedding, having been forced to attend by Sommerset. If he could listen to the woman in question's conversation without being involved in it, it may give him a clue as to how he should proceed. Maneuvering between people brought him to the wall of the ballroom just to the side of the ladies but within easy earshot of his quarry.

"Doesn't Lady Rose look splendid in that sky-blue dress? It almost seems to make her eyes sparkle."

"I agree."

Rose's friends were at least complimentary, if acutely boring.

"I'm not surprised by that." Lady Dorothea smiled. "According to Aristotle's theory of colors, it has to do with the amount of light. He considered black the absence of light. So though the dance floor resembles a rainbow, the dark clothes of the men certainly keep the colors apart. Do you think if men wore lighter colors, it would highlight the women's dresses more or less?"

The answer was obvious and he waited impatiently for one of the ladies to respond.

At first, silence greeted her question, then one of the ladies exclaimed. "Oh, my mother wishes me to attend her. I best see what is amiss."

"I will go with you. Perhaps I can be of assistance."

And with that weak excuse, Rose's companions left Lady Dorothea standing by herself. Curious as to how the lady would manage the obvious disinterest of the other two, he took a step forward to better see her expression.

Her lips remained lifted in a frozen smile, but her eyes clearly filled with tears.

His stomach tensed with anger at the two women who could neither answer the question nor create a legitimate excuse to leave. While in the same instant, he felt a strong pang near his heart, a strange occurrence since that particular part of him was rarely used. Not giving himself time to think it through, he addressed the now-alone Lady Dorothea. "Obviously, if all men wore such light colors as our acquaintance Lord Sommerset, the ladies' dresses would fade. Black attire like my own is what sets the colors apart."

"Oh, Lord Harewood. I didn't see you there." She surreptitiously wiped her eyes with the back of her gloved hand. "Do you truly believe the black enhances the colors?"

"Is it not obvious?" He pretended not to notice that she had high color in her cheeks, no doubt due to her upset. "As you stated, black is the absence of light, so what better canvas upon which to set light or partial light, as Aristotle would have us believe?"

"I would have never thought of it in quite that way. I wonder if that is why I much prefer darker blues, deep purples, like this dress, and even maroons in my choice of evening wear while my friends prefer more light in their colors. Or mayhap they are simply choosing what will bring out their features more. I've never really thought about if my dress complements my person, per se. I rather choose the color I enjoy seeing. But that doesn't make sense now, does it, since I don't actually see what I'm wearing unless I take a seat and stare at my lap, which would hardly seem proper and rather odd. Though I very much doubt that would be the oddest behavior seen at a ball. Still, it would not do to be so preoccupied with the color of one's clothing, as it may be interpreted as being preoccupied with oneself. Of course, that could be viewed differently depending on which philosophy of *self* one subscribes to, would it not?"

He barely kept from lifting his lips into a smile, which would not do, but her quick intellect was rather refreshing, as it forced him to pay attention to understand how she moved from one thought to the next. It was hardly logical, yet there was a pattern of some kind that he couldn't quite identify. "Indeed it would. While Locke would have us believe we are no more than our conscious intellect, far older and wiser men have already determined we are much more complicated."

Her hazel eyes lit with the very light she'd spoken of not a few moments past as they widened in excitement. The flush on her cheeks had changed its hue and her small frame seemed to vibrate with energy. "I have often wondered at that. Do you think Locke came to such conclusions by studying Descartes or by his powers of observation? I do not discount that he was a great mind, but that he came by his assertions only through human reason is a bit disconcerting, as opposed to Socrates, who had his daimōn. I am more apt to accept Socrates. Though much has come to light since his teachings. It leaves one in a bit of a muddle."

He had to cough to keep from laughing out right. To listen to such an erudite soliloquy, only to have it end in "a muddle" was far too humorous. "By muddle, do you mean as in the learned man's ever-present conundrum of the existence of the soul?"

Her eyes widened at his question. "No. To be truthful, I was thinking of the changes in human thought over time and how they resemble both a puddle and a tangled mess of yarn."

This time, his hard-won control was bested, and he grinned. "So, then, in your estimation, were a tangle of yarn to be dropped into a puddle, we would have a resulting muddle?"

"Yes, exactly." Lady Dorothea's smile was far too wide to be pretense. She obviously found such imagery to be important and worthy of discussion.

Though he didn't necessarily agree, he found her way of thinking entertaining. "And are there other words for which you have contemplated the appropriate imagery?"

Her smile faltered and her gaze dulled. "Do you play with me, my lord?"

The lightning-quick change caught him unawares. "I'm afraid I do not understand your question."

"Then allow me to be plain." She straightened her shoulders and looked him in the eye, despite being significantly shorter than himself. "I ask if you find my choice of topics silly and only wish to laugh at me."

He would have been affronted had anyone else accused him of such rude behavior, but it wasn't difficult to see that the lady spoke from experience. Her chin was tilted up in defiance despite the slightest trembling of her lower lip. "I assure, my lady, that what you suggest had not occurred to me. I am genuinely interested in any imagery you may have stumbled upon to better comprehend a particular word. With a very good friend who is an art collector, and whose wife is an artist, I am often searching for words to use which they might find easier to understand."

Her shoulders relaxed and she gave him a shy smile. "Then I owe you an apology, my lord. I fear my past experience had me making assumptions that were uncalled for. I hope you can forgive me." She dropped her gaze and her cheeks grew rosy.

If he were any other man, he would rush to assuage her guilt, but that was not his way. As the musicians finished their current song, an idea arose. "I believe I can forgive you if you would consent to this dance."

Her head came up as her gaze locked with his. "You wish to dance with me?"

"Yes." He found himself very curious as to whether or not she could hold a conversation while dancing. Since they would part and return, he wished to know if her thoughts would jump in the silence.

Just as she opened her mouth to answer, they called the dance, a waltz. She froze for a moment before licking her lips and swallowing hard. "I would gladly accept, but I must caution you that I have had little practice with the waltz."

Now his curiosity led him in a new direction, that of the woman's gracefulness. "That is of little concern, as I am an expert and will be happy to lead you."

Clearly nervous, she gave him a silent nod, and he offered his arm. As they strode toward the dance area, her grip grew stronger, far stronger than he'd expected from a lady of such small stature.

As they stood side by side, waiting for the first section of the waltz to begin, she leaned in so only he could hear. "I've never waltzed in company."

He lowered his head. "But you do know how?"

"Oh, yes. Lady Elsbeth—Lady Mabry helped me practice." She said the words as if that were all that was needed to prove her skill.

His gut tightened at the implications. It appeared conversation of any sort would be out of the question. He was about to make a fool of himself with a woman from Belinda's school and there was nothing he could do about it.

CHAPTER TWO

DOROTHEA LOOKED ACROSS the room at Elsbeth, who nodded encouragement. No doubt, Lord Harewood even now was regretting asking her to dance. She would just have to force her mind to focus on the odd beat. She'd done it before, until the turns. That was when she couldn't keep her mind on the counts. But she refused to make herself and the lord victims of ridicule.

He had been far kinder than she'd expected, based on her limited interactions with him in the past. She'd actually thought him a bit sinister since he always dressed in black, never smiled, and remained aloof, as if they were all far too boring and of little consequence. She had assumed that came from being very intelligent or very arrogant. But when he'd come to her rescue after Lady Rose's companions left her, he'd been kind, interested, and he had even smiled!

Grateful to him for that kindness, she would manage the waltz turns somehow, simply keeping her gaze on his and counting, even if she must do so under her breath. She'd never been asked to waltz before and Lord Harewood never asked anyone to dance. It was paramount she not disappoint him. If she stumbled, she would simply claim a twisted ankle, and he could escort her off the floor, no harm done to their reputations.

As the strains of the music began, she kept her gaze on the other dancers to start her count. But she needn't have worried because just as they were to take the first step, she felt his arm tense, cuing her movement. Pleased that his own movements could help her, she made it through the beginning of the dance with no missteps. In fact, she found herself relaxing into the beat instead of forcing it.

Thankfully, Lord Harewood did not attempt to engage in conversation because had he done so, she was sure she would lose her count. Then as the last pattern before the turns came to an end, he took her in his arms. Panic filled her as she stared at his chest and tried to remember the count as he moved. She stumbled, catching up, trying to keep in step.

"Look at me."

The command of his voice brooked no resistance, and she did as told.

"Now, relax and allow me to lead."

As she had lost the count completely, she held on tightly and let him move her about the floor. His gaze never left her, yet she could feel his arm muscles anticipating the next turn and his hand on her back moved her to the position she needed to be. It took a few minutes, but she began to feel the sway and rhythm and soon found herself studying the color of his eyes instead of paying attention to the dance. They were a bright green like new leaves bursting from their buds, but against that bright backdrop were darker shades that flitted about the edges like shadows. What kind of man dressed in black, kept himself apart from others, yet had such fascinating eyes?

Suddenly, they stopped, the dance over. She wanted to continue. She'd never felt so graceful. His arms left her, and she stepped back as appropriate, giving Lord Harewood her best curtsey. He bowed then held out his arm. "Allow me to escort you to your chaperone."

Immediately, panic of a different sort set in. She quickly searched the room, not surprised to see her mother slipping outside into the gardens with a man. Desperate to find a suitable chaperone in Lord Harewood's eyes, her gaze landed on Elsbeth standing with her husband, Lord Mabry not far from the musicians. Elsbeth wore a pale blue dress that matched her eyes and complemented her blonde hair. Her husband's very dark blue tailcoat complemented her dress just as Aristotle had suggested. "Lady Mabry is my dearest friend and serving as my chaperone this evening." It wasn't precisely the truth, but very close.

The lord's brows rose. "I would have expected your parents, or at the least, your mother. Did she not attend tonight's ball?"

She put her hand upon his arm. "My mother attends almost every ball, even those held on the same evening. Did you know that in one season, there can be as many as sixty-eight balls held, not to mention the various recitals? Just last week, I attended a recital of the Worthington sisters. They are truly talented. It will be a great loss when one of them marries and no longer graces us with her voice, but I imagine she will then be able to sing to her children. I know it's not common, but who else could she sing to? It's not as if she can go on the stage. What a scandal that would be, don't you agree?"

Lord Harewood stared at her as if he were unsure of her question.

She was about to repeat herself when he nodded. "That would indeed be a scandal. And so we, too, do not create one by remaining on the dance floor, allow me to escort you to Lady Mabry." He immediately guided her across the room.

Though she couldn't be sure, she felt that he was anxious to be rid of her, a feeling she was quite used to. She did not cast blame, as she was quite aware it was her fault. If she could stay on one topic for more than a couple of sentences, both ladies and gentlemen wouldn't be in such a hurry to relieve themselves of her company. But alas, that was not within her abilities, so she was actually grateful that Lord Harewood had not only conversed with her, but had continued in her company through a dance. Though, to be fair, she hadn't spoken a word during their time on the dance floor and so it wasn't that he had needed to follow her thoughts. Whatever would he think if he knew her thoughts on his eye color?

She smiled at the thought as they approached Elsbeth.

Her friend returned her smile, before addressing her escort. "Lord Harewood, thank you for returning Lady Dorothea to us."

As the lord in question released her, she stepped next to Elsbeth. "Thank you for the dance. I believe I now have a better understanding of the waltz."

The man did not smile, but neither did he frown. "And I, Lady Dorothea, have a better understanding of a muddle. I hope you enjoy the rest of your evening." With that, he strode away.

She watched as he made his way to Lord and Lady Sommerset, who stood near the entrance of the ballroom. It was rather awe-inspiring how quickly he could move through the crowd while avoiding conversation with anyone. Then why had he conversed with her?

"Dory, you must tell me everything. How did you garner a dance with Lord Harewood?" Lady Elsbeth stepped in front of her, blocking her view of the interesting man.

She wanted more than anything to crane her neck to see if he spoke to Lord Sommerset about his time with her, but she'd been taught her manners well. Instead, she focused on Elsbeth. "I didn't. He asked me."

Elsbeth winked, much like their teacher, the Duchess of Northwick. "I guessed as much, but how did that happen to occur? Did he stride up to you and ask? Did he accidently bump into you? Did Lady Sommerset and her husband approach you with him in tow?"

She grinned as she remembered his kindness. "He answered a question I had posed to Lady Rose's companions. They couldn't answer, but he could. He's very intelligent. We actually conversed for quite some time."

"You did?" Elsbeth's light-blue eyes widened in evident surprise. "Do you mean to say he followed your ideas?"

She nodded, her smile growing wider. "He did." To have someone follow every word she spoke had never happened before. Her classmates understood her in pieces and were not shy about asking her to repeat herself, which she gladly did. It had been refreshing to find ladies of her own age who were willing to listen. Her mother said she prattled far too much and her father wished her to be silent at all times, which she tended to be when he was present, even if her mind continued to think about various and sundry ideas.

Elsbeth patted her arm. "I, for one, am quite pleased for you. You even did well in your waltz. Have you been practicing?"

She grimaced as she remembered Elsbeth practicing with her. "No, but Lord Harewood told me what to do and when."

Elsbeth's brows rose. "Now that is not surprising. I understand the man can be very particular about things."

"I did admit to him when the dance was called that I had not danced the waltz in public before."

Lord Mabry, who stood next to his wife, chuckled. "I imagine the stodgy Lord Harewood was quite taken aback by your honesty."

She didn't know why she felt the need to defend him, but she did nonetheless. "Actually, he appreciated my honesty."

"I imagine he preferred to be forewarned, then." Lord Mabry nodded, as if that made the most sense.

The bell for dinner was rung, and she looked toward the garden doors, but her mother was not there. While she wished her mother would behave in another manner, she also understood she was deeply unhappy.

"Come, you must dine with us." Elsbeth hooked her arm.

Thankful that her friend understood her dilemma as they had talked about her mother's activities at length, she moved forward with them, making their way to the dining room. As they entered, she was relieved to see numerous tables were set with no particular seating order, which allowed her to remain with Elsbeth. It was always a bit awkward when the seating arrangements placed her next to or across from her mother and her mother was not present.

As they ate their meal, she couldn't help glancing toward the table with Lord Harewood. He sat with his friends the Earl and Countess of Sommerset, his sister, Rose, and his parents, the Marquess and Marchioness of Enderly. Though he was quite solicitous of his family, he did not smile once. She found that rather odd. Did he not find anything amusing? The others at his table smiled. In fact, he was a stark contrast to them, not only in his clothing, but also in his demeanor. Did he dress so to allow them to be noticed more? He *did* say that black helped to bring out the beauty of brighter and lighter colors.

"Dory, if you keep glancing at Lord Harewood, people will have you two married by the end of a fortnight."

At Elsbeth's whispered words, Dory whipped her head around to face her companions. "I did not mean to be noticeable in my interest. I just find Lord Harewood to be a puzzle."

Her friend groaned. "Not another puzzle. It would be best if you left this one unsolved. Remember what happened when you didn't understand why the vicar allowed the curate to perform the Sunday service at Easter?"

She felt heat rise to her cheeks. She'd been so sure it had been because he would surprise them all with a special guest, like the bishop. Hearing he was at home had prompted her to pry far too much, only to discover he'd decided to take the day to tup not one, but two townswomen. "You are correct, of course. I will allow the puzzle of Lord Harewood to remain just that, a puzzle."

"I'm relieved to hear that. Now, do tell me about the play last night. I've never seen *Macbeth* performed. Only read it. Was it as bloody as it sounded?"

As she described the play, she had to force herself not to look at Lord Harewood's table. Unfortunately, that made her discussion wander a bit. When she finally paused, Elsbeth had the usual look of bafflement on her face. "I confused everything, didn't I?"

"Yes, but I caught enough to know that I would enjoy it very much." Elsbeth's kind smile was a balm to her soul.

"Since I am trying to keep my attention here, can you tell me if you see my mother?"

Elsbeth nodded sagely. "Of course."

As her friend surreptitiously reviewed those in the room, Dory took another sip of her wine, daring a quick look toward Lord Harewood's table, only to discover he was no longer there. If he had left the ball, it would make it much easier to avoid looking at him.

"I do not see Lady Preston. When did you last see her?"

She shrugged, not surprised her mother was still missing. Her mother's growing dissatisfaction over the years had manifested in her penchant for finding other bed partners, but she was usually a bit more circumspect. "After I danced with Lord Harewood. She was making her way out into the gardens." She kept her voice low, as not a few people seemed to be finding a great interest in their table.

"Not to worry. You are welcome to be our guest tonight. You did wish to see our new portrait."

She'd all but forgotten that Elsbeth and Lord Mabry had had their portrait painted by Lady Sommerset. The lady's paintings were becoming quite sought after. "Is little Marianna in it?"

Elsbeth's face softened at the mention of her stepdaughter. "She is." She leaned in to whisper. "Lady Sommerset said she would add the baby after it arrives."

"She can do that?" It was not well known yet that Elsbeth was to have a child. Once it was, Elsbeth would withdraw from all public social events, which could make things difficult for Dory. It was fortunate that the season was almost over.

"Yes. She planned for it when she decided how we should be arranged."

"Be honest." Lord Mabry's lips quirked up. "This is dear Lady Dorothea, after all." He turned from Elsbeth to her. "I did not know how particular my cousin could be. She had us in three different poses, all sketched, before finally deciding which was best." He shook his head. "I am thankful that I have no such tendencies toward perfection. Except, of course, in my choice of a wife."

Elsbeth waved off her husband's flattery. "Truly, Teddy, there is no need to sing my praises. I am your wife now."

"All the more reason." He grinned. "It reflects rather well on myself."

At the banter between the couple, she couldn't help but feel a bit left out. She couldn't imagine what it must be like to have a loving marriage. Her own parents proved it was not the norm, as did most of her classmates' parents. It must be particular to the Mabry family, as they all seemed quite happy. For herself, she simply wished to make a match before her mother forgot herself and caused a serious scandal. Unfortunately, she had no offers.

"There you are, Dory."

At the sound of Eleanor's voice, she turned, just as Ellie, Sophie, and Georgie converged on their table.

Her classmate continued. "I know you want to fix your hair. Come with us."

It could be hard to gainsay Ellie, but in this instance, she was happy to join her friends. She looked to Elsbeth. "Do you mind?"

"Of course not. Go. You can find us in the ballroom when you have finished tidying up. I'm sure you have much to discuss." Elsbeth winked.

Grateful for Elsbeth's understanding, she rose. "Thank you." Though her words seemed to indicate only that she was allowed to leave, both she and Elsbeth understood they encompassed so much more. It wasn't the first time her newly married friend had suddenly become her chaperone.

Georgie linked her arm in hers. "Wait until you hear what Ellie did."

The whispered words had Dory hurrying up the grand stairs of the Stocktons' home and into the ladies' retiring room.

When they all arrived, there was one other woman of many more years than they, retying the ribbon in her hair, so they each set out to fixing their own appearances, everyone except Sophie, who simply sat in a chair and waited patiently.

As soon as the woman left, Ellie turned. "Lord Harewood?"

Surprised by the question, Dory shook her head. "I thought we were going to discuss what you did."

Ellie's cheeks flushed. "It was nothing."

"Oh, but it was something." Georgie put her arm around Ellie's shoulders. "She was so brave."

When Dory thought of bravery, she imagined a knight in battle, so she immediately pictured Ellie brandishing a sword in the ballroom. "Please, tell me what happened."

Ellie's gaze turned shrewd. "Only if you tell us how you came to be dancing with Lord Harewood."

That was fair. "Agreed."

"Very well, then. I set down Lord Ferriday." Ellie gave a strong nod to punctuate her statement as if to say that was that.

Georgie stepped away from Ellie and gestured to the air. "Do not allow her to be so humble. She didn't simply scold him. She boxed his ears!" Georgie clapped her two gloved hands together in front of her to demonstrate. "She was magnificent."

Ellie, who rarely shrank from anything, seem to shrink from such praise. "He was acting like a child, so I treated him like one."

Her heart sympathized with her friend. "Whatever did he do?"

"He thought mocking our host and his limp would impress me. When I failed to find him funny, he called me a prude."

"He didn't." How could anyone say such a thing? Ellie had the biggest heart, looking after all of them like a mother hen.

"He did. So I boxed his ears. He was quite stunned. I told him if he continued to act like a child, then he should return to the nursery."

Dory was well aware that Ellie spoke her mind, but she held herself in check while at social events. So it was a bit difficult to believe. However after looking to Sophie, who nodded her head, it confirmed the truth of the event. "Then he well deserved it. I suggest that should he ask any of us to dance, we refuse him."

"Agreed." Georgie crossed her arms, answering for all of them.

"Now, Dory, tell us how you came to dance with Lord Harewood." Ellie pulled her over to a settee and made her sit down with her. "That man never dances with anyone. We are not the only ones who noticed."

"Yes, do tell us, Dory." Sophie grasped her hand.

"I believe he was simply being kind." Quickly, she stated the events as they'd unfolded so she wouldn't wander off the topic. She didn't want her friends to become irritated with her.

"Hmm, I wonder if it wasn't more than being kind." Ellie shook her head. "Lord Harewood is not known for his kindness. He's a stodgy curmudgeon, in my estimation."

She was aware of his reputation but was still of the opinion that it had been kindness nonetheless because what else could it have been? "You can't be insinuating that it was an interest in me that led him to ask me."

Ellie's brow furrowed as if she wanted to believe that but couldn't.

"I'm at a loss." Georgie flounced down onto another chair. "You did tell us that you met him at Elsbeth's wedding. Did he bring up that subject?"

"No. He didn't refer to that at all."

Sophie squeezed her hand. "Maybe he was curious."

"Curious? How curious?"

"I've noticed that Lord Harewood watches people." Sophie blushed. "I do too, which is why I took note of his behavior. I would suggest that in seeing those ladies walk away from you, he may have been curious as to why and so engaged you in conversation."

At Sophie's suggestion, she found herself relaxing. That had to be it. The puzzle of Lord Harewood had been solved. "I do believe you're right. That explains it very nicely."

Sophie released her hand and smiled. "I'm so pleased I could help."

"Well done, Sophie." Ellie rose. "I suppose we should return to the ball now."

"I hear music." Georgie rose quickly, brushing out the skirts of her dress. "I'm hoping I'll be able to dance once more. I so enjoy dancing."

They were all aware that Georgie loved dancing. They also knew she only seemed to be asked once at every ball. If she were to be asked again, it would most definitely make her season. None of them were much sought after, which was odd, especially since Elsbeth had married.

She'd thought that would help the reputation of her school, as had her mother. "I'll be quite happy to watch you. You do dance beautifully."

Georgie hooked arms with her. "Thank you, Dory."

As the four of them descended the grand stairs, she secretly hoped no one would ask her to dance. Dancing was not one of her better skills. Neither was conversation, for that matter. Now that she thought on it, she wasn't quite sure she *had* any skills. It was definitely something to ponder. Since skills were required in a wife and she wished to be one, she needed to inventory those she had. Perhaps she could become an expert in a few. Why had she never realized her lack of skills? The answer was obvious. She rarely contemplated herself when there were so many other people and subjects about which to think upon. Why, just the other day she had wondered why the Serpentine had been created…

CHAPTER THREE

"FELTON, DID YOU hear me?"

At his mother's irritated tone, Felton set his half-eaten toast back on his plate and directed his gaze toward her. What had she been going on about again? So lost in his musings over the quandary of Lady Dorothea, he hadn't paid that much attention. "Of course I heard you. I was just waiting for you to be more specific."

His mother widened her eyes incredulously, which unfortunately made them the largest feature of her face, giving her a birdlike appearance. "What more specificity do you need beyond asking for your presence at our house party starting next weekend at Sunnydale?"

Just when he'd thought the tedious season was over, it appeared he must endure one more fete. "As you know, I have much to attend to at Denton Hall. What days in particular do you require my presence?"

"All of them." His mother's words came out in an angry huff. "Whatever business you need to accomplish, do so at another time. To ease your mind, it is only a fortnight and the guest list is quite selective. I even included Lord Sommerset to keep you from being a bear. Your support of your sister will be much appreciated."

He glanced at Rose, who sat across from him as they broke

their fast. Her cheeks colored prettily.

"Need me for more introductions, do you?"

Despite her embarrassment over being the sole reason for the party, she stuck her tongue out at him like she had when she was just a child.

He chuckled. "Very well. I shall do all in my power to set you on a pedestal before my peers. Just try not to drool."

He turned to his mother just as a napkin hit his chest. He glanced sideways at Rose, letting her know with a look that he'd be returning the favor at another time. "Mother, it will be an honor to advance my sister's marriage prospects. Do you have a list of those who have accepted the invitations? I still have a sennight to make the acquaintance of those I may not know yet."

His mother put down her cup of cocoa and patted at her lips with her own napkin before replying. "There may be one or two on the list with whom you are not as familiar, but it is difficult to know who is a member of your club and who is not." The censure was clear in her tone. She had no use of gentlemen's clubs, assuming they were like the gaming hells of London. He was quite sure his father, who was unusually absent this morning, had made it seem so on purpose, and he had no intention of enlightening her.

His mother rose. "I will retrieve the list from the parlor desk. The keys are in your father's study."

As soon as she left the dining room, a scone bounced off his cheek. "Damnation."

Rose slapped her hand on the table. "'Drool'? Truly? You can be such a bore."

"And you, sister, can be such a child."

She grinned even as she lifted another scone from her plate. "It's my prerogative as the youngest."

He held both hands out in front of him to defend himself from the missile about to be thrown. "I appreciate your position, but I don't think Raleigh will enjoy cleaning my waist-coat...again."

"Very well." Setting the scone back on her plate, she sighed. "I wish Mother weren't holding this party. I know she means well, but ever since Father said I could attend the Belinda School for Curious Ladies if I have no proposal by the end of the season, she has been almost *desperate* to see me proposed to."

He stiffened as dread filled him. "Father cannot allow that." They couldn't let Rose attend the Belinda School, especially when he hadn't created a plan yet to make the ladies there sought after.

"I know. To be sure, I don't think he'd accept a proposal at this late date, anyway. Thank you for seeing my dilemma. There is always next season. Maybe then, after a term at the school, I will have something of interest to convey in a conversation. We all know I'm quite boring."

He'd been about to exact a promise from her to refuse to go, but her words had him snapping his mouth shut. What he should do is reassure her that her conversation was engaging, but that would be an outright lie. He loved his sister dearly, but he never lied to her. Instead, he focused on the school. "Are you sure the school will enhance your chances for a proposal? Only one of their students has married."

She shrugged. "I was hoping you'd have a better perspective on that. I've come to know a few of the ladies from there over this past season and enjoy their company very much. They have so much to say that is quite interesting and hardly any of it is gossip." She sighed. "I've learned everything Mother has taught me and she states that I am proficient, so I'm not sure what else I should do. Could it be my appearance?"

His jaw tightened that his sister could think herself anything but beautiful. With her fashionable blue eyes and chestnut hair, she stood out from many. He waved his hand dismissively. "You are perfect on that account. No need to worry. You are obviously sought after. How many times did you speak to a gentleman at the Stocktons' ball the other night?"

She blushed once again. "I believe is was eight."

"Ah, then there are at least eight men interested in better

making your acquaintance. Perhaps one of them will be calling on you today."

"One has already spoken to me today." Her lips quirked up on one side.

"What?" He glanced at the clock. It was not yet noon. "Who would dare?"

Her smug expression gave her away before she could answer.

He shook his head. "You cannot count me as one of the eight. Still, seven is respectable."

"I suppose." Her shoulders slumped. "But I do not expect any callers today. I simply have nothing to say to my dance partners. I'm quite sure if I learned about something, anything besides how to stitch a hem or arrange seatings at dinner, I could become interesting enough to pursue."

It had never occurred to him that a man might want a woman who was interesting. Having already loved the best woman to walk the Earth, he had since planned on finding a woman very much like his sister for that inevitable day when he must marry and produce an heir. At a score and six, he still had years before contemplating such an arrangement. Not even mildly interested in considering such an event at the moment, he turned his attention to his sister's reasoning. "What subject would you be most interested in pursuing? Sommerset tells me each student decides upon a particular field of study."

His sister sat straighter and her eyes lit with excitement. "I don't know. But I'm to understand that my first year will be in all the general studies, an introduction, so to speak, on each of the many possibilities. Lady Mabry said that even if there was a subject not investigated the first year that excited me, I could find another that made my heart beat faster."

"She was referring to a topic and not a man, correct?"

Rose narrowed her round blue eyes at him. "Yes. I spoke to her before she left for the Continent when she was Lady Elsbeth Rawley. She said that geology makes her heart skip a beat and that I would know what I was most interested in when I stumbled upon it."

"As she finds rocks of interest, I can see why she would stumble." He smirked, pleased with his wit.

A scone hit him on his nose before bouncing onto the table. "You little minx." He lifted a honey cake from the platter on the table, fully planning to fire it off at his sister, when his mother entered.

"Felton, I thought you disliked honey cake immensely."

He placed the offending cake on his plate. "I thought to confirm my dislike of it."

His mother's brow furrowed, but rather than ask the obvious, she handed him a piece of paper. "Here are the guests who have accepted the invitation. If you wish to add any, please let me know today, and I'll have invitations delivered post-haste. Many people have already started leaving the city, though."

He took the proffered paper and began reading it.

"While you peruse that, I must have a word with the butler. Do find me when you are finished here." Without waiting for his agreement, his mother bustled out of the room, already thinking about her next task, no doubt.

"You wish to confirm your dislike? Truly?" Rose grinned at him, the twinkle in her eyes very becoming.

Could her lack of suitors truly be due to her lack of knowledge? He looked down at the guest list and shook his head. That made no sense.

"Is there someone on the guest list you don't like, then?"

He lifted his gaze to hers once again. "Not, not specifically. A few chaps are a bit boring and one not someone I would suggest, but as long as they can dance and play pall-mall, they should do." He'd talk to his mother privately about not inviting Viscount Leighhall. He studied the list again. There were some ladies missing, and one in particular who could aid him in his quest to make Belinda's school a success. "I don't see any of the ladies from the school you hope to attend. Do you not wish them here?"

"What?" She held her hand out, an unspoken demand for the list.

He let her have it.

Her brows lowered in consternation. "Do you think Mother left them off the list purposefully?"

He did, based on what she'd told him. "I cannot say what is in our mother's head. However, if you tell me who else should be invited, I'd be happy to relay that to Mother." He lowered his voice. "She does listen to me so much better than she does you."

"Brother, you best behave or I'll box your ears."

He chuckled. "I don't doubt you would. So whom would you like to add?"

Rose set her chin upon her knuckles. "Lady Mabry said the Stockton ball was her last event this season, as she is moving into the dowager house on the grounds of the school. Lady Eleanor's mother has them visiting her sister this month, and I know Lady Sophie won't attend anything without the others."

He wanted to suggest Lady Dorothea, but Rose needed to think of her first. "Are those the only students you know?"

She stared down at the table as if the pattern in the platter that had held the scones could help her. "I've only just met Lady Georgina and Lady Dorothea, so I'm not sure if they would attend."

"The only way to discover if they are interested is to send them an invitation."

She moved her hand from beneath her chin and took his. "You are correct. Thank you for helping me I don't care what the ladies say about you. They don't know you as I do." She let go and grinned like a cat who had just swallowed a mouse.

"What do they say about me?" Not that he cared, but he could see she was quite excited to tell him.

She rose, still grinning. "Only that you are far too serious and if you tried to smile, you would shatter into myriad pieces like a broken mirror."

He stifled a chuckle, not wishing her to know how much he enjoyed having such a reputation. "Myriad pieces? Not a hundred, or perhaps triangular pieces?"

Evidently put out that her attempt to deflate him had missed its mark, she pouted prettily. "Yes, myriad. Truly, you are quite lucky I am your sister."

When he simply raised his brows in question, she gave a heartfelt sigh and rose.

"Because, my dear brother, no other woman would have the patience for you." Then as quick as a sparrow, she threw half a brioche bun she must have been hiding in her skirts, hitting him square on his left cheek. As she raced for the door, she laughed. "Don't forget our shopping trip."

And with that, the little urchin disappeared.

Wiping the crumbs from his face, he tried to remember a time when she hadn't thrown food at him. Though it was not a regular occurrence, it was a longstanding one. If he didn't miss his guess, it began while she'd still been in napkins. He'd think a woman in her twenties would have grown out of such a deplorable habit, but he recognized it for what it was. It was her only defense against his superior intellect.

He set the dirty napkin on the table and rose. That did beg the question as to whether the Belinda School could indeed help stimulate her mind. Though Rose was sweeter than honey, her observational capabilities into human behavior were sorely lacking, as had been made painfully obvious last year when she'd brought home the widow Lady Garmoyle for the holidays.

He shivered at the memory. How could a woman like that engender a proposal and his own sweet sister not. He'd always felt protective of Rose, but now with his mother's and father's agendas for her in conflict, he needed to fully focus on what was best for her. Her wish was to go to the damn school, and as much as he didn't care for that idea, it could, possibly, aid her, especially if he could find a way to make those ladies popular.

He strolled through the archway to the parlor before slowing to glance toward the ceiling. "My dear Belinda. By opening my heart, you have set me on a course I have no inkling how to navigate."

CHAPTER FOUR

D ORY LOOKED OUT the window of the carriage as if the scenery was riveting, but she didn't even see it. Her thoughts were like the sea in a storm, and she rode it in a dingy. After the Stocktons' ball, the last thing she'd expected was to be journeying to Sunnydale Manor, home of the Marquess and Marchioness of Enderly at the invitation of their daughter, Rose, whom she'd spoken to for the first time barely a fortnight past, though they had met last season.

To make her travels even more unbelievable, she rode there being chaperoned by none other than Lord Sommerset and his wife, friends of Lord Harewood. Though at first her mother had said it was impossible for her to attend. As it happened, her mother had other engagements already planned. Elsbeth, who had been calling and understood what a wonderful opportunity it could be, had suggested that one of her relatives could serve as chaperone. Dory had expected that person to be the Duchess of Northwick, who owned the school she attended. Her mother must have expected that as well and quickly agreed.

The note they received from Lady Elsbeth the following day simply stated the day to be ready for the journey. It wasn't until the carriage had arrived at their doorstep yesterday that she'd discovered her chaperones would be Lord and Lady Sommerset. Not that she was ungrateful. Much the opposite. Lady Sommerset was very amusing and seemed to understand her better than the duchess—at least that was how it appeared when they had all been to her house just outside Town for lessons on art forgeries. She'd never thought about paintings, except the one in the school of Lady Belinda, so it hadn't occurred to her that as a wife, she might be expected to purchase some. Just when she thought she knew all she needed to fulfill her role as a future wife, she was surprised by yet another skill that needed to be mastered. Not that she had yet to truly master any, but she was adequate. While she agreed that learning enhanced one's experiences, she sometimes wished she could simply enjoy the small pleasures of a newly bloomed rose or the sound of the rain hitting the window.

She glanced toward the sky. It didn't appear there would be rain before they arrived at the manor. A bubble of excitement started in her belly. She'd never been to a house party. Her father did not allow her mother to go away for that length of time, but he was happy to let his daughter go. She knew it was because he couldn't stand her prattle, as he called it. He said she talked in circles. She smirked. She preferred to think of it as squiggly lines. When she saw Lord Harewood again, she would tell him that was her imagery for her thoughts. He would appreciate that.

Thankfully, she had apologized for thinking his remark about her imagery was him having fun with her. That had been a terrible assumption on her part. Unfortunately, her own self-awareness made it obvious that she apologized far too frequently. She'd only been in Lord and Lady Sommerset's carriage a few hours since they left the quaint inn where they stayed the night, and she was quite sure she'd apologized at least three times. Elsbeth said it was not necessary, but that apologizing was an endearing trait nonetheless. However, Elsbeth was her dearest friend and might have simply been kind for that reason.

But a very good friend would tell her the truth, wouldn't she? *Was* apologizing endearing? She wished Lissette had agreed to come with her, but she'd said her grandmother wasn't feeling well and she needed to stay with her. Lissette might tell her the truth about apologizing. Then again, she didn't wish to point out her own faults to the one person who seemed genuinely interested in all her wisdom, such as it was.

Who would she talk to for a whole fortnight? She sincerely hoped Lady Rose was as nice as she seemed. They had both come out in the same year but had not been at many events together. She might be able to speak to Lord Harewood, but it wouldn't do to be seen with him too much. She did have her chaperones. She glanced at them. Lord Sommerset was far too handsome to look at with his golden hair and tawny eyes. Luckily, he found the scenery interesting as his wife slept with her head on his shoulder.

The carriage started to slow and turned a corner. She focused outside just in time to see the stately four-floor mansion before it disappeared from her vision since she sat with her back toward their forward progress. Still, she watched as the rolling lawns spread out from the main drive into the distant forest. There must be plenty of lawn for pall-mall, but if there was a hunt planned and the ladies were invited to watch, she would refrain. She could sit a horse well enough, but not for a jaunt over the countryside.

"It's time to wake." Lord Sommerset's voice brought her attention back to the inside of the carriage.

As he nudged his wife's chin, her eyes fluttered open and she lifted her head, yawning. She quickly covered her mouth when she saw they were not alone. "Oh, dear. I do apologize, Lady Dorothea. That's two days in a row I have been a poor hostess."

"Please do not apologize. I was quite content watching the scenery. I have never been to Bedford. Is it true your family is neighbors of Lord and Lady Enderly?"

Lady Sommerset smoothed out her Persian green dress skirts as she sat straighter next to her husband. "They are, indeed." She glanced at her husband. "And very glad am I that they are. It was they who hosted Lord Sommerset last year, and we were better able to deepen our acquaintance." The woman gave her a sly look. "Are you hoping to deepen an acquaintance of yours?"

"Oh, no. I doubt I will know anyone. But I am looking forward to meeting all who would be the marquess and marchioness's guests. They will only be strangers to me until they become my friends. Aristotle observed we have three types of friends, be it for utility, pleasure, or good. Just look at us. I did not know you before attending the Belinda School for Curious Ladies because I hadn't yet met Elsbeth or any of the other ladies who attend. Though I had met Mademoiselle Lissette. She is going to be a new student this term and has attended a few lectures and some teas." At the raised brows of Lady Sommerset, she had to assume she had wandered off topic again and closed her mouth quickly before commenting about one of the lectures they had attended.

"I am quite sure you will enjoy your time here." Lord Sommerset took up the conversation. "I have been a friend of Lord Harewood for near on ten years now and have enjoyed his family's hospitality many times. At the very least, you already know Lady Rose."

"Yes, of course. I also know Lord Harewood from our brief conversation at the Stocktons' ball."

"You conversed with Lord Harewood?" Lady Sommerset seemed hard-pressed to keep herself from smiling.

Not sure why that was, but also having become familiar with the lady looking as if she knew far more than others, Dory answered honestly. "Yes, I did. If I remember correctly, it was about self-reflection and muddles." She paused, fearing she had it wrong. "Or maybe it was about colors and muddles." She nodded, more confident that had been it. "Yes, colors and muddles, though I do think, Lady Sommerset, your expertise would have quite kept us from making a muddle of our discussion on colors."

Grinning happily that she'd tied it all together nicely, she gauged her chaperones' reactions. Lord Sommerset chuckled. His wife grinned before responding. "I have no doubt I would have been happy to be part of your dialogue."

The coach came to a halt and with it, the bubbles in her stomach felt as if they popped. Her first house party! She looked forward to it with both excitement and trepidation. Without her classmates in attendance, her old fears came back, but she shook them off. If Lord Harewood could follow her conversation, then surely, others at the party would, and she wouldn't be left by herself as she had so often in the past.

As Lord Sommerset stepped out before helping his wife to alight, Dory studied the footman standing nearby. His clothing was impeccable and his face didn't reveal any of his thoughts. If only she could be like that.

Quickly, she brushed out the skirts of her emerald-green traveling dress and tucked a stray hair behind her ear. Maybe this week, she would fall in love, or at the very least find a new friend. Trying to keep her mind on the many positive experiences upon which she was about to embark, she moved forward and carefully descended the coach with the footman's help.

"Lady Dorothea?" Lord Sommerset held out his other arm for her and she blushed. To be escorted by him into his friends' home was very thoughtful.

She gracefully took his arm, and they strode forward. They were halfway up the many steps when the doors opened and Lord Harewood stepped out. He was dressed in gray pantaloons, a white shirt, and his ever-present black tailcoat. In the sunlight, she noticed his hair appeared a very dark brown with deep-auburn strands that caught the sun and he'd trimmed his sideburns somewhat shorter since last she'd seen him. As the doors behind him closed, he was framed in the tan arch. He cut quite a fine figure standing there. She'd never noticed that about him before. But she had noticed his height, and standing there above them as they drew nearer just made him seem a giant.

"It's about time you arrived, Sommerset. Do you know how terribly boring it is to be here without you nearby to insult?"

Lord Sommerset, rather than looking offended, laughed. "I came as soon as I was able, always cognizant of how much you depend upon my presence."

Their host snickered. "And you say *I* have the large ego?"

They reached the top step and Lord Harewood turned to Lady Sommerset. "It is always a pleasure to see you, my lady."

"I do doubt that, but I will take your statement as a welcome."

Not a little surprised by the insults taken in such comradery, Dory wasn't sure how she should respond.

Lord Harewood finally turned to greet her. His lips lifted in that elusive smile of his. "Lady Dorothea. What a surprise. I did not know you'd be traveling in such sad company."

It was on her tongue to defend her hosts, but as that seemed far too serious for the levity of their welcome, she refrained. "Oh, dear. And here they had come so highly recommended as chaperones."

His lips twitched. "I must then doubt the source of their recommendation. But have no fear, you will be well taken care of while at Sunnydale."

She grinned, happy to have pleased him. "Thank you, Lord Harewood. You are ever gracious."

That elicited a snort from Lord Sommerset. "We best make our entrance before Lady Dorothea believes anything you say, Harewood. I'm sure Lady Enderly has heard of our arrival and is cooling her heels just inside."

Lord Harewood opened his arm to them all, and as they approached the doors, they opened once more to the very lady herself.

Lady Enderly held her hands out to Lord Sommerset. "There you are, Andrew. It's so lovely to have you here again and this time as a married man." As she smiled happily at the earl, Dory couldn't help noticing Harewood looking at the ceiling as if he were asking for patience from a divine power. Did he truly find his mother's statements of little worth, or was he simply pretending this was all a bore when it was obvious he was very pleased to have his friend near? Maybe she could watch his behavior this week, like Sophie said he did others, and then she could understand him better.

When Lady Enderly had finished welcoming Lady Sommerset, she finally turned to her. "Lady Dorothea. I'm very pleased you could join us. Rose is quite excited you are here."

Despite the kind words and smile, she could tell the marchioness was not as happy to see her as she claimed. Immediately worried that it might have to do with her mother's reputation, she vowed to be the epitome of a lady while at Sunnydale. "I'm quite honored that Lady Rose wished my company."

"Did I hear my name?" The lady in question descended the grand staircase in anything but a grand manner.

"Rose, do slow your step. You could fall." Lady Enderly's admonishment fell on deaf ears as Lady Rose seemed to practically run down to greet them.

Dory had the feeling if Lady Enderly wasn't present that Rose would either use the railing to slide down or at the very least jump to the floor from the third-to-last step. As it was, her feet barely touched the final stair.

Lady Rose strode directly to Dory and grasped her hands. "I'm so pleased you accepted my invitation. We have so much to discuss."

Not quite sure what they had in common beyond coming out in the same season, Dory nodded her acquiescence. At least her greeting by Lady Rose was warm and sincere.

"Rose. Do remember your manners and greet Lord and Lady Sommerset."

With a quick lift of her brows, Rose let go and did as her mother bid.

It was easy to see that the two families were well acquainted over many years, which was to be expected since Lady Sommerset's family lived nearby. As the others exchanged news briefly, Dory took the opportunity to view her surroundings. Much like many great country houses, this one boasted a central stair that spilt at the top. The house itself went off in opposite directions from where they stood. To the left was an open archway into what appeared to be a dining room, but to the right were two closed doors, which may signal a parlor, but it could as easily be a room for recitals and such. Her family had such a room, though it had rarely been used. She was acceptable at the pianoforte but not accomplished enough to gather a crowd.

If Rose was well accomplished, she would most likely give a recital during the party. At least, Dory thought so, but having never been to a house party, she wasn't entirely sure. She'd meant to ask Elsbeth about them but had wandered off track last they had spoken. If only she could keep her thoughts on one subject for more than two minutes.

"I'll show Lady Dorothea to her room."

At the mention of her name, she quickly looked to Rose, who grinned at her.

"Truly, Rose. We have servants for that." Lady Enderly shook her head as if corralling her daughter had long been a battle.

Dory found that odd, since Rose had behaved with the utmost decorum at the few events where she'd seen her. In fact, Rose seemed quite calm and serene. Her fine, straight, chestnut hair, which was never out of place, framed a square-shaped face with round, blue eyes, and a wide forehead. It could be she was different at home with few strangers present.

"Very well. Then I will show her to *my* room. Send someone to fetch her when it's time." Then, without giving Lady Enderly a chance to reply, Rose grabbed her hand and tugged her toward the stairs. By the third step, she had the presence of mind to look back at her chaperones in question. Lady Sommerset caught her gaze and waved her off.

As they reached the split in the stairs, Rose pointed to the right. "The other guests will be in that wing, but the Craufords are such close friends, they will be over here in the family wing and so will you."

Since Rose had let go of her hand before racing up the left set of stairs, Dory picked up her skirts and followed along quickly.

"This is my room. If you ever need me, I'm the fourth door down on the right. My brother stays in the room on the left, so don't mix them up." She shivered, as if that would be the worst event in the history of mankind, then opened her door.

Half-expecting a room covered in rose-colored wallpaper with tiny roses after her hostess, Dory was a bit taken aback by how yellow it was. The room was covered in a yellow wallpaper with tiny, yellow rose vines. The golden upholstery on the two chairs Rose pulled her toward matched the counterpane on the bed.

After taking the seat required by the slight push, she watched as Rose closed the door, locked it, and pocketed the key.

Immediately, the bubbles in her stomach started again. She truly hoped Rose didn't plan to impart any secrets to her. She wasn't the best at keeping them, as she sometimes gave them away without meaning to.

Rose returned and pulled the other armchair closer. "I can't tell you how excited I am that you came."

Quite flattered, she smiled warmly. "And I'm quite excited to be here. I've never been to a house party."

Rose's brows, which were truly the most expressive part of her face, rose high. "This is your first? Then we will make it the best. I will explain everything there is to know, but first, I'm hoping you can tell me all about the Belinda School for Curious Ladies."

The school? "Why do you wish to know about the school?"

Rose leaned in as if anyone could hear them. "My father has promised that if I receive no proposal this fortnight, then I may attend the school."

Pure pleasure ran through her at the thought of having another classmate. "Oh, Rose, that's wonderful."

"Isn't it? But I must avoid a proposal—not that I expect any. That's why I must attend the school."

Not a little confused, she frowned, as most of their mothers had threatened to pull them from the school if one of them didn't marry by the end of the season. Fortunately, Elsbeth had saved them all. Still, she wasn't sure attending the school could help Rose. "Why do you think the school will help you find a husband?"

Rose slumped back into her chair, as if all her excitement had drained from her like the juice of an orange for orange biscuits. "This was my second season and no one has had an interest in me beyond dancing. I am quite convinced that I'm boring."

Her heart immediately sympathized. "I'm sure that can't be true."

"No?" Rose pulled her knees up to hug them. "All I know to talk about are tasks of running a household and the weather." Her lips quirked up a bit. "My first season, the weather did provide quite a bit to discuss, being so cold, but then it stayed cold, so even that became tedious."

Dory couldn't imagine staying with only those subjects. She had so many topics swirling around in her own head, she could never seem to choose and so wandered from one to the next without stopping. "What about plays you've attended or recitals or museums, or other activities you've participated in? You can discuss those."

Rose seemed to squeeze her legs tighter to her chest. "I do mention them, but I don't know what to say about them beyond that I saw them or accomplished them." Rose rested her chin on her knees in defeat.

She stared at her hostess, not a little in shock. Did the woman not cogitate on her own experiences? How did one go through life without, well, thinking? "Let's try something. What did you do yesterday?"

Rose lifted her head from her knees. "I went into the village with my mother to visit the vicar. She always does so soon after we return to Bedford."

A visit to the village should yield many topics. This was the perfect place to start. "And what news did the vicar have?" She lowered her voice. "I'm sure he is the keeper of much information about the villagers."

Rose tilted her head, looking into the past. "He did state that the blacksmith has a new child; the baker has refused to make sugar plums anymore, as the children were stealing them from his shop; and that the inn has been fairly bursting at its seams with visitors. Is that what you mean?"

"Yes, precisely. That is so much fodder for conversation that I believe I could talk for at least an hour."

"You could? I would not want to bring any of that information into a conversation because I wouldn't know what to say next. What would you say?"

This time, she widened her eyes, unable to hide her surprise. No one had actually invited her to talk about something before beyond her classes at Silver Meadows. That she could actually be of help was quite exciting, but she forced herself to calm, knowing that she could often speak too quickly for others to follow when she was excited.

"Let's take the blacksmith having a baby. Now if it's a boy, I'm certain he is quite excited, as he would want to teach his son his trade and have him help. But if it's a daughter, he would no doubt be very protective of her and stand in the way of all but the bravest suitors. My brother is much older than I, and he has two boys, which he is pleased about, though his wife would like a little girl. I don't see him that often, as he doesn't come to Town very much and his estate is closer to Bath, so he prefers to go there. I have visited him there and it is a lovely place, though to be fair, I prefer a calm country lake to the wild deep ocean. I find it a bit intimidating. Yet the great Greek heroes, like Odysseus, Perseus, and Jason, all traversed the oceans. They had so much courage. It does make me wonder how one becomes courageous. Cicero said courage is 'that virtue which champions the cause of right.' Which does explain great heroes, but I'm not sure it would explain myself boarding a ship for the Continent. What cause of right would that be?"

Rose stared at her as if hypnotized before blinking. Dropping her feet to the floor, she clapped mightily. "Oh, that was wonderful. How do you do that? You are so intelligent." She clasped her hands together. "Do you think if I attend the Belinda School for Curious Ladies that I could hold conversations like yours?"

She felt the heat rise in her cheeks. She'd never had quite that reaction before. She was truly honored to be so revered but was also loath to lead such a kind lady astray. "We all converse in our own way. But if you do attend the school, I'm sure you will learn to generate plenty of ideas."

"It sounds perfect." Rose sighed, relaxing back into the chair. "And you will be there, so I will know someone. I admit to a bit of nerves. What should I expect in my studies? Is it painting, music, or maybe dancing?"

The naïveté of the woman before her immediately had Dory feeling protective. "No. Lady Northwick says we get quite enough of that at home."

Rose grimaced, making it clear she agreed.

"Instead, you will be taught how to think. Lady Northwick, the duchess, believes that all of life is experienced through thought and wants us to be able to comprehend everything and every experience, even if we haven't been taught about it, by drawing on our personal knowledge and using our minds. The duchess says understanding comes from that singular ability like the hub of a wheel. So your first year, you will learn how to think by drawing upon your life experience as you engage in a variety of subjects."

"That sounds exciting. What types of subjects, then?" Rose leaned forward, her eyes dancing with interest.

"Oh, there are so many, like arithmetic, literature, geography, astronomy, biology, animals, nature, and philosophy, which is my personal favorite. We also learn about estate management, the law, medicine, and self—" She stopped, not sure she should mention the self-defense classes.

"Self what?"

Quickly, she tried to think of what would fit. Landing on it, she grinned. "Self-reflection and physical activity."

Rose sighed. "All of those sound interesting." She slumped back in her chair. "I do hope no one proposes to me. I know that sounds terrible, but my brother, I know, has studied all that and more. He's very, very smart. I always feel silly when talking to him."

At the thought of Lord Harewood looking down his nose at his own sister, Dory bristled. "As your brother, he should not make you feel that way."

"Oh, no, he doesn't." Rose shook her head vigorously, as if the harder she did so, the more punctuated her statement would be. "He's so kind to me and very protective. He's a very good sport too." She grinned, obviously recalling something he'd done with her.

That Lord Harewood was a kind older brother relieved her. "He does seem quite intelligent, though we've only conversed a couple of times."

"You know my brother?"

"I would not say I *know* him, but I did—"

A knock on the door sounded.

Rose pouted. "I fear they've come to take you away from me. She stood and walked to the door, unlocking it with the key she had pocketed earlier. "Yes?"

"I've come to show Lady Dorothea to her room."

"Of course." Rose turned to her. "You will be nearby, so after you are rested, we can converse further."

Dory rose from her chair, surprised by the change in Rose's tone. She'd gone from sounding like an excited child to a refined young lady. It was a bit surprising. Dory walked to the door. "Thank you for the warm welcome. I'm looking forward to the coming days."

Rose smiled kindly but didn't say anything further.

Dory followed the maid down the hall closer to the stairs. As the woman opened the door, Dory peeked down the hall toward Rose, but she had disappeared back into her room.

"Here you go, my lady. Lady Sommerset is resting in the room next to this one. Is there anything you need?"

She stepped into the calm room and swallowed a sigh. The beige wallpaper was sprinkled with bluebells and the armchair by the fireplace was a deep blue. The quilt on the bed matched the walls, complete with blue flowers. "Just my trunk."

"Lady Sommerset requested that I hang your dresses in the armoire. Your trunk is next to it over there. I will return to help your dress for tea."

She looked to where the maid pointed and did indeed see a beige painted armoire. "Then that is all I'll need. Thank you and Lady Sommerset."

The maid bowed and slipped out.

She wandered over to the window to enjoy the view, only to discover that it was two doors. Pressing down on the latch, she stepped out onto a small balcony barely wide enough to set two settees side by side. The warm, late summer air enveloped her, and she quickly closed the doors behind her to keep her room cool. Taking the four steps to the stone railing, she surveyed the back of Sunnydale Manor.

Rolling fields disappeared into dark forests in the distance. Directly behind the house was a soft-green lawn. It appeared a pall-mall course was already set up, just past a towering hedge. Closer still was a narrow terrace that ran at least half the length of the house before becoming twice as wide. There were far fewer steps to the lawn at the back.

Looking to her right and left, she could see that each bedroom had its own small balcony to itself. No one else was about to enjoy such a pretty view. To the far right were extensive gardens as far as she could see. Her own family home boasted no such balconies, but her room did have a very large window with a window seat.

Leaning over the balcony a bit, she could see that the terrace had stone benches and planters as if it were a garden of its own. Did Rose enjoy the terrace? Had she used it to hide from her brother when she'd been younger? She could almost imagine a young Lord Harewood searching for his little sister.

She shook her head. Where had that thought come from? The earl was hardly the type to play games. He seemed a very serious sort, except when he smiled. Could he be like Rose, only relaxing when in the company of family and close friends? It did beg the question of what was real and what was not. Plato's allegory of the cave might apply—

The doors beneath her opened and footfalls followed.

CHAPTER FIVE

"I'M SURPRISED YOU didn't make some excuse to avoid this event." The voice clearly belonged to Lord Sommerset, who seemed to find much about life humorous.

"I had three at the ready, but as this greatly concerns my sister, I could not in good conscience beg off."

Dory grinned. That was most definitely Lord Harewood.

"Ah, so that is what this party is about. My wife was correct. Your mother wishes to extend the season for Lady Rose so that she might capture some man's heart."

"And yet my sister doesn't care to."

So Lord Harewood knew of his sister's desire to go to the duchess's school. She leaned over a bit more, wishing she could see their faces.

A chuckle emanated from Lord Sommerset. "I find that difficult to believe. All ladies aspire to find a husband."

There was a pause before Lord Harewood answered. "Need I remind you that one by the name of Lady Amelia was in no hurry to marry?"

"Yes, well, uh…what is the Lady Rose's hesitation? Surely, it can't be painting her masterpiece."

"Of course not."

When there was no further statement following that one, she pressed her feet against the concrete spindles on the railing. Even as she did so, she heard the tiny debris particles fall off the edge.

Quickly, she stepped back against the doors.

"What was that?" Lord Sommerset's voice moved closer to the building, away from where he must have been standing directly beneath her.

"It appears you have been dusted by a bird, or maybe…"

She held her breath as footfalls moved away from the building toward the end of the terrace. Lord Harewood would see her! She dropped to a kneeling position upon the balcony, hoping the angle would not give her away. If he descended the steps onto the lawn, she would no doubt be sent packing.

The footfalls halted. "It must have been a bird on the railing above."

She sincerely hoped he'd be happy with his conclusion.

"But to be sure. Let me take a further look."

Her heart stopped in her chest.

The sound of the terrace door opening caused her to groan silently. How many more people would come outside?

"Ah, there are you, Andrew. Felton, what are you doing over there?

"I was investigating a happenstance, Father."

"That's enough investigating. Your mother wishes you and Andrew to come inside for tea. We shall all humor her before slipping into the library for a real libation, right, Andrew? Port, if I remember correctly."

Lord Harewood's steps drew closer to the house until he was beneath her, but still, she didn't move.

"You are quite correct, sir." Sommerset sounded quite happy with the plan.

She listened to all three men's footsteps until they grew muffled as the door was closed. Still, she remained where she was, frozen with relief.

A muted knock sounded from inside her room.

Of course. They would send for her for tea! Jumping up, she stepped back into her room and ran toward the door with a sinking feeling that she would have to watch every step she took at this house party. She just hoped she lasted the entire week without drawing too much attention to herself. If only she knew how to accomplish such a feat.

LORD HAREWOOD STOOD at the fireplace, relaxed and pleased that his friend had arrived two days early, as he'd requested. What he hadn't expected was that Lady Dorothea would accompany Lord and Lady Sommerset. That, in his estimation, had been a fortuitous turn of events. It would give him the opportunity to learn more about her and determine the best way to make her quite popular with the men attending his mother's fortnight of activities.

He sincerely hoped he could discover some simple change that could then be applied to each woman in the school. What that change would be and how he would make it happen were still beyond his reach. But now, with his sister planning to attend the school, which was deemed scandalous simply by its goal of imparting young women of the peerage with knowledge and thought processes equal to that which was boasted of by Oxford and Cambridge, his task was even far more important. Obviously, the Duchess of Northwick had no knowledge of what other "lessons" young men availed themselves of while at school. No doubt her husband had kept those sinful activities from his wife, as any respectable gentleman would.

"You're smiling, Harewood. That does not bode well for the rest of your guests." Sommerset handed him the cup of tea his mother had poured, and he accepted.

"I am of the understanding that smiling is the preferred way to welcome others into one's home, is it not?"

"Normally, I would agree, but with you, my friend, I know there is much more behind that grin than a simple welcome.

Come, tell me. What is it that pleases you? It happens so rarely that something does."

He took a sip of the bitter black tea, the only way he could stomach it. "Perhaps I am simply content that the rest of the guests have yet to arrive and I still have two days to enjoy my childhood home."

Sommerset chuckled, as expected. Though many men might consider Sommerset nothing more than a handsome rival with far too much humor to take seriously, he knew his friend was not only steadfast in his loyalty to those he cared for, but also generous with a sharp intellect. Many a man had underestimated Sommerset, but he had recognized the man's potential even as a muscular lad at Eaton and had made it his first goal to befriend him. It may have been for self-preservation, as he had been a skinny youth back then, and Sommerset had had far more bulk to his build, so not the kindest motivation, but his instincts had been correct.

The parlor doors opened and Lady Sommerset and Lady Dorothea walked in. Sommerset immediately moved to greet his wife.

Harewood noticed that Lady Dorothea had changed from her traveling dress to a day dress of beige with tiny, dark-green leaves. He didn't like it. The few times he'd noticed her, she had worn deep tones. This dress reminded him of one of the guest rooms upstairs. Had his mother assigned her to that room? She definitely wouldn't become sought after wearing such mundane colors. But as she sat on the edge of an armchair next to his sister, she blended in with the others. Somehow, he was sure that had been her intent.

He studied the dresses of all the ladies, noticing that his mother's mauve gown was the darkest in the room. Lady Dorothea glanced at him, and he gave her a nod to acknowledge her presence. She nodded back before accepting her tea from Rose.

"Thank you, Lady Enderly." Lady Sommerset accepted a

teacup passed to her by Rose. "I'm anxious to hear what activities you have planned for us all."

His mother poured before answering. "I actually was hoping you might help me with one activity in particular."

"Of course. How may I be of assistance?"

His mother handed the next cup of tea to Rose, who passed it to Lady Dorothea. The latter took a sip as the other two women continued their conversation.

He had to grit his teeth to keep from grinning as Lady Dorothea blinked rapidly and her brow furrowed before she hid her reaction to his mother's overly sweetened tea. His mother thought everyone enjoyed her version of tea syrup, as he referred to it.

As the conversation continued among the ladies, he was content to observe. What he learned was that Lady Dorothea was well mannered and wished to speak more often than she actually did. When there was finally a lull in the conversation on painting and riddle making, he thought it best to join in. "Lady Dorothea, do you have any ideas for activities?"

Her eyes widened most likely at being asked directly, but she recovered quickly. "I admit to not being well-versed in house parties. However, I will say that I enjoy a stroll in the woods. At Silver Meadows, there's a beautiful waterfall and what's left of an abandoned mill. It is quite interesting to study the way nature is slowly taking back what man built long ago."

Before he could champion her cause, his mother responded. "We have no waterfalls here. Only the creek that feeds the pond. But I'm sure the men will enjoy a few boating races, don't you think, Felton?"

"I'm sure we will. But what of you ladies? A walk in the morning before the heat of the day might be pleasant."

Though his mother frowned, his sister quickly jumped on his idea. "Oh, yes. That would be lovely. There is that little path in the wood to the creek." She paused, looking to Lady Dorothea as if for support. "There are also the standing stones not far from the village of Marston Moretaine. Maybe we could take a ride there one morning and enjoy a light luncheon *al fresco*." She turned back to her mother. "We could make it an outing for everyone. I'm sure the men wouldn't mind giving up one morning to spend with us."

He grinned. His sister could be shrewd. It was clear his mother was not at first excited by the idea, but once Rose mentioned the men coming along, which would not have been the case usually, his mother appeared to see the potential in such an outing.

As he expected, his mother gave Rose a nod. "I think that's a splendid idea, Rose."

His sister linked hands with Dorothea. "Is that the type of activity you were thinking of?"

"That is even better than my suggestion. I have no doubt it will be one of the high points of the day."

Felton recognized how carefully the lady had worded her response. She both complimented Rose while not minimizing all the other activities his mother had planned. Whether that was because she attended Belinda's school or because she'd been well-trained in her etiquette, he didn't know, but he admired it nonetheless. "I'm sure with Sommerset's help, we can make it something to look forward to for the men as well. Maybe a contest of some kind."

"If you mean to see who can push down a stone first, you may as well sit with the ladies, Harewood." Sommerset's lips twitched. "I'm sure I would win handily."

"Brawn is rarely better than intelligence, so I wouldn't boast so."

"But it *is* handy in a pinch, wouldn't you say?" Sommerset raised his brows.

No doubt the man was thinking of the many times he'd defended them from the older boys at Eaton. "I do not argue that point. However, a majority of instances can be solved with a simple thought process."

Lady Dorothea opened her mouth then closed it, but her gaze was intensely focused on him. Surprised, he addressed her. "Do you disagree, Lady Dorothea?"

"Not at all. Seneca believed that the mind is what enables the body to have strength, for is it not the mind that determines how much to eat, exercise, breathe, and everything else that helps one to grow? Though to translate his words exactly, he did specifically refer to philosophy in particular, which is why I reread him often. How could one get on in life if the questions of life and why we live are not contemplated, dissected, and investigated? Without that, we are no smarter than the mules that turn the grist mill, going around in circles with no thought beyond our next meal and time to rest. There is no hardship but also no joy. It is simply to exist, which quite frankly seems a waste of life. After all women must go through to bring a baby forth, can it simply be to perpetuate the human race? But why? Have we accomplished much over the centuries? Yes, but to what end? It surely cannot be simply to accomplish an easier life of repetition, can it? I mean, if—"

The lady suddenly stopped, a red blush starting in her face and growing quickly down her neck to her chest. "I mean, it could be pleasant to have both physical and intellectual competitions, but as I said, I am not that knowledgeable on the usual activities your family enjoys."

The silence in the room made it obvious that everyone had stopped to listen to her. A quick glance made it clear his mother was appalled, his father riveted, his sister envious, and Lady Sommerset amused. Sommerset himself raised a brow at him, indicating it was his turn to reply, and so he would. "Lady Dorothea, you have made the argument so much more eloquently than I could. I appreciate your knowledge on the subject and think your idea of having both types of competitions an excellent one. It will give the men a chance to show their prowess in some way."

"And their weaknesses." His father joined the conversation

for the first time, his green gaze amused. "How else are we to see if these men are acceptable?"

His mother was not, as yet, ready to give up her primary focus. "We already know the men who have accepted our invitation are acceptable, my lord, or I wouldn't have invited them."

His father immediately capitulated. "Of course. I had forgotten that you had put so much work into the invitations. I am, as always, reminded of what a wonderful hostess you are and do beg your forgiveness."

His mother patted his father's hand on the arm of his chair. "Of course you are forgiven. This is why I must take care of all the details." She turned to Rose, whose obvious excitement over the idea of multiple competitions could be seen in the way she sat at the edge of the settee, keenly watching the interplay between their parents. "But I do suppose it would help Rose determine which would suit her better."

Felton was quite sure everyone in the room relaxed at his mother's pronouncement. "Then may I offer my services as well as Sommerset's in devising the competitions?"

"Oh, and you must allow me to aid you in the endeavor." Rose turned to Lady Dorothea. "And you must help us as well. I do believe this will be the best house party of the year." She faced her mother. "And you and Father can be the judges."

Their father nodded his approval and even his mother smiled. "I do believe I would enjoy being a judge. Maybe I can keep all competitions from becoming too serious. I would not want anyone to be hurt."

"And what of I?" Lady Sommerset cocked her head, her usual secret smile on her lips.

He had no doubt she knew exactly what she would do.

Her husband laid his hand on her shoulder. "You can help us create the competitions."

"Absolutely not. You will need a third judge to avoid a tie. That is, if you don't mind, Lady Enderly?"

"Amelia, I would enjoy that immensely. I do believe we will have quite an active two weeks."

He would have to applaud his sister in private for how well she helped him avoid an embarrassing moment for Lady Dorothea. But he couldn't be around the lady constantly. He needed to talk with her further in private to discover her reasons for her soliloquies. "Now that we have that settled, I believe Father had promised to show Sommerset the new painting."

"Yes. Yes, I did." His father rose much faster than he normally moved. "What do you say, Andrew?"

"I say if the ladies do not mind our absence."

The marchioness waved at them. "You know my lord is always anxious to be out and about. Off with you three. We ladies have so much more to discuss that will absolutely bore you."

He motioned to Sommerset to precede him. "What that means is that they plan to talk about us."

Sommerset bent to give his wife a kiss on the cheek before walking toward the door. "I, for one, am quite pleased about that."

He shook his head as he followed his friend and father out of the room. Love had definitely changed Sommerset...for the better.

CHAPTER SIX

DORY FOCUSED ON her food, trying to ignore the conversation around her. She'd pled a headache as soon as tea was over, hiding away in her room. How could she have brought up childbirth? And in mixed company! Even as she thought about it for the twenty-second time, she felt her cheeks heating. No one had mentioned her terrible blunder, but they were all aware. They heard her. The only way to survive until the other guests arrived was to keep silent.

She had tried the same tactic at the Mabrys' ball, the Worthington sisters' recital, and the lecture at the Royal Institution—and had failed. But she was determined to remain quiet until the first guests arrived. Or maybe until the first three guests arrived. It would be easier to not draw attention to herself with many more people.

To her benefit, she had been seated between Lady Sommerset and Lord Harewood instead of next to Rose, which made it easier to keep from joining the conversation. She had found herself far too comfortable with Rose. Lady Sommerset kept Lady Enderly engaged and with Lord Harewood, though he seemed to have knowledge on almost every subject, his cool manners made it easy not to interject, though she would have liked to many times, and they were barely halfway through the meal.

Lord Harewood put down his glass. "I predict all theatres will be gaslit by the end of the next season. That type of lighting is appropriate for those venues. While walkways at Hyde Park, which are hardly used at night, should be one of the last areas to receive gaslights."

Lord Sommerset shrugged before waiving a servant over. "I doubt there will be a logical reason for the order in which gas lighting of public places is installed. To me, it makes sense to start from one point and move outward, but that does not appear to be the case."

Dory quickly took another bite of the salmon pastry to keep from adding to the conversation. She tried instead to listen to the conversation on her left.

Lady Enderly commented, "I believe the gardens would be the perfect place to set up an out-of-doors painting session. We can schedule it for directly after we break our fast. If you wish, Amelia, we can go there tomorrow morning at the time I was thinking. Perhaps you can suggest the best spot for the easels."

Already bored with that conversation, Dory refocused to hear Lord Enderly declare the advent of gas lighting to be a step forward for mankind.

Thankful that his comment seemed to have ended whatever mild debate had been ensuing, she set her fork to the side, having finished her pastry, and lifted her wineglass to her lips.

"Lady Dorothea, which technological advance do you think the most advantageous to mankind?"

Having not expected to be addressed directly by Lord Harewood, she swallowed far more than she intended and quickly set her glass down as she covered her mouth with her napkin, trying not to cough. When she felt able, she turned her head to find the earl focused on her, his green gaze rather distracting at such a close distance. "I'm not sure that I could offer any insight, as I doubt very much that I am aware of all the great advances."

She didn't look to her left, but she was quite sure she heard a relieved breath come from Lady Sommerset. Proud of herself for avoiding the question, she smiled.

"Come now. Surely, you have learned of enough of them at your school to have an opinion."

Her smile froze. This would hardly make her more acceptable to his mother. Why did Lord Harewood save her from embarrassment in one moment and then draw her out in another? "To be honest, I have not thought upon the subject before, so I doubt I can add anything of substance."

Pleased with herself once again, she turned away and lifted her glass.

"Then tell us what first comes to mind."

What first came to mind was that she wished she had a plum to stick in his mouth to keep him from asking any more questions of her. Slowly, she set the glass down, not unaware that everyone at the table was now awaiting her response. "Very well, then. Let me see." She paused as she thought then turned toward him. "The first advance that comes to mind is the wheel."

His dark brows raised over his stunning eyes. They were as distracting as if he'd had a wart on his nose. Then again, if she stared at his nose, she might appear as if she needed glasses, as that would be the wrong focal point of his face.

"Pray tell me, why the wheel? That is a rather mundane and rudimentary advancement that has been used for millenria."

She refocused by looking across the table to Lord Sommerset and Lady Rose. "Precisely."

Lord Sommerset lowered his brows. "The wheel, you say."

"Quite." She turned back to Lord Harewood. "The wheel has been used since before the ancient Greeks. It is still in use, proving its importance to mankind. Nothing has replaced it, and it is used for everything from that cheese trolley over there to the new steam locomotive. It allows items and even people to be transported great distances."

The man's gaze became so intense at her words that she turned her head to talk to the rest of the table. "It was simply the first item that came to mind."

Surprisingly, everyone picked up the topic. Everyone except

the man sitting next to her. Finally, unable to resist, she turned to look at him and found a sly smile on his face. She simply had to ask. "Is that what you'd hoped I'd answer?"

"No. I had predicted something else entirely. You surprise me, Lady Dorothea."

Instinct told her that the man was not surprised often, but she couldn't be sure if he liked being surprised or if she'd insulted him once again. If it was the latter, it would be best to make amends. "What did you predict I would say?"

"I thought you might say cloth, since clothing has been in existence for quite some time and you did remark upon clothing colors at the Stocktons' ball." He appeared to find his answer amusing. "In fact, that burgundy color suits you very well."

She wasn't sure if she should feel complimented or insulted. Something in the way he phrased his statement along with his tone made it sound as if he were instructing her on what to wear. Surely, he wouldn't presume so much. "While what you say about cloth is—"

"Ladies, I suggest we retire to the parlor." Lady Enderly rose from her seat at the end of the table. "These gentlemen obviously have much to discuss involving progress and such." She gave her husband a pitying smile. "I'm sure they will join us as soon as all is decided."

Lord Enderly grinned. "I assure you, my lady, that we will set the world aright in due haste."

"Very good." As the marchioness started for the door, Rose also stood and turned to follow.

Rising herself, Dory waited for Lady Sommerset to pass before following her, not unaware that Lord Harewood frowned quite ominously. As she continued out of the room, she couldn't help wondering if she was the cause of his upset.

She didn't have long to wait to discover her answer, for it was barely an hour before the men joined them. Though she found the hour to be quite revealing. Anytime Lady Sommerset mentioned anything beyond paintings, sewing, or others in the *ton*, Lady Enderly guided the conversation back to her favorite three topics.

Since she had little interest in those subjects, having long ago learned all that was necessary, she didn't feel a need to become an expert in any of them. This made it far easier to remain silent, or to simply nod in agreement. Was this why Rose didn't know what to say in society? How absolutely boring her life must be.

As the men filed in, Dory felt a certain relief that they would take some of Lady Enderly's attention, but a new tension started in her belly that she must guard her tongue once more. Lord Enderly took the wingback chair next to his wife as he had at tea. Lord Sommerset did not move to his wife but instead to a painting across the room that he pointed to. Lord Harewood joined him. As the painting was quite close to where Dory sat on the settee with Rose, she angled her head to peruse it.

Sommerset's finger moved. "See here. This is not the left bank of the Seine. It may have all the markings of being painted in Paris, but an artist who painted in Paris would never leave off the wall along the river across from Notre Dame."

Lord Harewood examined the section referred to. "It could be there under all that greenery."

Sommerset chuckled. "Must you always argue a point?"

"Would you prefer I agree? What would our conversations be like if I did agree? Would we ever truly understand a topic if I agreed?"

Lady Enderly interrupted. "Felton, must you always answer a question with three more? You fairly make me dizzy with all that." She waved her hand as if swatting a fly.

"Must I?"

At his rejoinder, Dory placed her hand to her lips to stifle a laugh.

Lady Sommerset rolled her eyes at the earl. "Lord Harewood, do leave off teasing my husband. For those in the room who are unaware, the painting was done by an Englishman from memory. He did visit Paris but did not paint while there. It is authentic and executed passably well."

"There you are, Harewood." Lord Sommerset clapped the other earl on his back. "An authority who cannot be questioned."

Lord Harewood opened his mouth, but before he could speak, Lady Sommerset did. "And there is nothing more to be said about that."

The earl actually closed his mouth and nodded his agreement.

Dory was quite sure she did not understand the undercurrent of the relationship between Lord Harewood and the Craufords. It was rather puzzling. They seemed to get on well, but sometimes, they spoke quite harshly to each other or put each other in their place. Was it a friendly rivalry?

"I do believe we have thoroughly confused poor Lady Dorothea." Lady Sommerset gave her a sympathetic look. "Pay us no mind. We are simply comrades in deciphering life."

Lady Enderly hmphed, clearly not impressed.

Feeling the need to divert attention, Dory rose. "Might I see what you were commenting on?"

"Of course." Lord Harewood stepped aside as Lord Sommerset moved to take a chair by his wife.

As the conversation turned once again to the coming guests, she stepped before the painting and studied it. Lady Sommerset had taught them about forgeries at Silver Meadows. It was well known at the school that she could tell an authentic painting from a forgery in minutes and that her husband collected art.

Studying the painting and in particular the area in question, Dory could easily see why Lord Sommerset had questioned its authenticity. But he would have known it was not a forgery, so he had teased his friend apurpose. She almost sighed at how wonderful it would be to have a friend like that. Elsbeth and she were very close, but it was mutual respect and love that made it so, not jesting and teasing. It seemed a very fun kind of friendship.

"Do you see my point?"

Lord Harewood's breath brushed passed her ear, which caused an odd tingle down the back of her neck. She stepped to the side to put distance between them. "I do. I also see Lord Sommerset's point."

"So you do not wish to take a side?"

Before she spoke, she reminded herself not to wander. "I feel that it is a moot point, as I know that Lady Sommerset is an expert in identifying forgeries. The piece simply is not a forgery based upon her assertion it is authentic. However, if that were not the situation, I would still bow to her better judgment. But if she were not present, I would examine it further as she taught us at school and mostly likely come to the same conclusion she has. So in essence, I would agree with you because you were correct according to my own knowledge on the matter. However, if my knowledge were faulty, I might as easily disagree with you because Lord Sommerset was quite correct. Despite your assertion there is a wall beneath the greenery, there most certainly is not." She gave a small nod, pleased that she'd stayed on the subject.

His gaze softened. "I am very pleased that I'm not the only person who appears to talk in circles."

At the appreciation in his eyes, she felt her cheeks heat. "Actually, I prefer to think of it as squiggly lines, like a meandering river with its tributaries, but since in this case I did remain on topic, I would agree it appears to be a circle, though perhaps a wobbly one?"

This time, the earl laughed.

Immediately, she felt the eyes of everyone in the room upon them despite the fact that her back was to most of them.

"Felton, what do you find so humorous?" His mother did not sound pleased.

How odd. Wouldn't a mother enjoy her son's laughter? Unless, of course, she found it offensive in mixed company.

"Nothing of great import, Mother. I was simply comparing thought processes with Lady Dorothea and I found her description rather droll."

"'Thought processes'? Really, Felton, do leave that for your club. I'm sure Lady Dorothea has little use for such conversation."

He gave her a quick wink before responding to his mother. "I'm sure you are correct. I apologize for bringing such an inane subject to your parlor."

If he hadn't winked at her first, she would have taken offense, but it was obvious he was humoring his mother. She had thought her family odd, but the Ambroses were far more complicated.

"Lady Dorothea, do ignore my brother and come sit. I would very much enjoy your opinion on a contest I have devised."

Happy to be of service to Rose, she moved back to the settee both pleased and a little disappointed to leave the earl's company. Lord Harewood was proving to be an interesting study. Unfortunately, as such, he was a great distraction and if she wasn't careful, she would make one too many missteps and find herself in a coach headed for home.

CHAPTER SEVEN

JUMPING DOWN FROM Nyx, Felton gave his tar-black thorough-bred a couple of pats. "Well done this morning." Then he turned to the approaching stable hand. "Give him a good rub down and extra oats. He earned them."

At the man's nod, assuring him his orders would be followed, he strode from the stable and across the side yard. Bounding up the few steps to the library doors, he opened them and continued through the room, his intention to steal a few rout cakes from Cook before seeking out their guests.

"You seem particularly cheerful this morning."

At his father's voice, he turned. "I believe it was the ride. The air is crystal clear and there is not a cloud in the sky." Adjusting his direction, he sat in the armchair on the other side of the small table, which boasted a plate of rout cakes. Snatching one up, he took a bite, the slight orange flavor mixing with the currant inside forcing him to pause before continuing. "I must have Cook teach my cook how to make these in just this way."

His father put down his newspaper and shook his head. "She'll never tell. She enjoys sending you off with a basket of them far too much. Last I heard, your mother wanted to use them as a way to make you visit."

He hmphed at that as he chewed on his second bite, though he couldn't deny his mother's plans could possibly work. "It looks like the grounds are ready for the deluge of guests Mother is expecting. I noticed the gardener was just finishing a few places on the hedge in the gardens."

His father sighed. "As to that, she has something planned out there for this morning with the ladies. I must thank Andrew again for coming early. Brilliant idea, that. It has definitely distracted your mother and allowed me some peace before the coming onslaught. I'm grateful also to you for suggesting that."

As he had just taken another bite of his rout cake, he simply nodded, pleased with both his father's acknowledgment of his superior idea and the deliciousness in his mouth.

"Rose's friend seems a bit unusual, don't you think?"

A need to defend Lady Dorothea caught him unawares as he swallowed before answering. "Do you mean in the fact that she can speak upon subjects other than the latest fashion and gossip?"

"Yes, I suppose that's it. It's rather refreshing."

Pleased that his father wasn't being critical, he quickly explained. "I believe it's because she attends the Belinda School for Curious Ladies."

His father's eyes widened at that before his gaze moved to the cold fireplace before them. "That's the school Rose wishes to attend, is it not?"

"Yes." He didn't want to sway his father either way. He didn't like the fact that his sister's only two options were getting married or going to that particular school.

"You should know Rose is set on going. Your mother is facing a serious challenge, and I told her as much." His father steepled his hands. "The Duke of Northwick oversees it, and I have been impressed by his intellect, but I'm not convinced how that relates to women. Then again, the duchess, our former neighbor, has always been a proponent of education. What do you think of this school?"

Now that was a topic he wasn't in a hurry to discuss, so he rose. "Having learned of Rose's interest in it only last week, I've just started my inquiries, but I assure you, sir, that I will give you my full opinion by the end of this fete."

"You are always thorough. I appreciate that. Do share your findings with me when you have concluded your analysis."

"I would be honored to. Now I must fly to my sister's rescue. If Mother has something planned in the garden this morning, it could well be anything." He strode for the library doors, which were both open. As he crossed the threshold, his father chuckled and mumbled something under his breath. It sounded very much akin to the fact that his mother most definitely had something stewing.

He didn't wish to enlighten his father on his jovial mood, as it had nothing to do with the morning air and everything to do with his quest. A quest he'd decided not to share with Sommerset, despite their close relationship, never mind his father. Fortunately, he was quite capable of unraveling the puzzle of the students of Belinda's school on his own.

His morning ride had given him the time to contemplate his challenge, and it occurred to him that it may be that each lady was unique. Lady Elsbeth Rawley before marrying Mabry had been the epitome of all that was expected of a single woman of the *ton* except for her interest in geology, and though Lady Dorothea appeared similar, her penchant for roundabout soliloquies made her far different. The other ladies of the school of whom he had some knowledge had other quirks that made them unusual, and while that made his mission more difficult, it did give him two possible plans of attack. He could either make their individual qualities popular or find a way to help them conform. Though he still wasn't sure which track would be easier, that he had narrowed his plan down to two paths had him feeling quite accomplished. After all, it been but an early morning spent in the open air with Nyx that had brought him thus far.

His pace slowed as he navigated through the house. The garden could be accessed by both the dining room and the ballroom. If he knew his mother, which he did, she would use the ballroom as her exit, no doubt discussing how the guests could best spend their time there. He turned and opened one of the doors to the empty ballroom. The room was cavernous, his boot heels echoing through it like a pack of anxious duck hunters shooting at a flock.

Stepping through the glass doors to the garden, he halted at the top of the steps. The voice of his mother had him turning to his right before descending onto the embedded walkway. Sunnydale's gardens were his mother's pride and joy, boasting no fewer than a dozen fountains, a large variety of flowers, and at least twenty gathering places. She'd even had different stone laid for the paths, be it underfoot or as borders. Some of the hedges were quite tall, while others barely reached his knees. He gladly admitted that he saw no logic or reason for the large variety, but as it kept her busy, it was a boon to his father. It would seem that the secret to a harmonious marriage was diverse and separate interests.

As he passed by a particularly high row of hedges, high in that he couldn't see over them, while he could with most of the others, he found his quarry by peering between the branches. His mother pointed to something near what he referred to as "the fish fountain" and spoke to Lady Sommerset. Moving farther down where the hedge was lower, he searched the alcove still two courts away, and found Rose and Lady Dorothea sitting beneath a cherry laurel tree, their heads together, no doubt whispering about subjects of which his mother would not approve.

Though he'd been headed for his mother, he changed direction and moved into the section directly behind his sister and her friend. He could easily see them both between the branches, but the hedge was high enough behind them that it hid him from their view. The two sat facing each other on a stone bench. He was keen to be able to study Lady Dorothea without her knowledge.

"And what if there is no subject in particular that interests me?" His sister's shoulders fell in defeat.

He did not like that she already anticipated failure. Had she so little faith in her own abilities? She'd mastered being a lady beautifully.

Lady Dorothea set her hand on Rose's. "Do not worry. You will most likely find many subjects of interest and have a difficult time choosing. Whichever you choose, you will be encouraged. This year, we have women studying birds, literature, philosophy, the stars—and my good friend Lady Mabry studied rocks."

"Rocks? I didn't know people did that."

Lady Dorothea nodded sagely. "Oh, yes. Even rocks like the standing stones you mentioned can be studied. Anything can be studied. But first you must do well in the general studies. That's where your curiosity will be encouraged and you'll learn the basics about the main subjects to better prepare you for your focus in year two. You'll be in those classes with my friend Lissette. She's from France, but she studies in English very well." Lady Dorothea's face grew serious. "She witnessed the ravages of Napoleon's war and lost most of her family. She already knows so much about weapons because of her life there, but I'm sure once she's in the first-year classes with you, she will find other interests, and I hope be distracted from her past experience. Though one's experience cannot be discounted if we contemplate it."

"You will be there even though we are not learning the same topics, won't you? I would feel so much braver if I knew you would be near if I needed help."

The lady in question's hand came to her chest as if honored by Rose's request. "I promise that while I remain at the school, I will always be available to you should you need me, even if it's just as someone to take a walk with or sit next to at dinner."

Something in the sincerity of Lady Dorothea had his chest tightening. He was quite sure she did not know his sister well and yet already planned to help her adjust. If she was an example of the character of the women who attended Belinda's school, then they already honored Belinda's name. That should be enough for society, but he was well aware that such honesty and loyalty were neither valued nor desired when competition for mates grew fierce.

"Thank you, Dory. You have made me feel more confident in my decision. Now I just need to avoid a proposal, which should be fairly easy. Though I am worried that some of the gentlemen my mother has invited are anxious to consider me for a wife because of my dowry."

Dory? That was a rather unusual pet name, but then again, the lady was unusual.

Lady Dorothea responded. "Are they all known to your family? Do you think Lord Harewood would encourage them in their pursuit?"

Rose smiled warmly as she shook her head. "Oh, no. He was appalled by the idea when I told him. I have his full support for attending school with you."

Lady Dorothea pulled her head back, her brows lowering as her doubt became clear even before she spoke. "Are you sure? Your brother appears to be rather, um…traditional."

It was all he could do not to snort at the obvious euphemism for his character. His sister, though, felt no such compunction and laughed outright.

"Oh, you can say it. He's stiff and stodgy and acts like an old man. He wasn't always so, truly. I've made it my life's goal to make him smile and laugh. He really is a good fellow."

"I do admit to seeing him smile on occasion." Lady Dorothea crinkled her nose. "But sometimes I believe it's because he finds me amusing, though not in a positive way. It's more like I'm laughable."

Rose's smile didn't waver. "He would never be so cruel. If you make him smile, then you are one of only a few of us, and it makes me happy. I believe if he would at least smile more, he wouldn't scare all the ladies away."

He could remain silent no more. "So I scare the ladies away, do I?"

Both women jumped up at the sound of his voice. His sister

laughed, but Lady Dorothea blushed, as if he'd caught her saying something she shouldn't.

Rose peered through the hedge then placed her hands on her hips when she spotted him. "You know better than to eavesdrop on someone, brother. Mother would box your ears if she knew."

"I thought boxing my ears was your domain?"

"And so it is." Without a by your leave, Rose climbed upon the stone bench she'd been sitting on and held out her hands. "Now come over here and receive your punishment like a good boy."

He chuckled, his sister's antics always finding a way to amuse him. "If I were indeed a 'good' boy, there would be no need to box my ears. No, I appreciate the sentiment, but I'm quite happy with my ears as they are."

Rose pouted and dropped her arms. "You are far too intelligent for me to spar with and well you know it. It's simply not fair."

Her blue eyes twinkled with laughter, despite her apparent defeat.

"Rose, where are you?" His mother's voice floated across the garden at least three fountains away.

Rose turned toward the sound. "I'm here!"

"Well, do come here. Lady Sommerset has a question for you."

Immediately, he sensed his sister's intent to jump from the bench. "No. You stay right there until I help you down." He strode along the hedge, quickly rounding it, and headed for the bench.

"I climbed up here by myself. I see no reason why I cannot step down by myself."

He reached her and stood directly before her. "Hands on my shoulders."

"Oh, very well." She did as she was told, and he grasped her waist and gently set her down.

"I don't see what the fuss is about." His sister frowned, clearly not happy with him now.

"It's about you twisting your ankle and Mother being furious for the next fortnight."

Rose turned to Lady Dorothea. "See, I told you he supports me. You really don't want to see Mother in a full-blown fury."

"Rose, are you coming?" Their mother's voice had become insistent.

"Yes, Mother." Rose turned back to address her friend. "Stay here. It will give me an excuse to leave sooner. After all, you are a guest." With that, his sister spun about and was past the hedge within seconds. She was far more intelligent than she realized. Maybe she would flourish at Belinda's school. That possibility surprised him.

"I hope I did not say anything that was inappropriate." At Lady Dorothea's words, he gave her his full attention, which he completely enjoyed. Unlike his sister, who had dressed in a pale-peach day dress, Lady Dorothea wore a sky-blue day gown that brought out the lighter-blue specks in her hazel eyes.

"Why? Do you often make inappropriate statements?"

Color rose in her cheeks. "Not apurpose. But sometimes I may inadvertently forget myself."

Seeing that she truly was concerned, he motioned toward the bench for her to sit. "No, you need not worry. Please."

She sat on the bench and self-consciously arranged her dress. "For that, I am relieved. I am much better at watching what I say when there are more people about."

Now *that* was interesting. If he remembered correctly, and he always did, she had been left standing alone at the Stocktons' ball before he had addressed her. "So you are anxious for the other guests to arrive, then?"

"Yes. I mean, not that your company and that of your family is not perfectly lovely." The color rose in her cheeks yet again.

How fascinating. She blurted out what she wished to say, then reflected upon it and attempted to fix the problem. That could be something he could work with. "I understand completely." He set his foot on the bench and bent his knee. "In other words, you will be less likely to be noticed and judged by my mother."

She bit down on her lip, but the corners of her mouth still curved upward. That simple movement epitomized her character—honest, but attempting to stay within the norms of what was expected. It was that conclusion that decided his path. He would mold her to be more in line with what was expected. Though her hair wasn't the typical blonde that was so popular, she was quite beautiful in her own right and knew how to be a lady. She just needed a bit of polishing with her conversation.

"Have I been that obvious?" She looked up at him, not through her lashes like a maiden, but by meeting his gaze directly.

"I would not say *obvious*, but as I have foreknowledge of my mother's and sister's feelings and the fact that you are from the school Rose wishes to attend, it has not been difficult to conclude as I have."

"You are very observant, my lord. That is a rare quality in those I have met. Only my classmate Sophie has the level of skill that you have. I have often envied that, for as Hume suggested, observation can bring us new knowledge through induction. I believe that these newer poets, such as William Wordsworth, see observation of nature to bring an almost spiritual knowledge, which does seem to supersede logic. However, I understand their meaning when I walk at home and the only sounds are those of the birds and the only sights are those of the trees and leaves swaying in the breeze…"

As she continued, he understood it was this very penchant for prose that kept her from being marriageable. While he thoroughly enjoyed following her thought process with its variety of twists and turns, as it was much more challenging than simple logic, he recognized that most men looking for a wife would find it confusing at best and tedious at the worst. So if he could find a way to help her focus and shorten her communication style, she may very well land a husband and make Belinda's school for ladies more promising. But how was he to do that when she didn't pause for such long periods?

"…I often wonder if there are specific colors or sounds that speak to the human soul. If so, which colors and which sounds? Perhaps that is what William Congreve meant when he wrote that music has charms to soothe a savage breast. I can believe there are sounds that soothe and conversely, there must be sounds that excite or anger, though I'm not sure which of those could be…"

He could think of only one way to politely silence her, but it was entirely inappropriate. Yet the longer she spoke, the more he was convinced it was the only way.

"Perhaps that is why when we attend a recital of the pianoforte, if the young woman playing strikes a wrong note, we grit our teeth at the sound, though she may be quite pleasant to look at. Therefore, chaotic sound may well overcome a sight—"

Leaning down, he kissed her.

Her lips were soft and though he had only meant to interrupt, her open mouth was an invitation he couldn't ignore. Slipping his tongue inside, his first impression was chocolate and then a unique flavor and texture hit as her own tongue met his. A shock of desire sped to his groin, recalling him to his senses and he straightened.

Her eyes rounded for a moment before she spoke. "Though I do believe the green of your eyes would overcome any strident sound."

He should apologize, but the words stuck in his throat. He had only wanted to stop her discourse in the politest way possible. "I have not thought my eyes a particularly peaceful shade."

"Oh, yes. They are like new leaves uncurling on the buds of trees in the spring."

He stared at her, for the first time speechless himself. He just kissed her, which was in all actuality, highly uncalled for, yet she continued to discuss her topic as if nothing had happened, albeit more briefly. "It appears you are observant as well."

She cocked her head as she thought about his statement. "I believe I am observant about those items which stand out. Your eyes are unusual in their color."

He waited for more, but she seemed to have finished what she meant to say. Where was her prattle about leaves, nature, or even the kiss? "Do you mind that I kissed you?" Even as he said it, he wished he hadn't.

"No." She didn't blush, yet she blushed so often.

"Then am I to assume you are often kissed?"

Chuckling, she shook her head, genuinely finding his comment comical. "Hardly. You are the first."

Completely confounded by her odd reaction to such a momentous occasion in a young woman's life, he needed to understand. "Were you surprised, then?" He refused to ask if she enjoyed it.

"Most certainly. I did not think of you as a suitor."

"I'm not." He dropped his foot from the bench and took a step back, a mild panic starting in his gut. "I was merely hoping to refocus your attention."

Her brows raised, but her gaze left him. "I see. I do think it worked." She turned her head to look at him. "Yes, it most definitely did." She grinned, her happiness seemingly unbound. "By the beard of Zeus, you've fixed me."

She rose, coming closer, and he backed up a step.

"I'm beholden to you. If only I had known a simple kiss would make my prattle disappear. You simply don't know how wonderful this is."

Simple? He took umbrage to the word. It had not been simple. It had been complex, trying to kiss her while she spoke and then taste—"I'm pleased that I could be of service, though I would caution you from kissing every man you meet in order to converse in a more typical manner."

She stilled at that and the smile left her face, which he found he didn't like. Her eyes when she smiled seemed to glow, making her even prettier, and her cheeks rounded in, dare he think it, an adorable way. Maybe if she smiled mostly, she could also attract a husband.

"So you think it might be you in particular who must kiss me?"

He silenced a groan. "As much as I would like to accept the honor you so generously bestow upon me, I am not convinced that my action had anything to do with you concluding your dialogue. It could be that you had simply come to the end of your statement."

She contemplated his remarks, turning away as if she needed a moment of privacy. That did not bode well. How could such a simple solution to a temporary problem become complicated? Maybe if he could find another way to distract her, he could signal her from across the room, so as—

"I think you should kiss me again, then."

As she wasn't facing him, he wasn't sure he'd heard her correctly. "Did you say something?"

She turned to him and advanced. "Yes. I said that in order to determine if your kiss had an effect on my dialogue, we must kiss again. We learned in school that an experiment must be repeated more than once to glean any empirical data from it. So you must kiss me again."

She closed her eyes and puckered her lips.

What he wanted to do was run, but even in her ridiculous pose, he found it hard to resist her full lips. "But circumstances are quite different, as we are not having a conversation. Besides, I do believe that it was not the kiss itself, but the distraction that helped you focus." He had no reason to believe that were the case, but he needed her to open her eyes and stop offering him her lips.

As he hoped, she opened her eyes and relaxed her mouth. "I do see what you mean. Then I suggest that we start another conversation and if I begin to ramble, you can bring me back with a kiss." She gave a quick nod. "Yes, that would repeat all the elements of the first occasion nicely."

He was not one to panic, or to be of a frantic disposition, but at the moment, his gut burned as if it were being used as a grindstone and the resulting powder were acid.

She moved back to the bench and sat. "What topic should we choose? Oh, or should I stand? Would that be easier? No, then we wouldn't be repeating the same circumstances. I understand that is of the utmost importance." She patted the stone bench beside her. "And I do believe you had your foot up here?"

For the love of Jove, she could not honestly believe that he would kiss her again to prove to her it was or wasn't his kiss that had caused the end of her vocal wanderings?

"Dory?" His sister voice had never been so welcome. "Dory, are you still out here?"

Lady Dorothea's shoulders slumped, proving the extent of her disappointment. "I'm here."

He turned to see his sister in the adjacent court. "Rose, keep heading toward the lawn."

His sister's head snapped up, but she couldn't see him over the hedge.

"Was I really so far from you?" Rose finally came into view. "I do apologize, Dory, for leaving you so long with my brother, but wait until I tell you what we are doing tonight."

As his sister brushed by him to sit next to her friend, he took the opportunity to leave. "I'd best return to the house. I'm sure Sommerset is awake and I must fulfill my duties as his host."

His sister waved him off, but Lady Dorothea looked at him with determination.

Damn, he needed to discover what else could be done for her before she caught him alone once again. Adjusting his direction, he strode past the ballroom to the terrace outside the library. There had to be something in there that would help.

CHAPTER EIGHT

DORY COVERTLY WATCHED Lord Harewood as he engaged Lord Sommerset in conversation after dinner. His kiss earlier in the day had been a shock, but a far from unpleasant one. She was anxious to kiss him again for two reasons. The first was that she'd been so taken by surprise that she hadn't truly had time to observe all the nuances of the kiss. His pine scent was what she remembered the most, followed by the texture of his tongue. But just as a warm feeling started in her belly, he pulled away and her mind suddenly cleared with the utmost precision. It was this very effect that was her second reason for wishing for another kiss. She truly believed he could cure her penchant for prolonged oration.

He'd also sparked a riotous mickle of thoughts in her head as to his intentions, feelings, and suitability as a husband. No one had ever kissed her before. She'd worn more dresses than had dances, and no one had ever walked with her in the garden anywhere. To have Lord Harewood, known as a rather cool and stilted fish, be the one to kiss her was surprising. She equated him with a black lamppost in the daylight, with his dark clothes and hair. Could he actually have fire in his head like a lit streetlight? She stifled a chuckle at her own image but sobered quickly as she wished to find out. But how?

Just then, the butler entered the parlor. "My lady, the garden is ready."

The marchioness lifted her chin. "Thank you, Haggett. We will remove ourselves to there presently."

Rose grabbed Dory's wrist, her eyes sparkling. "I do believe Mother's vision will be magical."

Having been the recipient of all the details earlier in the day, she too anticipated the spectacle Lady Enderly had planned. Tonight was to make sure all would be perfect for when the rest of the guests would see it.

Lady Enderly rose. "Come, all. I need everyone to take a portion of the gardens to ensure we have the perfect effect. If you see any area unlit, be sure to come to me at once. Lord Enderly and I will inspect the six middle courts. Lord and Lady Sommerset, if you would take the most eastern seven? And, Felton, you can take the ladies with you to inspect the western courts. We have but an hour before the lights will go out, so be thorough but expedient." She looked pointedly at Rose, who silently nodded.

Lord Harewood walked to the settee and gestured with his arm toward the door. "May I suggest we exit by the library doors to start at the beginning of Mother's spectacle?"

Rose grabbed her hand and forced her to rise, not that she was hesitant to go. She was quite anxious to both see the lit gardens and be in Lord Harewood's company again.

Without answering her brother, Rose pulled her out of the room and down the corridor to the library, which had its doors open and a few lamps lit. Rose quickly led them out the French doors and across the wide but shallow terrace Dory had seen from her balcony. In no time, they were at the entrance to the gardens, which had very tall hedges and a beautiful arched bower, but in the dark of night, the bower was lit with very small lanterns, making it feel as if they'd walked into a faerie world.

"I love how Mother arranged this." Rose let go of her and fairly *skipped* into the first gathering area, what Lady Enderly called courts.

Dory walked beneath the lit bower and stopped, in awe of the beauty of the garden. This court boasted a small fish fountain, only the water did not flow because the fish held a lantern in its mouth, lighting the detail of the sculpted figures. Lanterns of all sizes hung from the three small trees and the hedge itself had small enclosed lights seemingly embedded in them.

"It's quite spectacular, is it not?"

At Lord Harewood's low voice behind her, she shivered, the sound so close to her that she felt it down to her toes. She didn't turn, though she wanted to. "It takes away my very breath."

He stepped up next to her. "Mother is quite proud of her garden. She lights it about every three years for some fete or another."

She wasn't sure whether she found it hard to breathe because of the beauty before her or the man beside her, but making any response was beyond her.

Rose, who had been inspecting all the lighting, came back to her. "This area is perfect. Let's proceed. Mother won't have it relit until the culmination of our first week of guests."

She nodded but couldn't seem to move.

"May I escort you through my mother's very own Vauxhall?" His tone made it clear he thought his mother's creation somewhat tedious, even as he offered his arm.

Did the man not appreciate the beauty and joy in life? That concerning thought loosened her tongue. "This is far more beautiful than Vauxhall. The detail and placement of every light has been carefully thought out. Do you not see the splendor of this creation?" She finally looked at him and wished she hadn't. The soft lighting made him seem far less stiff and much kinder than perhaps he was.

"If you take my arm, I will be happy to reply."

Very much wanting to know his thoughts, she laid her hand on his arm and allowed him to walk her forward, but she would not be thwarted. "Now, as to your appreciation or lack thereof."

"I can understand your wonderment. However, having seen this sight since a child, the wonder has faded. It is simply lanterns in a garden to me."

"So do you look at a sunrise or sunset in the same way? If you see *Timon of Athens* performed for the third time at the Theatre Royal in Drury Lane, is it then just another evening about Town?"

He stiffened slightly beneath her hand but otherwise gave no other indication that he was insulted by her words. "I'm afraid that is the case." He paused, but she sensed there was more. "Once I saw life as you do, a new daily adventure of discovery and joy. But I am jaded, older than my years, as my mother complains. The entertainments that so many of my peers find enjoyable are simply a way to spend time for me."

The sting of tears hit her eyes, and she blinked them back. He could not be more than a handful of years older than she. Surely, it was not because he was a man. Even Lord Sommerset, his contemporary, appreciated the nuances of life.

"Dory, could you make sure all twelve lanterns are in the tree over the bench?" At Rose's request, Dory reluctantly released the earl and stepped up onto the low bench.

He set his hand under her arm to steady her, though she was quite well balanced, despite her unskilled display of the waltz. Quickly, she counted the lights. Turning back toward the court, she caught sight of Rose heading into the next one. "There are exactly a dozen."

When Rose didn't reply, Dory looked to Lord Harewood, who was almost as tall as she standing on the bench, which made her feel much more equal. "So a new dish or aria does nothing to engender happiness for you?"

"No. However, that does not mean I am not pleased to go through the paces of life. My heart simply does not beat faster for anything in particular. I suppose that means it will last much longer." Though he chuckled, there was something in the sound that seemed sad to her.

Suddenly, she remembered what Rose told her about Lord Harewood betting on Lord Sommerset marrying a Mabry. "Do you not feel joy when a bet you set down comes to fruition despite everyone else betting against you?"

His eyes widened in surprise. "My Lady Dorothea, I'm shocked you would mention such an activity." Though the words were to be expected, the amusement in his eyes was not.

Understanding that he teased her once again as he did his friends, the Earl and Countess of Sommerset, had her cheeks heating, not in embarrassment, but in pleasure. "No more shocked than I was to learn you participated in such. Do tell me. Does winning when no one else sees what you foresee cause your heart to beat faster?"

He grinned, and in the light, it made him appear far more handsome and approachable. "It would seem you have found me out, though to be honest, I had not thought on it before."

That he could find joy in something, even if it was betting, relieved her. It was as if that small presence of humanity meant there could be more buried beneath the surface. "I wonder if perhaps it is the uncertainty."

"No, I am quite certain when I place a bet on what will occur. That cannot be it."

She searched among her knowledge of philosophy. The three ancient ones—Plato, Aristotle, and Socrates—had much to say on happiness, but even as she thought through what she knew, she could not find what she sought. "Perhaps, then, it is the satisfaction of being correct despite, shall we say, the odds. To go against the norm and be considered odd or worse, unacceptable, only to later be revered as brilliant, must indeed engender a feeling of happiness. Perhaps it is a feeling of happiness with oneself, or it could be a happiness of intellect in knowing what others do not know and cannot see." A small part of her recognized she followed another squiggly line, but it was far too intriguing to stop. "That does bring up the question of whether an intellectual happiness is possible and of equal value to an emotional happiness. As much as we like to believe that as human beings, we can think without emotion, that is far from the truth and some think with emotion far more than they think without it. So, then, is there such a possibility as an intellectual happiness?"

His eyes twinkled with evident amusement as he listened intently.

She wanted to stop but couldn't. "On the other hand, it could well be that the intellect is fully engaged, which brings about that satisfaction or emotional happiness. In that instance, it would be a happiness that is triggered by the intellect and—" Without thought, she grabbed his head and pressed her lips to his to stop her own dialogue.

His closed lips were firm yet soft, and she licked at them.

He sucked in a breath, and she thrust her tongue past his parted lips. Immediately, her thoughts flew away and her blood pounded in her ears. His hands found her waist as he stepped closer, his tongue now tangling with hers and causing a million faeries to flit throughout her body, making her far warmer than usual. A desire to draw closer had her taking a step, except she found no purchase.

As she fell forward, she was lifted to the ground and his mouth left hers.

She looked up at him, startled, her ideas flying back into a neat line in her head. "...manifested in emotion."

His brows drew down, but his lips curved upward as he stared at her in puzzlement and amusement. "My Lady Dorothea, I do feel somewhat put upon."

"I apologize, my lord. Did you not like the kiss?"

His lips flattened, all sense of humor disappearing. "Why would you ask that? Because I feel put upon? Or is there another reason?"

His mother was right—he did answer a question with multiple questions. "I ask because it seemed to me, novice that I am, that you enjoyed the kiss as much as I. Therefore, I do not understand why you would feel put upon." The warm, fuzzy feeling she had begun to feel in her belly had cooled considerably at his attitude.

"Ladies do not go about kissing men. As a lady and student of

Belinda's school, you must know that you could tarnish its reputation with such behavior."

Indignation rifled through her that he had that very afternoon kissed her with little thought to the consequences, yet when she kissed him in relative darkness, it was suddenly of the utmost insult to propriety? How dare he presume—oh. She felt her cheeks flame anew. He must know of her mother.

Shame washed over her. Unable to bear it, she lifted her skirts and strode into the next court, catching sight of Rose before her vision blurred. Had she accomplished what even her mother hadn't been able to? Had she tarnished her own reputation? Taking a deep breath, she moved closer to the fountain of Neptune that rose at the center of the gathering area.

Rose, examining the hedge at the back, noticed her. "Could you make sure all the lanterns about the fountain are working properly? Mother is very particular."

"Of course." She managed to speak with no catch in her voice and forced herself to look at each and every lantern, from those below the stone basin to the ones suspended above it from a tree. It was quite ingenious, and if she hadn't just kissed a man and ruined herself, she would further investigate. Unfortunately, her thoughts were firmly placed on the damage she'd perpetrated upon herself.

As she came back around to where she started, she halted as Lord Harewood stood with arms folded, watching her. Ignoring him was her only option, so she continued past, determined to examine the lights above the archway that led to the next court.

"Lady Dorothea."

Blast, he could not mean to continue their conversation. But to continue to walk away was far too rude, so she halted. Lifting her chin, she turned around. "Yes, Lord Harewood."

"I believe you were discussing the satisfaction of the intellect causing the emotion referred to as happiness."

She blinked. Happiness? By the beard of Zeus, he did mean to continue! Well aware that Rose was within hearing distance, she folded her own arms. "I was unaware that you were familiar with such an emotion. If I remember, you did say that happiness was not part of your life."

Rose sucked in her breath audibly, but the earl simply raised his brows. "And so I did. How good of you to remember."

The last was said with such sardonic intent that Dory barely kept herself from marching over to him and slapping his face. "I assure you, my lord, that my memory is quite remarkable and my intellect equal to your own."

A soft giggle came from Rose, who now bent over by a bench doing who knew what.

The earl dropped his arms and took two steps toward her before stopping. In the shadow cast by the limited lighting, it was now more difficult to see his face. "And I can assure you that my state of happiness, unhappiness, anger, or pique are all quite in harmony."

"As I can hardly attest to that, I will accept your word on that subject. My curiosity about it was merely to pass the time."

He opened his mouth to answer her obvious insult when she heard rustling behind her. She turned in time to find Lady Enderly bearing down on them.

"Felton!" The lady strode into the court, glanced over the area quickly, then turned on Dory. "What are you doing alone out here with my son?"

Surprised by the accusation and not a little guilty for kissing that very man just moments earlier, she took a step back.

"Mother."

Lady Enderly turned on her son. "Why must I keep saving you from scheming women?"

Her heart stopped in her chest. She tried to breathe, but the shock of such an insult caught her off guard.

"You don't." Lord Harewood's voice remained calm, but with an edge as sharp as honed steal to it, and there was a slight tick beneath his right ear. "As similar to the last time, you are wrong in your assumptions."

Realizing there was more to the current event than what she knew, Dory took a deep breath at last and lifted her skirts, anxious to leave.

"No, Lady Dorothea. Please stay a moment." Though he said it kindly, she could sense his anger just beneath the surface. "I feel it only fitting that you witness my mother's embarrassment."

Lady Enderly pulled air in through her teeth. "*My* embarrassment? Felton, you—"

"He means me, Mother." Rose stood from her crouched position. "The *three* of us were inspecting your creation, as *you* requested. Dory, did you find any lantern lights amiss on the fountain?"

She quickly answered. "All were lit, but the one from above was weaker than the rest. I wasn't certain if that was purposeful or not." She wanted nothing more than to be away from the situation.

Rose walked toward her with a smile. "I believe my mother can decide that. Since we have finished our inspection, let's go inside. I know Cook made baked apple pudding and I'm quite smitten with autumn apples."

As Rose took her hand and pulled her along, Dory glanced backward once to see that Lady Enderly and Lord Harewood both stood frozen in place. Despite the warm, summer night air, she felt chilled by the whole episode and shivered.

Rose leaned in. "You won't want to know what is said. They can go on and on. When I was little, I'd hide in the kitchen. They will both be in a sour mood all day tomorrow."

She nodded as if she understood, but she didn't. She was particularly confused by what his mother had said. "Has your brother been caught alone with a lady before?"

"Yes. Well, no. Actually, it was all my fault." Rose let go of her hand as they stepped through the French doors of the library. She stopped to make sure no one was about. "We don't talk about it, probably because Mother doesn't wish me to feel horrible, but I still do."

This time, Dory took Rose's hand and pulled her to the closest piece of furniture, which happened to be a chair behind a large desk. "Sit. You must tell me. Maybe it wasn't as horrible as you imagine it."

Rose slumped into the chair. "Oh, it was. You see, I felt bad for Lady Garmoyle, who had recently lost her husband. She was quite nice to me, so I invited her to spend the holidays."

"That doesn't sound horrible. That was very kind of you."

"Yes, but as it happened, she didn't want to spend the holidays with me. She just wanted to have access to my brother and Lord Sommerset to seek her revenge."

Now, that was much more concerning. Not having anywhere to sit, she leveraged herself up on the desk to listen. "What was the revenge for? Did she succeed?"

"Almost." Rose looked toward the fireplace that was across the room. "I wasn't quite sure how she'd been insulted, but from what I gathered, she'd tried to trap Lord Sommerset into marriage by luring him into the garden alone. But since neither he nor my brother trusted her, my brother secretly strolled through the garden with the lady's mother. When Lady Garmoyle tried to claim Lord Sommerset had taken liberties, Felton and the lady's mother were witnesses to the lack of such actions. So despite having later married someone else, she was still angry that she'd been foiled."

Why a person would go to such lengths for revenge after being married and widowed was far beyond her comprehension. "So based on what your mother stated, the widow thought she was alone with your brother?"

Rose's head snapped around to look at her. "Oh, no. It was much worse. She thought she had succeeded in maneuvering my brother to be alone in this very library with Lady Sommerset! Of course, she was Lady Ameila last year and would have been forced to marry my brother."

Knowing a bit about both the lady and Lord Harewood, Dory's belly tightened into a ball no faerie could puncture. Did

Lord Sommerset call his good friend out? "Please, tell me quickly. What happened?"

Rose gave her a questioning look before she continued. "As it happened, unbeknownst to Lady Garmoyle, Lady Sommerset's father had secreted himself away in the library and was sitting in that chair right there." Rose pointed to one of two wingback chairs that faced the fireplace so their backs were toward the doorway to the corridor.

That the earl had indeed not been forced to lose his only friend for even a short while was reassuring. "I imagine your brother was quite relieved."

Rose shrugged. "He had not been worried, as he'd noticed Lord Wakefield immediately because Lady Amelia had been talking to her father when my brother had entered. *I* was the one who felt horrible. Yet, as Lady Garmoyle protested, I still believed her. I fear I was so desperate to have a friend who liked my company that I did not question her motives."

"I quite enjoy your company, as you are so easy to converse with and have such a warm spirit." Dory laid her hand over her heart. "And I promise you, Rose, I have no such motive of revenge against your brother."

Rose's lips twitched. "Well, at least one of us doesn't."

Surprised, she widened her eyes. "What has he done to you?"

Rose sat up in the chair, her grin quite real. "What hasn't he? He's teased me my whole life. He wins every debate because he is far too smart and I can't keep up." Her smile turned to a smirk and she wiggled her brow. "I have managed my own revenge over the years. Once I discovered that the unexpected unbalanced him, I have done everything from spilled gravy on his clothes to put thorns beneath his sheets."

"You didn't." She was quite shocked. She'd never had such a relationship with her older brother. "What did he do?"

A soft look came into Rose's eyes. "Nothing. Oh, he grumbled to me and swore retribution, but he never followed through. And when our mother asked how his face got scratched or why his pantaloons were wet, he made an excuse, never revealing the truth."

Dory's heart warmed at the obvious implication. He loved and protected his sister. There was a kind and sweet person somewhere beneath the Earl of Harewood's boring and stiff exterior, which made her even more curious as to why he had such a hard shell. He was like a macaron that was hard on the outside and soft in the middle. She did so enjoy those. Which reminded her of Rose's suggestion. "Did you not say that your cook made baked apple pudding today?"

Rose jumped from the chair, her good humor restored. "I did, and we must have some. I like to have cocoa with mine."

"I've never had cocoa with them. I usually have tea."

Rose headed for the library doors. "Well, do be quick. I'll have Haggett send everything to your room and we can enjoy them without the rest of my family."

She hopped down from the desk and strode out after Rose, but she had already disappeared. Quickly ascending the stairs, Dory found her thoughts straying back to Lord Harewood. His fury had been palpable, but it hadn't been directed at her and for that, she was thankful. Though he'd been irritated with her, his feelings toward his mother were difficult to explain, but if she were the marchioness, she'd duck and run because the image of Lord Harewood that came to her mind was that of a well-loaded cannon.

CHAPTER NINE

FELTON STOOD ON the terrace outside the library, refusing to partake in the niceties of welcoming guests to his home, or rather, his parents' home. He had his own, not far from Sunnydale. Was he punishing his mother? Yes. Should he? That was a moot question. Her attack upon Lady Dorothea, whom he was quite positive had never even contemplated being so devious as to trap a man into marriage, had infuriated him. That his mother assumed he couldn't master his own affairs on top of it had caused a rift in his feelings for his parent that he wasn't sure would ever be bridged.

It was not that his mother was a mean person by nature, but her overzealous need for societal approval would sometimes make her forget that at her core, she was a good woman. Rose was like her, but Rose simply handled society differently by playing the role. It saddened him because he wished her a man who could look beneath the surface she presented to society and treasure her for the warm, good-hearted person she was.

There was only one woman he'd ever known who had been able to be warm and caring while at the same time be what society expected, even though she'd never debuted. He'd fallen in love with Belinda as a young boy and by the age of sixteen, couldn't refrain from kissing her. He smiled softly as he thought back to that afternoon when they were in the village at a traveling fair. They had walked behind the puppeteer show to see how it was done and were disappointed to find a wall between them and their answer. Noticing they were alone, he couldn't help but kiss her.

He'd received a well-deserved slap for his trouble. But even as she ran off in a huff, he'd been quite proud of himself, though explaining his red cheek to his mother had been a bit difficult.

The sound of the French doors opening behind him had him stiffening even as he scowled that someone would search him out when he obviously didn't wish to be found.

"Ah, so here you are. Hiding."

At the sound of Sommerset's voice, he relaxed. "Not hiding. Making a point."

Sommerset stepped up next to him, appearing to study the lawn where pall-mall would be played. "Looks like pouting."

He faced his friend. "I do not pout. I make a point in whatever way is necessary."

"I'm assuming you are not happy with your mother once again since she has been greeting the guests without you by her side."

"That would be correct." He didn't miss the use of the word "again." It did seem as if he and his mother had been at odds his whole life. No, that was not true. Only since Belinda had passed and she'd started trying to encourage him to choose another Mabry lady to marry.

"I don't know what caused the argument this time, but she is being very solicitous to Lady Dorothea. So much so that not only did my wife notice it, but so did I, and you know these things usually pass me by with little acknowledgment."

He harrumphed at that. Sommerset was almost as observant as he was.

"Did the argument perhaps have something to so with Lady Dorothea? As one of her chaperones, I should probably be informed."

He considered his answer carefully, not wanting to reveal too much. "Suffice it to say, my mother made accusations with no facts, and I scolded her for it."

Sommerset chuckled. "I gather she thought something was about between you and the lady in question. I would think she would know you better. Lady Dorothea is hardly the right match for you. She is far too warm, innocent, and kind, if a bit of a rambler."

His friend's description of the lady sounded so much like Belinda that he took umbrage, but with the last descriptor, he was able to let it pass like a bird heading south. "Yes, she does appear to enjoy talking in squiggly lines."

Sommerset's brows rose. "Squiggly lines? Not circles?"

He barely held back his smile. "No, she assures me it's squiggly lines."

At Sommerset's laughter, Felton felt his pique vanish. "Mother is not happy that the lady is here because she's afraid that Rose will wish to attend the Belinda School for Curious Ladies even more than she already does."

"I didn't realize Rose had such high aspirations."

"You consider the school of high quality, then?"

Sommerset pondered his question for a few moments before answering. "I do. Though to be truthful, at first, I did so simply because my wife lectures there on occasion, and no, she doesn't teach painting. That's not one of the classes. But the more we visited, and the more I came to know the Duke and Duchess of Northwick, I came to understand the purpose and quality of the education."

His friend's opinion held a lot of sway over him. "Then I must ask you, since you know the school and my sister, do you think Rose would benefit from attending?" Though barely a few seconds elapsed, his stomach knotted, far too anxious for the answer.

"I'm not sure what you mean by 'benefit.' Since it's a school on par with Oxford, though much stricter since it is for ladies of the peerage, by definition, it benefits the minds of those who attend."

"But would it make Rose more sought after by appropriate men?"

Sommerset's brows rose. "Is that why she wants to attend, to make herself more popular among the men?"

At his nod, Sommerset's brows furrowed. "I thought Lady Rose would be having to choose among multiple offers her very first season. I'm stymied why that isn't the case, so I can't say if attending the school would benefit her."

It wasn't what he'd hoped to learn, but he appreciated his friend's honesty. "I believe her inability to garner a proposal has to do with her ability to be accepted."

"I understand. She is like two different people. Do you think if she showed society who she is, she'd have more offers? It's not as if the *ton* encourages eccentricities like Lady Dorothea."

Felton's immediate reaction was to defend the lady, but his logical side had to agree. In fact, it was that very unusual part of her he was hoping to rectify. "I don't consider my sister to be that eccentric."

"Yes, of course. Throwing food and tipping tea trays is really quite the norm." Though Sommerset kept a serious face, his tawny eyes laughed at him.

"She only acts in that way among those she knows won't judge her."

"Exactly."

Since his path of inquiry had led him to a dead end, he posed the question that he most wanted Sommerset's opinion on. "Do you think my sister will *lessen* her chances by going to the school?"

"Now, that is a difficult question to answer. It could since people were beginning to think the women there bluestockings until Lady Elsbeth married Lord Mabry."

Having maneuvered his friend onto the subject he was anxious to pursue, he continued his inquiry. "Is it simply that these women have an education or is there something else? Is it that they are considered unusual simply for attending?"

Sommerset shook his head and opened his mouth but then closed it. Finally, he spoke. "This is only my own observation, and I do believe my wife would have far more knowledge on the matter, though I'm sure she is biased, but it appears that these women, all of whom have rather unique flaws, have brought closer scrutiny to themselves *because* they attend the school and so their uniqueness, shall we say, becomes far more of a problem in a potential wife."

He was pleased that Sommerset had confirmed his own suspicions, yet not pleased that his own task for both his sister's sake and Belinda's good name seemed far more monumental than he had first thought. "I appreciate your candor. I will seek your wife's counsel as well on this matter since if my sister does not receive a proposal by the end of this house party, my father has given permission for her to attend the school."

"Then wouldn't it behoove you to meet the many young men who are arriving and judge which would make your sister a good husband? Then the issue of the school would no longer matter."

As tempting as that suggestion was, he knew his sister's wishes. If that wasn't enough motivation to not help suitors for his sister's hand, Lady Dorothea's future was now at stake, and he was quite determined to solve that problem. "If I were to meet those men now, that would be far too agreeable to my mother. No, I believe I will simply support my sister in whatever she wishes to do."

"You are a better sibling than I." Sommerset shook his head. "I am forever at odds with my younger brother."

Sommerset's younger brother, Christopher, was just that…younger. "Is it that mistress he had while at Oxford?"

"If only that were the problem. Despite my warnings and our father's example, a mistress alone would be a blessing. I'm worried I'll find him dead in a gutter one day."

He clapped his friend on the shoulder that had slumped. "Do

not worry. Remember our misspent youth in the brothels and gaming hells. We made it through alive, much to your wife's satisfaction, I guess."

Sommerset smirked. "True. But we were first born. He seems hellbent on laughing his way through life."

Felton chuckled, unable to stifle it. "I had the same thought about you after we left Eaton for Oxford."

"You did? I was not so rakish as that."

He raised his brows and stared at his friend. "Weren't you?"

"I most certainly was not. And before you say another word, I'm going to return to my wife before she grows irritable at my absence." With that, Sommerset turned on his heel and strode back into the library, leaving the terrace doors open.

"Coward." Despite his good humor, his mind returned to the dilemma of Lady Dorothea, or rather the school's reputation. He'd spent the morning skimming through a few of his father's books on the human mind. He'd hoped to find a malady like the one Lady Dorothea had, but nothing was remotely similar. Most of what he'd read was merely theory. It appeared it was up to him to discover how to help her stay within the confines of a normal conversation. Trial and error were not the most efficient way to experiment, but it was what he was left with, so based upon his reading, he'd formulated a plan.

Of course, first, he'd have to make it clear that there would be no more kisses between them. For him to remain in control of his mother, he could not allow any more of such behavior, no matter how much he enjoyed it. He dared not give Lady Dorothea hope that there could ever be a relationship between them. Perhaps he should—

The sound of the library doors opening and closing reached him.

Now who was it? Quickly, he stepped out of sight. Not hearing a conversation, he concluded it had to be a single individual, most likely his father, skipping away for a quick drink and some quiet. Cautiously, he looked inside. At first, he didn't see her, as her deep-blue dress matched the velvet of the wingback chairs exactly.

Lady Dorothea. Perfect. Striding in, he moved to the fireplace before which she sat.

"Oh." She sprang up. "I didn't know anyone was in here. I'll go." She turned away and headed for the doors.

"Wait. I wish to talk to you."

She looked about. "I cannot. Your mother has been so nice to me today. I do not want to incur her wrath again."

Devil it, she was correct. "Then I'll have Haggett fetch Lady Sommerset. Perhaps you could wait on the terrace?"

Still uncertain, she hesitated.

"I promise you, I have no argument with you. My upset was strictly with my mother."

Finally, she nodded and scurried across the room and outside.

Striding out of the library, he found the butler in the foyer. After telling him to fetch Lady Sommerset, for Lady Dorothea needed her assistance, he waited in the corridor.

As Lady Sommerset exited the parlor, and he could hear the sound of many feminine voices. After the door closed and she searched the immediate area, he stepped from the shadows. "Lady Sommerset, this way."

The lady, dressed in a lilac day dress, shook her head. "I should have guessed you were involved. What have you done with Lady Dorothea now?"

He straightened to his full height and frowned. "I do not know what I've done to engender such a remark, especially when I have asked you to attend her. I wish to speak to her, but she needs her chaperone."

Lady Sommerset's secret smile appeared, which was never a good omen. "Of course. That is my role during our stay. Where is she?"

He offered her his arm and she took it. "This way. She was in the library but decided to wait on the terrace. She is particularly concerned about incurring my mother's scorn."

"I don't know why. Your mother seems to have taken a sudden liking to her."

"Yes, well, that was not by her choice."

"Hmm, why do I have a feeling this is all connected to you leaving your parents and sister alone to greet the guests as they arrive?"

He halted at the closed doors to the library. "Because, my lady, you are particularly astute."

Lady Sommerset laughed even as she took her hand from his arm and opened one of the doors herself. "Flattery will get you far, Harewood." Striding forward, the lady stepped outside and spoke to Lady Dorothea, who nodded before entering.

Not wanting anything to appear improper, he met her halfway. "May we speak, then?"

She looked over her shoulder to make sure Lady Sommerset was within sight then nodded. "Yes. What do you wish to discuss?"

Her manner was somewhat reserved, and he didn't like it. "First, why did you seek the sanctuary of the library? Did my mother cause your wish to escape?"

"No. As I said, she's been very kind. It was simply that there were so many women. I don't believe I've ever been in a parlor with that many. Even at school, there are only the five of us. And I only know these women by acquaintance, so it is difficult to converse, not knowing what subjects they have an interest in that I might know something about."

As she spoke, she relaxed. He was pleased that she could speak freely with him. "And what subjects *were* they discussing?"

"Well, there are the many activities that Lady Enderly has planned, which has spurred conversations on appropriate clothing, the latest fashion, the travel experience from when each came, and the men who have arrived or will be arriving."

He stifled a grin. "Then I'm to assume my father has the men out and about?"

"Yes. They are in the stables at the moment, though—they

have been there for hours. I imagine they went for a ride, but how could they if he doesn't know when the next gentleman will arrive? I have never been to a house party, so I'm still assimilating to the protocols."

Assimilating to the protocols? He found her phrasing intriguing. "Today is only the first day. I'm sure you will find this party very educational."

Her face brightened and the lighter specks in her eyes seemed to dance. "I never thought of it that way. Here I was feeling awkward and out of place, but if I approach this party like a class at school or a lecture at the Royal Institution, then I'll feel much more comfortable. No, not a lecture. It must be something where I am a part of it. If I think of this like going to a Panorama or Vauxhall or a museum, then it will be much more familiar. I hadn't thought about this experience that way. The way we approach events creates the pathways we take in life. Each one offers us…"

He grinned, unable to hide his pleasure in her ideas. Part of him disliked it that he would try to help her better fit into society's expectations, but if he was to make Belinda's school a place that was revered, he had to. Still, if she proved able to make the necessary changes, he would miss this. Her mind was truly beautiful and far too many men would never see that nor understand it. She was like the rose that cross-pollenates and blooms not red and not white, but a mixture of both, beautiful in its uniqueness. Yet it would be dug out and discarded because it did not bloom the color that was wished for.

"…that is why making mistakes is so important. They are our most valuable lessons, yet there are many places where these are not accepted."

A warmth filled his chest, and he found himself smiling even as she continued, completely unaware of how delightful she was.

"We must all be perfect, but that is not part of our creation. We are born imperfect and to aspire to such is fruitless. In addition, if we were to achieve such perfection—"

He pulled her to him and kissed her. Her lips were open and he slipped his tongue between them.

She responded with something close to glee and opened wider, grasping him around the middle and pressing her bountiful breasts against his ribs.

Not immune to the feminine curves in his arms, he deepened the kiss, tilting her head and inhaling the lemony scent that was her and her alone. It wrapped around his senses, leaving him in a cocoon of her making.

Her soft moan filled his mouth, and he snapped his eyes open. What was he doing? He pulled away, even stepping back as if she were a siren who had magical powers, but he could still taste her.

She opened her eyes. "…we would be boring." She grinned, very pleased at something.

He, on the other hand, was anything but. His reaction to her was far from appropriate, especially since he hoped to get her married off post-haste. That she somehow linked him to being boring did not sit well with ego, either. "Boring?"

"Yes. If we were all perfect, I do believe it would be utterly boring. There would be nothing to critique. Can you imagine our conversations?"

He prided himself on being able to follow her, but devil it, he couldn't seem to concentrate. How could she rattle on after that kiss? "I just kissed you."

She nodded. "Yes, you did. Again." She glanced toward the terrace doors, where Lady Sommerset stood, her back to them, no doubt purposefully. "I find it so very helpful."

Helpful? His wits must be addled, but he found himself asking, anyway. "How is a kiss helpful?"

"It's hard to explain."

"Try." His tone came out harsh, but he didn't care one wit. The woman was beyond baffling.

She looked at the ceiling, as if it could help her figure out her own thoughts. "I think the best way to describe it is like a tangled mess of twine."

Bloody twine? He just frowned, his patience wearing away.

"Yes, that's it. My thoughts form a tangled mess of twine in my head, and when you kiss me, or I kiss you, the twine shoots skyward and disappears. Then when you stop, it comes back down in a neat line in my mind, and I can speak upon one idea at a time."

As much as he wanted to growl, he refrained because her analogy actually made sense in an odd way, though why he would expect it to be a normal way, he didn't know. He stepped back further, behind a small table as much to avoid the temptation of her now rather plump lips and rosy cheeks as to contemplate what to do with this new revelation.

When he didn't reply, she clasped her hands together. "Is that not a usual reaction to a kiss?"

Her question had his body heating again as it remembered how much he enjoyed the sensation of kissing her. Though irritated by his own response to her, his pride was somewhat soothed by the description of her reaction to him. That his kiss caused her to lose her many ideas was telling. "Yes, it is common to lose all thought during a kiss." But what to make of the rest of it?

"Then I simply must kiss you more often."

Even as he stiffened, she frowned. "But that is highly improper." Her hazel gaze found his, and he could clearly see the sadness in her eyes as tears gathered there. "Then there is no hope for me. I must ramble my life away or be silent. If I can just be silent long enough to attract a husband before..." She turned away, not finishing her sentence.

Before what? Before her fourth season? Before she graduated from the school? Before she made a fool of herself in public? Before—It hit him hard as he suddenly understood her fear, her reaction to his mother's accusation in the garden, to him being in the library alone when she'd come in.

He was a fairly observant fellow and had not missed her

mother slipping into the garden at the last ball, or her noticeable absence when supposedly chaperoning her daughter. It always seemed the Mabrys came to her rescue. It was obvious she needed to marry before her mother caused a scandal and made all chances of marriage disappear. Unfortunately, she was correct. Men would assume she would be similar, yet he alone knew the innocence of her first kiss.

The same protective feeling he felt for his sister rose up into his chest. He also was obligated to make things right, as her innocence would be questioned the first time another man kissed her. Even at the thought of their kiss, his body reacted again. Devil it. "I may have a solution." Even as he said the words, he was well aware it was nothing more than an experiment, but if it worked, they both would be pleased with the outcome.

She sniffed but didn't face him. "What kind of solution?"

Reaching into his pocket, he took out a handkerchief and forced himself to walk to her and offer it.

She accepted and wiped her eyes, then crumpled it in her hand and turned to face him.

He returned to his place behind the table, not wanting to allow for any appearance of impropriety. He glanced to the open doors and found Lady Sommerset sketching. She held a wooden board no larger than her hand with a sheet of paper on it and used a small pencil. She was a terrible chaperone.

Turning back to Lady Dorothea, he found her lips quirking. "Lady Sommerset is always prepared to capture the beauty of the moment. It makes her happy."

Her remark reminded him of what she'd said in the garden about being happy. She was right—he was happy when he won a bet. From now on, he would be more observant of his own instances of happiness. But at the moment, he wished to make her happy. "After much research," which had yielded him nothing but had instigated his own ideas, "I have a way to help you stay in a conversation without losing your compatriots—and without kissing me."

Her eyebrows rose. "Truly?"

He would not lie, as he could not be sure. "If you can keep any response to three sentences at the most, it will curb your thoughts and eliminate more robust, hmm, squiggly lines."

"It will?" The excitement in her face made him uncomfortable. "How?"

"The reason this can work, and I say *can* because only you can do it, is because it forces you to focus on two items at once. You will focus on not only what you wish to say, but also on how many sentences, thereby forcing you to choose the best statements to make a point. Both parameters will help you limit your replies."

"That does make sense. It would keep the twine to three strings at most. How tangled could they possibly get?" She grinned and held up three fingers.

He understood that she had just responded in three sentences. Pleased by her effort, he nodded approvingly. "Well done."

Her smile faltered. "And if I go over the allotted three? What should I do? There need to be ramifications, don't you think?"

The thought of that did not please him at all. "Is that what they do at Belinda's school?"

She waved his words away, looking toward the terrace doors once more. "Of course not. But this is far more important than the Pythagorean theorem or Copernican principle. This is about my future."

"What do you propose?"

Her brows lowered then she snapped her head back to meet his gaze. "If I fail in my goal, I will be silent for the rest of the event, whatever it will be." She pointed at him. "But you must promise not to draw me out when I am silent, as you are wont to do."

The back of his neck pricked at her deduction of his actions over the last couple of days. "I agree to respect your silence."

"Good. So no more kisses and only three sentences."

Even as he imagined what the fortnight would be like if she

succeeded, he squelched the inclination to tell her she needn't be that way with him. Her success would be the beginning of his success and that of Belinda's school, and all the students there would benefit, including his sister. He could not ask for more. It was a simple solution that put all the work firmly on her small shoulders.

Even as guilt snaked its way into his conscience, he pushed it aside. Lady Dorothea would benefit as well, perhaps even garner a proposal. It stood to reason that she would make the change for the better.

But was it truly for the better?

Lady Dorothea moved toward him. "Thank you for thinking of me. Your sister said you are very different from what everyone thinks of you, and I can see she was correct. I'd best gather Lady Sommerset and begin practicing my new conversation skills." She snapped her mouth shut and grinned, then strode outside.

For some reason, the triumph he'd expected to feel was missing. This was definitely not one of those moments of happiness, but it should have been. Not willing to contemplate the feeling any longer, he left the library and made his way down to the billiard room. He would help his father with his hosting duties and observe the men his mother hoped to pair with his sister. Perhaps one there could appreciate Lady Dorothea as well.

CHAPTER TEN

DORY HAPPILY ENJOYED the first course, white soup. She had come to dinner quite pleased with herself, and to celebrate had worn her favorite blue dress. It helped bring out the blue flecks in her hazel eyes, which made them more the norm.

She'd spent the rest of the afternoon with the ladies, most of whom seemed quite nice and many of whom she had spoken to during the season. She'd had to silence herself twice. It would have been once, but as Lady Arabella had asked her a question to involve her in the conversation, it would have been rude not to answer. She'd allowed herself many replies, but upon a longer response, promptly stopped conversing again.

Perfection had never been her forte, nor did she wish it, so her two lapses were a very good beginning. It had been difficult, though, and when sent to her room to rest before dinner, she'd found herself falling asleep almost instantly. But now refreshed, she was quite ready for the challenge of the meal, which should be much easier since they did all have to eat. It also helped that the Earl of Dearling, a handsome man with light-brown hair, dark-brown eyes, and a quick smile, was seated to her right. She'd never encountered him before he arrived at Sunnydale, so she could make a good first impression.

Unfortunately, on her left was Lord Leighhall, a viscount she'd spoken to before, but who had walked away from their conversation. He was quite handsome with his blue eyes, blond hair, and rather long sideburns, but his fair looks hid a poor disposition, in her opinion. He was the oldest of the single men by at least ten years. She planned to speak to him as little as possible, which made her exercise in conversation rather easy. In addition, across from her was Lord and Lady Sommerset, a Lord Manning, whom she knew of but had only been introduced to earlier, and Lady Arabella, whom she quite liked after getting to know her better in the parlor. The lady, with her chestnut hair and brown eyes, was unremarkable in appearance, but her demeanor was lively and very engaging.

However, she was not a little disappointed that Lord Harewood had been placed much farther down the table of twenty-four, next to his mother. She glanced his way to see him talking to the lady on his right. She had hoped he could witness her success at dinner, only because it was at his instruction that she engaged in such a difficult exercise.

"Tell me, Lady Dorothea. Can you give us a hint as to what activities we should expect over the coming weeks?"

Lord Dearling's address had her turning her attention to him.

"I'm to understand you arrived early and perhaps have been privy to what entertainments Lord and Lady Enderly have devised, besides billiards, of course." He smiled warmly at her, his interest in her reply absolute.

"To be sure, my lord, I'm not certain if I am to tell, but I can say that there will be many of the usual amusements, with a surprise or two." Pleased she kept her answer to one sentence, she lifted her wine to take a small sip.

"The usual? Would you say you excel at all these usual activities?"

She set her glass down while shaking her head. "Oh, my, I fear I am quite horrid at pall-mall. I do think I may simply watch. I could not imagine anyone would wish to partner with me, for they are sure to lose." Lord Dearling's eyes widened in surprise, making her re-count her sentences, but she'd only spoken three.

However, discussing her shortcomings wasn't perhaps the best course.

"Then I hope you will allow me to offer you some instruction. We could be partners, as I find the enjoyment of the game is in the playing of it, not in the triumph."

"And well you should, Dearling." Lord Manning, who sat across from Lord Dearling, smirked. "As I recall, last time you played, more than one ball went missing in the pond."

Lord Dearling frowned, obviously not as comfortable with his own shortcomings as she was with hers.

She wished to make him feel better about them. "Lord Manning, there is no need to worry about anyone's balls falling into a pond, mine included."

The man raised his dark eyebrows is question but didn't speak. Though he had darker hair than Lord Dearling and brown eyes to match, he was far lighter than Lord Harewood.

"That's because there is no pond for them to fall into." She smiled, quite pleased with her rejoinder.

Lord Manning gave a pleased nod and lifted his glass to her. "Then I say, it shall be a very good game."

As Lord Dearling had become engaged with the lady to his right, she instead focused on finishing her soup.

"Lady Dorothea, I was surprised to see you attending this grand fete." Lord Leighhall's statement required a response, so she placed her spoon back in her bowl and forced herself to politely reply.

"Why, my lord?"

"As I don't see your mother here, I didn't expect you to be. Is she quite well?"

She moved her hand beneath the table as her fingers curled into her palm at the uncomfortableness of his remark. "My mother is quite well. I will be sure to tell her you inquired. She is home with my father. Lady Sommerset offered to be my chaperone."

Before Lord Leighhall could respond, Lord Sommerset spoke.

"As did I." The stern look he gave the viscount, made her feel much safer.

"I am quite grateful for you, sir." She nodded to her chaperone then turned to Lord Leighhall. "You see, Lady Sommerset has lectured at my school many times. She is knowledgeable on so many topics."

The man gave a nod of respect to the countess. "I have heard many praises of the lady's work. I can only assume that you have been learning how to paint, then."

Dory barely kept from grinning at his assumption. "Oh, no. I already know how to paint, though not nearly as well as Lady Sommerset. Painting is not one of our courses at the Belinda School for Curious Ladies. No, Lady Sommerset taught us about how certain colors come from certain plants and the process to extract them in one of our science courses. She also lectured on observation, a skill required of artists but also critical to navigating life itself. After all, life—" She halted, recognizing she'd gone far over her three-sentence limit. Guiltily, she glanced down the table to find Lord Harewood looking at her. Blast. "Life is so colorful."

"Observation?" Lord Leighhall snorted, which did not become him at all. "I've never given observation much thought. So do you mean to say that you could tell me what color pocket watch I wear tonight?"

She glanced across the table to find that Lady Sommerset was indeed listening to the conversation. As their eyes met, the lady's lips formed a secret smile even as she gave the smallest of nods.

"Of course, my lord." She would have remained silent, but as her instructor had been insulted, she had to make an exception. "You wear a silver pocket watch, much like Lord Harewood, while Lord Dearling wears a gold one, as does Lord Sommerset." She kept a serious face, though she wanted very much to laugh at his surprise. She wasn't the most observant of her classmates, but she did pay attention when she wasn't speaking.

He lifted his head to look down his nose. "Well, that's very good to know. Now if any of us misplace our hat or our cane and someone else takes it by mistake, we'll know whom to ask about it." The words were said with such insult that the air caught in her lungs.

"I, for one, am quite pleased that I can count on Lady Dorothea to help me keep track of my belongings." Lord Dearling's voice had her turning toward him. "I consider it a great skill you have and would be honored if you would let me know if I accidently take someone else's hat." He nodded toward Lord Manning. "Or, perhaps, hit someone else's croquet ball."

Relieved by Lord Dearling's kind response, she gave him a grateful smile. "I will be happy to keep you from misappropriating anyone else's belongings, but I admit I may not be of much help with the croquet ball."

He cocked his head as if they were discussing the latest bill before Parliament, so serious was his visage. "And why is that?"

Holding back her own humor, she replied in an equal vein. "Because if your hit is to our advantage, I may willfully ignore your misstep."

He gave her a serious nod, though his lips twitched with mischief. "I do believe we will make a superb team."

"Do you hear that, Lady Arabella?" Lord Manning addressed the lady on his left but lifted his glass toward them. "We will have to watch these two closely if we are to have any chance of winning."

Lady Arabella's eyes grew wide. "I was not aware we were partnering for this game."

As Lord Manning turned to the lady to request that very thing, Lord Dearling leaned in. "I am so pleased I offered to play with you. I'm quite sure Lord Manning would have if I hadn't been so quick about it."

Dory felt her cheeks heat at the thought that both men wanted to be in her company, even though she was such a poor pall-mall player. She'd never had such an experience before. She gave the man a genuine smile before turning back to her soup. As she took another sip, she looked toward Lord Harewood, only to find him watching her. His face did not reveal his thoughts, but she hoped he approved. The time would go by very slowly until she could tell him all that had transpired because of his suggestion.

As the dinner continued, she had to go silent twice more, but since the first time was when the duck was served, a particular favorite dish of hers, and she was expected to eat, anyway, it was not a hardship. Then the second occasion occurred just as Lady Enderly stood to gather the ladies to retreat, so it had not been too difficult. What had been difficult was ignoring Lord Leighhall. He didn't engage her in conversation, but he spoke on subjects that made her want to argue with him. Her other companions, though, had made the time go by in a pleasant manner.

As they all stood, she glanced once more at Lord Harewood, but he was speaking to the lady he had been seated next to.

"Lady Dorothea, I look forward to furthering our conversation in the parlor." Lord Dearling's kind words had her turning toward him.

She opened her mouth to give him a polite response.

"As do I." Lord Manning grinned at Dearling.

Lady Arabella chuckled. "Come, Lady Dorothea. We must prepare our topics of conversation while these gentlemen discuss their favorite scotch whisky and horses."

Dory leaned toward Lord Dearling and whispered. "The best is truly from Littlemill." At his look of surprise, she quickly walked past to link arms with Lady Arabella and proceeded toward the parlor. Even as they entered the room, she wished she hadn't mentioned the scotch. No doubt Lord Dearling thought she imbibed now, when in actuality it was the Duke of Northwick, the owner of the school, who had mentioned that particular libation.

As the ladies all entered, Lady Rose intercepted her and pulled her toward two chairs by one of the windows. "I greatly missed your company at dinner. I don't know why Mother seated you so far away."

It most likely had to do with the fact that she attended the Belinda School, but she didn't wish to mention that. "I have no doubt that since you and I were able to spend so much time together over the last few days, she simply wanted you to converse with more of your guests."

Rose glanced toward her mother, who was speaking to two ladies and their chaperones. "Or rather converse with the gentlemen she invited. She made it appear that I am accomplished in absolutely every possible way and my brother is the epitome of a peer."

"Your brother. I did not know he sought a wife."

Rose waved her hand as if it were a forgone conclusion. "He is much like me. Neither of us is interested in what our mother wishes for us, at least not yet."

"I thought you wished to attend the school so you could have better conversations and attract a husband? Does that mean if a man was truly interested in you as you are, you would not consider it?" She, herself, would be thrilled by such an opportunity, though she would miss her classmates, but Rose had not yet attended.

"To be honest, that was my first intention, but after hearing all that you have related about the school over the last few days, I admit I'm anxious to attend. It would be such a grand adventure." Rose clasped one hand in the other against her chest, her excitement clear in her eyes.

If Lady Enderly heard such talk, Dory was quite sure she'd be sent home immediately. That Rose wished an experience beyond what she had so far was not entirely surprising.

"Then mayhap you can help *me* find a prospective suitor." At her friend's excited look, she quickly held up her hand. "I caution you, it will not be an easy task."

Rose grabbed her hand and squeezed. "I would very much enjoy that. I've never done anything of the sort. You must tell me how I can help."

"Let's see. I believe the first would be to observe the men

who are here and their qualities, both good and poor. The second might be to remember anything that is said about me, again good and poor."

"Oh, no one could say anything about you that is poor. You are a lovely person."

Her heart warmed at Rose's enthusiastic endorsement. If only all others felt that way, she could have her pick of a gentleman. "Most importantly, they should be someone interested in marriage."

Rose smirked. "That leaves every man except my brother."

Unfortunately, that was true. "There could be others here who are in no hurry to marry as well, so listen carefully."

"I do believe you just made the next fortnight much more enjoyable for me."

Pleased that she had made Rose happy, she couldn't help feeling uncomfortable. "Just be sure to report everything to me and not say a word about my interest in any of the gentlemen here."

Rose lost her smile and nodded. "I understand. I can be quite circumspect when needed." Even as she said the words, her relaxed manner changed and she sat straighter in her chair. "Lady Matilda please join us."

Looking over her shoulder, Dory understood the full change in her friend's demeanor. Lady Matilda approached, obviously curious about their conversation. It was just as well, as she needed to practice her three-sentence skill so she had more to report to Lord Harewood when they spoke.

For the rest of the evening, she only had to keep silent once, but she had not been able to converse with Lord Harewood at all. It wasn't as if he were flanked by many of the women, but more that, he stood aside from everyone, only speaking with his father or Lord Sommerset. Not once did she see him speak to his mother.

Her evening was still pleasant as Lord Dearling, Lord Manning, and Mr. Retford, with whom she'd danced the quadrille that very season, had kept her entertained. By the time she crawled into bed, her mind was ready to sleep after such a challenging day.

The following morning after breaking her fast in her room, she was ushered downstairs by Lady Sommerset to sew with the other ladies. Unfortunately, she had no choice but to sit next to Rose's two friends who had left her standing by herself at the Stocktons' ball. Though she didn't hold any ill will toward them, as there had been so many others who had done the same, she was not inclined to join their conversation and instead focused on her embroidery.

Lady Sommerset, who appeared to be adding the Sommerset crest to a handkerchief, noticed her focus. "Are you deep in thought over your prospects?"

Dory moved her gaze from the handkerchief to the lady, somewhat confused. "My prospects?"

Her chaperone gave her a secret smile as she set down her needle. "You appear to have many men quite interested in you."

Her cheeks heated and she kept her voice low. "I'm not as certain as you, though I did have lovely conversations with Lord Dearling and Lord Manning yesterday eve."

Lady Sommerset lowered her voice to match. "And don't forget Mr. Retford and Lord Harewood."

"Lord Harewood?" She tried to ignore the jump her heart gave, which did not make sense, as the man was not in the market for a wife. "I didn't speak to him all day. Why would you think so?"

"Perhaps because you spoke to him quite often before the others arrived. Or rather, more telling, *he* spoke to *you*."

"Yes, that is true, but our conversations did not lead me to imagine he has an interest." That was true, but his kisses led her to believe he did, not that she could admit that.

Lady Sommerset shook her head and sighed. "I'm disappointed to hear that. Both my husband and I had thought maybe there was an interest. It is our wish that he can open his heart to another someday."

"Another?" Her curiosity bloomed. "Has he been interested in someone before?"

Lady Sommerset stuck her needle in the material stretched tightly over her loop. "I forget that many people are not aware of the connection between the Mabrys and the Ambroses. Lord Harewood had his heart broken over ten years ago. I'm not sure he will ever care for another woman again, but we do hope it could happen."

Ten years ago? He couldn't have been more than a lad. A sadness filled her that someone could have turned away such a unique man. "Did the woman marry another? I do hope it wasn't you."

Lady Sommerset chuckled. "Hardly. He and Lord Sommerset are opposites in many ways, just as I and my sister were."

"Was Lord Harewood in love with Lady Northwick then?"

This time, Lady Sommerset laughed, drawing the attention of others in the room. "Lady Dorothea, how adorable." The words were said loudly enough for all to assume some *on-dit* had been shared and nothing was of great import. Then the lady lowered her voice again. "No, Joanna and the lord would have never been a match, nor would Mariel. It was my sweet sister Belinda who caught Lord Harewood's fancy and he hers."

The softness in the countess's gaze caused a tightening in Dory's chest for both Lady Sommerset and Lord Harewood. Lady Belinda was revered by the Mabry sisters and even by those who attended the school. They all knew her story. She'd been kind, gentle, giving, and very understanding. Despite Lady Northwick nursing Lady Belinda through scarlet fever, she never regained her strength and faded away.

She and her classmates referred to Lady Belinda as "the Angel." The life-like full-sized painting of her, created by Lady Sommerset, graced the parlor of Silver Meadows, where the school was housed. Many of her classmates admitted to talking to the portrait, which seemed so real.

She tried to imagine the stiff Lord Harewood with the Angel. "Did they truly love each other?" She couldn't quite see it.

Lady Sommerset nodded. "Indeed, they did. He was just waiting for her to come out before asking her for her hand. Some say they were too young to know what it was to love, but I disagree. They were well matched, perhaps too well matched. Her passing changed all of us, but the most drastic change was in Lord Harewood. As a young lad, he was much like my husband, full of mischief and smiles." She sighed. "Very few are witness to that side of him now. And for years, it simply did not exist, as if it died with my sister. I like to credit my husband for helping Lord Harewood find that piece of himself again."

Dory had a feeling that Rose also had a hand in helping him with that. "Do you think that means that he will love again someday?" She wasn't sure why the countess's answer was so important, but it was. Perhaps because he had helped her, she held a sympathy for his loss.

"I do not know." The lady gave her usual smile. "But I do hope. In fact, I had noticed his interest in you and so I needed to ask."

She almost laughed herself, even as a deep disappointment settled in her belly. "I am so far from being like Lady Belinda that to posit such a notion is humorous." Was that why Lady Sommerset had turned her back on them when they'd been in the library? Best to make it clear that the earl in question had no intentions toward her. "No, our conversations centered on people's thought processes and happiness."

Lady Sommerset rolled her eyes. "That sounds like a conversation with Joanna. Ah, well. But what about the other men I mentioned?"

Ignoring her feeling of disappointment over Lord Harewood, even though she hadn't realized she'd had any hopes in that direction, she thought about the men who had shown her interest so far. "Today is only the second day, but I do believe there may be some mutual interest. It is difficult to know a person in just a couple of conversations. Perhaps I will better be able to answer that in a fortnight."

"That sounds like a pragmatic approach. I will listen carefully and let you know if I think any the men are ones to stay clear of. After all, that's what a chaperone is supposed to do, or so I've been told."

"Thank you. I'm already avoiding Lord Leighhall. He's never liked me because of my mother. Do you think you can influence Lady Enderly into not seating him next to me again?"

"I'd be pleased to do so. He hasn't endeared himself to me, either. Lady Enderly did say she was going to change the seating every night. Maybe I'll have him seated next to me tomorrow." Her lips lifted in a particularly impish smile.

Dory almost felt sorry for Lord Leighhall, but not quite. "I am most grateful for your kindness toward me."

Lady Sommerset waved away her comment and picked up her needle again.

As she returned her attention to her own embroidery, her thoughts wandered to Lord Harewood. Now her heart ached for him, though not enough to suggest him to another woman. Did that mean she had some small feeling for him? If so, she needed to disperse it post-haste. But she did wish to help him in some way, like he had helped her. Perhaps she could convince him that he could be happy. Yes, she liked that idea. Maybe then, he could let himself fall in love again. She had no doubt that he would feel happy to see her succeed by following his suggestion, which gave her more motivation. She was just thankful that in her head, she could wander along her many squiggly lines to her heart's content.

CHAPTER ELEVEN

FELTON FOCUSED ON his hit and drew back the mallet. The black ball ran along the lawn and smacked into Leighhall's ball, sending it off the course and leaving the pathway clear for his own partner, Lady Matilda.

"I say, Lord Harewood, that was a particularly harsh stroke."

He shrugged at the man, not at all unhappy with his shot, which should put them in the lead, if Lady Matilda continued to show her skill at the game. Taking his second stroke, he passed his ball through the wire hoop and stepped back. "It is your turn, my lady."

"Thank you, Lord Harewood. You cleared the way nicely." Taking aim, she hit the ball, sending it through the wicket. She turned toward him. "I do believe we will take this contest."

She was a slender lady, with light-brown hair, nondescript eyes, dressed in a typical white day dress. She had a strong competitive streak, which he had noticed at dinner the other night. He gave her an approving nod before moving off toward his ball.

Rose blocked his way. "Truly, brother, you take unfair advantage of us."

"I do not. You are as skilled at pall-mall as I." He nodded toward Leighhall, who stood at the edge of the game lining up his mallet. "It is your partner to whom you should complain."

She sighed. "True, but that would hardly be fitting." She moved aside and let him proceed. His sister always put propriety before her own wishes. Though she would prefer to win against him, she would encourage the man he'd nicknamed "the braggart." He hoped she had no true interest in him.

By nature, Felton was competitive, which was why he'd started betting at White's Gentlemen's Club. He planned to win this game and the one after with the winner of the next set playing behind them. But his pleasure at soon winning the game was quickly being overshadowed by Lady Dorothea and Lord Dearling. The two of them were still at the second wicket as the man attempted to instruct the lady on aiming, which was hardly fitting since he didn't seem to be able to find the wicket himself. That would not have bothered Felton at all. In fact, he'd usually find it mildly amusing.

However, Lady Dorothea's laughter was distracting. That she could enjoy losing so thoroughly rubbed at him like a rock in his boot. It didn't help that not only did she look lovely in her green dress and matching bonnet, but Lady Arabella and Lord Manning appeared to be purposefully miss-hitting to make her feel better about being such a poor shot. They were enjoying the game far too much despite their lack of progress.

"Lord Harewood, I believe it's your turn." At Lady Matilda's call, he lined up and struck, his ball easily rolling through the next wicket and lining up on the next one.

The lady clapped her gloved hands. "That was a wonderful shot. I do hope I can do half as well."

It was obvious she was looking for a compliment, but as he prepared to answer, Lady Dorothea squealed, causing him to look back. She sat on the ground, as if she'd fallen. His instinct was to come to her aid, but Lord Dearling had everything well in hand, if Lady Dorothea laughing as the man helped her to stand could be considered well in hand.

"Do you think I should set up my fall or attempt the angle?"

Though Lady Matilda spoke to him, Lord Leighhall answered. "The angle is tricky, but you would be sure to win if you made it."

Forcing himself to refocus on the game, Felton stepped to where Lady Matilda's ball lay and studied the line to the hoop. "In my opinion, you'll have more success if you set up the shot."

"Even if it takes an additional stroke?"

"Yes." While the lady had skill, even he would have difficulty with the angle, something Leighhall was sure to know.

The lady took another look as if actually contemplating Leighhall's advice. Finally, she lined her mallet up and hit, setting the ball up directly before the hoop and in the way of his own shot.

Leighhall laughed. "Now, that, I didn't expect. Excellent setup, Lady Matilda."

Felton gave the man a bored stare before glancing at his sister, who shook her head. She knew exactly what to do were it her turn. But it wasn't, it was his.

Standing behind his ball, he examined the line and the distance between Lady Matilda's ball and the arch he must send his ball through. Determining the best angle, he hit the ball toward the ground and watched as it jumped over Lady Matilda's ball and through the hoop.

"Oh, that was marvelous!" Lady Matilda clapped her hands as Lord Leighhall stared.

"Where did you learn to do that?" Leighhall shook his head. "That can't be fair."

His sister looped her arm through Lord Leighhall's. "Actually, my lord, it is. But I do believe it is our turn."

As his sister and Leighhall determined their shots, he glanced back toward the third hoop to find that foursome talking as they waited for Lady Dorothea's group on hoop four. Was he the only person who cared about winning? If so, he'd be loath to play the game again.

"Tell me, Lord Harewood, are you equally skilled in hunting?"

Surprised by the question, he gave Lady Matilda his full attention. "I am. I do not like to fail."

She looked up at him from beneath her lashes. "That was the impression I was under."

For Jove's sake, did she really think he had an interest in her beyond the game? If that was to be the case, he'd ask another lady to partner with him for the next activity. "And what of you? Do you excel at something other than pall-mall?"

She laughed daintily, her gloved hand half-covering her rather thin lips. "I do, but it is hardly attractive to brag. However, since you ask, I'm excellent at the pianoforte and sewing. I've also been given many compliments on my dancing ability."

Surprised, not by her list, but by her forthright revelation of said accomplishments, he barely kept from asking how she was at kissing, as he would have with Lady Dorothea. Fortunately, the thought of Lady Matilda wanting to demonstrate that ability with him made it possible to refrain. "That is quite impressive."

"My mother has been very insistent that I be well-accomplished. I was tutored by the very best governesses. You see, my father, the Marquess of Stamford, is well attended and expectations for me are quite high."

And he thought Leighhall a braggart? "No doubt they are."

"Brother, can you please take your turn? I'm parched and wish for a lemonade."

Happy to have his sister interrupt, he studied the field to find his ball far from where he'd left it. Looking to his sister, he caught an impish gleam in her eye. Finally, a challenge. "I would not wish to keep you from your refreshment longer than required."

It was obvious by the position of the balls that she expected him to jump her ball, but he had a far better plan. Lining his mallet up, he smacked it hard into her ball, sending it off the course. It did leave him with a terrible angle, but it was worth it to see her open mouth.

"Oh, dear, Lord Harewood. I'm not sure you will make this next shot."

At Lady Matilda's statement, he almost wished he was with Lady Dorothea's group. At least they found their game entertaining, while he thought he may die of boredom before he finished his. Though he knew it wasn't the most gentlemanly action to take, he hit his ball so it glanced off Lady Matilda's, giving it just the angle he needed for it to fly through the final hoop.

Leighhall stepped next to him. "You're in for it now."

Lady Matilda's mouth turned down and her upper lip plumped out in a pout.

Ignoring her reaction, he held his hand out toward her ball. "Though we've just won, I believe it's your turn."

She looked askance at him, clearly not happy, but didn't say a word as she lined up and brought her ball within range.

After his sister and Leighhall made their attempts, his sister also clearing the final hoop, Lady Matilda sent her ball through. Leighhall completed his game last. Or rather, last in their group. He turned around to check on the group behind them. Lady Dorothea's quartet was just starting hoop five, with the next group close on their heels.

"You seem a bit out of sorts, brother."

He didn't turn at his sister's comment as she stepped up next to him. "I find myself unusually disappointed in my own accomplishment."

She hooked her arm in his. "Maybe it's because it was far too easy an accomplishment?"

He glanced down at her, his lips quirking up. "I see you couldn't seem to let Leighhall win."

"No. I tried. I truly did, but he was so conceited at the idea that he could play better than I, I grew bored."

"As did I." He looked over her head to see Lady Matilda and Lord Leighhall walking arm and arm to the tent set up on the lawn where the elders sat.

More laughter from Lady Dorothea's group had him turning his head back toward the course. "Did you wish for that refreshment, or would you prefer to discover what makes pall-mall so amusing?"

"Oh, I'm all about learning new things. My lemonade can wait. Let's do investigate."

"And so we shall."

At Rose's laughter, his mood lightened, and they strolled back the way they had played to find out what was so damned humorous about sending balls through hoops. As they approached, the foursome stopped talking. Lady Arabella and Lord Manning smiled, but Lord Dearling and Lady Dorothea looked sheepish.

His sister cocked her head. "Do you need instruction on playing pall-mall?"

Lord Manning answered, grinning. "Not at all. We all know how to play. We just have a couple of us who are, let us say, less skilled."

He couldn't let that pass. "Then perhaps we can be of assistance. My sister and I are quite adept at the game."

Lord Manning and Lady Arabella turned toward Lady Dorothea and Lord Dearling. Lady Dorothea's cherubic cheeks were flushed as she laughed. "I could use some assistance in retrieving my ball."

"To be fair, I did hit it quite by accident." Lord Dearling pointed to a red ball in the distance. The man must have hit it like canon fire to send it so far.

"And I may have kicked Lord Dearling's ball back a bit." Lady Dorothea pointed past the third hoop, appearing quite proud of herself.

He did notice *she* didn't say it was an accident. "Then, Lady Dorothea, I suggest we retrieve your ball, and I'm sure my sister would be happy to aid Lord Dearling."

"That would be most appreciated." Lord Dearling bowed toward Rose.

As Rose left, Lady Dorothea joined him. "I do appreciate your help." She gave him a shy smile, which added to her already flushed cheeks and shimmering eyes.

He held out his arm, and she moved her mallet to her other hand before taking it. He didn't look at her as they began the long walk toward her ball. "Am I to understand that you kicked Lord Dearling's ball out of the way purposefully?"

She giggled. "I did. But to be truthful, he deserved it for hitting my ball so hard, and it wasn't even with his ball. He thought to prove a point about decisiveness versus accuracy and accidently hit my ball with his mallet when he completely missed his own. Truthfully, my lord, if he goes hunting with you all tomorrow morning, I highly suggest that you don't allow him a weapon."

At her statement, he laughed. "I assure you, I will keep that in mind or keep myself far away from said gentleman."

"Very good. I would not want anything to happen to you or anyone else."

His curiosity about their play refused to remain unsatisfied. "With Lord Dearling doing so poorly, did you not find it frustrating to continue the game?"

"Frustrating?" She thought for a moment. "No, I don't believe I did. However, it was quite amusing, as was my own play. And then when Lord Manning and Lady Arabella began to play terribly, it was all quite comical."

"And you enjoyed this?"

She stopped walking, forcing him to halt. "Of course." She looked back over her shoulder before facing him once again. "Have you finished your game?"

"We did. My partner and I won." He smiled, pleased he could tell her of his accomplishment.

"And you enjoyed winning."

"Yes, of course. Wouldn't you?" He was puzzled by her question. That was the purpose of any game, to win.

"I'm not sure, but I am enjoying the game nonetheless." She leaned closer, her citric scent wafting upward into his nostrils. "To be fair, I doubt very much that I will win and I am not disappointed by that fact at all. We are having such a lovely time, anyway."

Her answer puzzled him, but he took a moment and looked back over his shoulder to see that Dearling's ball had now somehow rolled under a hedge. The foursome waiting to play the hoop didn't appear to be concerned as they talked to each other, the men with their mallets slung over their shoulders. He turned back and started their stroll again. "It appears that the group behind you is content to converse while we retrieve your ball."

"You sound surprised by that. I'm not because those four were talking quite a bit in the parlor last evening. I believe the game is simply an excuse to have more conversation. Perhaps they find each other more interesting than the game."

They stopped before her ball, and he bent to retrieve it. He stared at it as if it could solve the puzzle of her ideas. "In your estimation, then, the purpose of pall-mall it not to win, but to play?"

She shook her head, causing the pale-green bonnet to fall a bit to one side. "Not simply to play, but to *enjoy*. For what is a game's purpose but to spend the time in a different manner for enjoyment? For some, such as yourself, the accomplishment of being the first to reach the game's goal is what is enjoyed. For others, like myself and Lord Dearling, it is the enjoyment of sharing laughter with others who have poor skills. Still, for those behind us, it is the pleasure of each other's company. I imagine for still others, it is the camaraderie of a shared purpose and for some, it may be simply the enjoyment of honing a skill. It was Francis Bacon who said we need to cultivate our natural abilities so as to—" She dropped her mallet and pressed her hand to her mouth.

"What is it?" Concern for her welfare flared through him. "Do you feel faint?"

She shook her head but didn't remove her hand.

"Tell me what is amiss. Perhaps I can help."

She dropped her hand and her shoulders slumped. "I'd been doing so well all day until now." She let out a heavy sigh and looked at him. "That was far too many sentences. I broke your rule, and with you, of all people. I'm sorely disappointed in myself."

His rule? "Oh, you mean my suggestion."

"No, don't say that. If it's not a rule, I won't follow it." She shook her head emphatically and the bonnet, already lopsided, fell more to the right, which on any other woman would have looked ridiculous, but on Dorothea seemed to be just right.

"Very well, if it's my rule, then I do believe I can make an exception when you speak to me."

Her brows lowered as she cocked her head. "I'm not sure. I was doing so well with my new skill. No one was turning away from my conversation."

That his idea was aiding her filled him with pleasure. "I'm very pleased to learn that. But also remember, I never turned away from you when you spoke more than three sentences. In fact, if I recall, it was that particular habit that engaged me in our first true conversation."

Her eye's brightened and she stood straighter. "That's true. So with everyone else, I must stay with three sentences or be silent, but with you, I'm free to follow my thoughts."

He smiled, feeling oddly honored. "Yes."

"I do like that I can relax when speaking to you. Do you think we can make Rose an exception, too? She seems to truly enjoy it when I ramble."

Her request for permission had his chest filling with warmth even as his mind recognized he was not her tutor, though in some aspects, perhaps he was. "I think that would be acceptable if it doesn't make it more difficult for you to limit your conversation with others."

"Hmm, perhaps I can only follow my squiggly lines with Rose when we are in private." She gazed directly at him. "I will have to do the same with you as well. It will be too much to think about if it's not the same."

"Agreed. That is an excellent plan."

"Dory, did you find your ball?" The shout from Rose had them both turning.

He held the ball aloft. "Shall we return you to your game?"

"Yes. I do so enjoy it."

"Then let us walk back to your group post-haste." He bent and retrieved her mallet for her before walking her toward his sister, pleased that Lady Dorothea enjoyed the game in her own way. He had learned more from her in the few days since she arrived than he had from anyone in the last year. He found himself looking forward to more insights from her in the coming days.

Lord Dearling approached. "Lady Dorothea, I do believe it is your turn."

Letting go of Felton's arm, the lady in question held her hand out for her ball. Reluctantly, he returned it, as there was no reason to stay longer. She handed it to Dearling and the two set off to the spot she needed to hit from.

"I think I'm ready for that refreshment now." His sister linked her arm in his, forcing him to look away.

"Of course." He led her toward the tent deep in thought. Lady Dorothea had shown him that he did feel happiness when he won a bet. That could mean that the happiness he felt while they spoke was because she related her success so far with his suggested method of conversation. It was a different feeling of accomplishment than the former, but if people could enjoy a game of pall-mall in myriad ways, he could certainly feel happiness in more than one way as well.

It was not how he'd felt when with Belinda. Nonetheless, it *was* happiness.

CHAPTER TWELVE

L ADY ROSE POINTED out the coach window. "There's the lake I told you about."

Dory rode in the coach with only Rose and Lady Enderly, the men preferring to ride their horses so as to have a friendly race with which to entertain the ladies later. She leaned forward to look. "So we are not far, then?"

"Not at all. I cannot wait to spend the day outside."

She agreed. The last three days, the weather had not cooperated, forcing them to remain inside. Though the men had been able to hunt every morning, the rains had come every afternoon, forcing all the ladies to stay in the house, while the men played billiards and whatever else they did. She was not privy to the arrangements. The evenings, though, had been fun with charades, whist, and buzz, with which she found she had particular skill, though she'd never played it before. Though some of the men, particularly Lord Harewood, Lord Sommerset, and Lord Enderly, had not participated, choosing to simply watch. There had even been a skit performed by some of the ladies.

But she was much more excited for today. She'd worn a bright-blue dress to complement the sunny skies. They were traveling to the standing stone called "the Devil's Stone." It sounded quite ominous, but Rose said it was just old folklore and it really wasn't that large. Supposedly, there had been two others, but only one remained. In her opinion, the best part of the day would be eating *al fresco*, as the Italians called it. She'd never eaten in a field before, though she'd taken a meal outside at a table many a time at home and at other events.

The coach slowed, and she craned her neck to see the venue, but all she could see was a row of trees with a field beyond on Rose's side and a building on her side. On the building, a sign hung above the door boasting what looked like a pedestal and over it in an arch were the words *The Jumps Inn*.

"Rose, I want you to spend some time getting to know Lord Manning." Lady Enderly pulled on her gloves. "He is heir to the Duke of Richmond, and according to your father, he has good views."

Rose nodded dutifully. "Will I be seated next to him tonight as well?"

"Of course. And, Lady Dorothea, you will be seated next to my son tonight. I apologize that it could not be someone else, but the rotation wasn't working any other way."

Not unhappy about the news, Dory nodded, holding back a grin. "I understand. I will endeavor to engage those around me to the best of my ability."

"Good." Lady Enderly rose as the door to the coach opened.

Rose grabbed her hand and squeezed before whispering. "At least I know Lord Manning isn't interested in me. That is a relief." She let go and moved forward as her mother exited the coach, following her out with the help of the footman.

Finally, Dory moved forward to the opening.

Lord Manning, dressed in a brown tailcoat and beige pantaloons, stood just outside the conveyance and held his hand up. "May I help you down, Lady Dorothea?"

She jerked her gaze to the right to see Lady Enderly's back was turned as she walked toward the next coach with Rose in tow. Relieved the marchioness hadn't noticed, Dory met Lord Manning's gaze. "I would be most grateful."

Once her feet had made it to solid ground, Lord Manning

pulled her hand to his arm. "If you would allow me, I thought you would be interested in seeing the standing stone."

Immediately, her curiosity rose. "I understand there used to be three stones."

He started them forward in a leisurely stroll. "To be truthful, I do not know. I suggest we discover the truth for ourselves."

She glanced around the area to see everyone moving in the same direction in groups of three and four. She did not see Lord Harewood anywhere, but Rose strolled arm and arm with Lady Arabella. "I think that's a lovely idea."

"Now, I did talk to the stableboy and he said there was only one stone, the Devil's Stone."

She looked askance at him. His lips were turned up as if amused by his own story. Though she had already been told the name of the stone, she was interested in what he had discovered. "The Devil's Stone."

"Yes, the tale goes that the Devil caught a man in this very field playing the game leapfrog on the sabbath. The Devil joined the man and on his third jump grabbed the unholy soul and took him to hell. The three stones sprouted up where the Devil had jumped."

She pressed her hand to her chest. "What an awful tale. Should we even go near the stones? Might we too be in danger?" She barely kept from smiling.

Lord Manning slowed their walk and looked at her, his brows knit in concern. "I would not allow anything to happen to you. I promise."

She finally grinned, chuckling. "I do appreciate your kindness, but as it is not Sunday and I do not believe I can play leapfrog in my dress, I don't believe we have anything to fear."

Understanding dawned and his brows lifted. "Very good observations. Also, there is a church nearby, so I believe we will be safe." He pointed to the north, where she could just see the top of a bell tower.

"I fear that we may be too far from such holy walls, but as we are with so many others, I'm sure we will be safe."

He nodded, evidently still not quite understanding her humor.

They came to a stop with the others in a circle around the stone, and she was thankful only half of the party had arrived yet because the stone was so unimpressive as to be fairly engulfed by them all.

Rose stepped forward, bent her knees a bit, and laid her hand on the top of the stone. "This is the Devil's Stone. It's just a wee one, so there is no need to fear."

The gathering laughed before turning back the way they'd come. Obviously, this had simply been an excuse for an outdoor journey, and no one seemed to mind.

But Dory wished to investigate further. Slipping her hand from Lord Manning's arm, she crouched down to examined the stone, which came to no more than two feet high. "It does look old. Maybe the other two stones are even smaller and so not as noticeable." She rose, looking around as she did. "Maybe only the tops of them are above the soil."

"Do you mean to say the Devil has uneven jumps?"

She looked over her shoulder at him to see his brows raised in question. "Or mayhap he jumped too hard the first and last time." She pointed toward the north of the stone. "I'll take this side. You take that side."

He didn't look pleased with that idea. "Why don't we both take the same side?"

She set her hand to her hip. "Because we can cover more area my way." When he continued to frown, she shook her head at him. "Don't you want to get back to the activities?"

He shrugged. "I'm perfectly happy here."

Heaven save her from stubborn men. Exasperated, she gave up and began walking the ground looking for anything that could resemble the stone. After going a ways alone, she turned back to find that Lord Manning was doing the same. At least he was helpful. "Did you find anything?"

"No." He didn't look at her, continuing to walk in a pattern.

That was probably what she should have done. "How far do you think a devil jumps?"

He stopped at that. "Now that I think upon it, the next jump could be in the next town."

She shook her head. "No, you said the Devil came upon a man in *this* field." She looked north and then south. "This is a very big field."

"Yes, it is, and I'm growing hungry. Would you be willing to leave the search for a while so that we may eat?"

"I would be amenable to that arrangement."

"Excellent." He held his arm out to her, and she lifted her skirts and strode toward him.

She hadn't quite reached him when Lord Harewood walked up. Despite the sunny day, or maybe in honor of it, he wore gray pantaloons, but his tailcoat was still black. She halted. "Oh, you *are* here."

Lord Manning turned. "Lord Harewood. Did you ride in a coach?"

"No, I headed out earlier than the rest of you, as I had to make arrangements with the inn across the lane for tea for the ladies and spirits for the men."

"That was thoughtful. Lady Dorothea and I were just about to return to the trees for our meal." Lord Manning looked around the earl. "I see they have laid out tablecloths for the occasion."

"Yes, they have. My sister has set up one for you. And I am to escort Lady Dorothea for the meal."

Lord Manning opened his mouth then closed it. He obviously didn't like his plans undone. Finally, he nodded. "Of course." Turning toward Dory, he gave a nod. "We can continue our search later, then."

"I look forward to it." Though actually, she was quite convinced now that there were no other stones.

Without another word, he turned on his heel and strode past Lord Harewood in search of Rose.

She smiled warmly. "I admit it is a relief to see you here."

Lord Harewood raised his brows. "Indeed?"

She took the last steps that brought her to him. "Yes. I was worried I would have to count sentences the entire day. You don't know how tiring that is." She rolled her eyes like she'd seen Lady Northwick do at school.

His lips twitched. "So you are only pleased to see me because you can relax and say what you please for as long as you please?"

Surprised by his question, she wasn't sure how to respond, but as his lips lifted in a smirk, she understood. "Of course. I can think of no other reason. Can you?"

"Ah, Dory, I can always depend upon you saying something I couldn't predict."

Knowing his pridefulness regarding his predictions, it was a high compliment. "Thank you, my lord."

A chuckle escaped before he offered her his arm. "Shall we join the meal?"

She studied the ground one more time. "I suppose."

"What is it you look for? Lord Manning said you searched for something. What did you lose?"

She set her hand on his arm. "I didn't lose anything, but it appears the Devil lost two of his jumps."

"You've heard the tale of this stone, then?" Instead of walking her toward the others, he walked her back to the stone.

"I did. Lord Manning got it from the stableboy."

"I see. Then I should tell you that you will not find the other jumps."

She stepped away to see his face. "How can you be sure? Did you search for them?"

He bent and patted the stone. "I would have, but I had a very intelligent tutor, one who refused to allow me to search until I researched the origins of said stone." He stood straight again. "I'm thankful I didn't walk this entire field looking for them as well."

"What did you discover that had you leaving off the search?"

"Men far more advanced than I in archeology determined two very credible origins. One is that this is the remainder of a Celtic Cross that was broken."

She studied the stone. That could be, considering how weathered it was. Even if it had been a hard break, after six hundred years in the elements, it was bound to be rounded by wind and rain. "And what was the second origin?"

"The second scholar determined that it may be a Roman mile marker."

She moved her gaze from the stone to him. "A Roman mile marker?"

He nodded, his face absolutely serious.

She studied the stone closely. "This is much shorter than any marker I've encountered, Roman or otherwise. Why would an archeologist suggest that?"

"Perhaps it was simply to be different. Or it could be he was from the area and wished the local area to be known for something of value."

She crouched down again, trying to discern if there were indeed any marks on the stone at all that could lead one to believe it had served such a purpose. She ran her fingertips along the face of the stone, hoping she would feel an indent even if she couldn't see it. She didn't find any. Looking up, she found Harewood's arms crossed as he studied her. "What?" She looked at her dress to make sure nothing was amiss, but finding nothing, she rose. "Is there something wrong?"

"No. I was just curious."

When he didn't continue upon that which he was curious about, she guessed. "I believe I know which is the correct origin."

"You do?"

She crossed her arms and nodded. "I do. Tell me. Which scholar had the better reputation?"

He frowned, moving his gaze from her to the stone and back, then his face lightened. "Of course. Whichever scholar had the most experience is most likely correct. I'm not sure I still retain that research, but it wouldn't be difficult to obtain, as I found it in my father's library once, which means it would be no large task to find it again."

"I would be very interested in knowing if I'm correct. From my brief study of the stone, I believe it is the remains of a Celtic Cross. First, because of the dimensions. It has the right length and width of ones I have seen that are still intact. Second, I could find no indentations or markings on the stone, which we know are common on Roman mile markers. Granted, the stone could have been weathered so much as to erase them. However, the other markers I have come across all had marks of some kind upon them, even though equally as old as this one.

"Then again, an argument could be made for the location in an open field with fairly young trees, as in under one hundred years old, and therefore, the stone could have been beaten upon by Mother Nature, exposed as it is. Yet even were I to accept that, the height of the stone is far shorter than any I've seen. Not that I've visited them all. I do not know how many there are but have heard it is well over one thousand.

"Still, based on the knowledge I have, this stone is far too short to be a Roman mile marker by at least one foot. Therefore, I believe it to be the remains of a broken Celtic Cross. Now you may ask, where is the rest of the cross and that is, indeed, a mystery and the answer to that could well be lost forever. Perhaps someone decided to use the top of the cross as a headstone, as we are near sacred ground. Or a poor country boy with artistic talent decided to drag the rest of the stone home so that he may sculpt it into his vision. For all we know, the rest of this stone could be the cornerstone of the inn across the lane."

She stopped talking when the earl's smile grew wide, too distracted by his lips and how his face appeared more attractive when he smiled.

"I agree."

She raised her brows in astonishment. "You do?"

He lowered his arm and walked toward her, stopping next to

her to examine the stone. "I do. Your logic makes sense. I am now of the firm belief that this is the remains of a Celtic Cross."

She warmed at his agreement. When he said it, it made it sound absolutely true.

He offered her his arm. "Now that you've solved the puzzle of the standing stone, are you ready to eat? That did take quite a bit of reasoning."

She linked her arm with his and glanced at him to see if he teased, but there was no smirk on his face as he led her back toward the others, who were already sitting beneath various trees. "Though the mystery may be solved, it is not nearly so endearing as the story of the Devil playing leapfrog. I don't believe The Jumps Inn will be willing to change its name to The Broken Cross Inn, as that does not sound nearly as appealing a place to stay."

"Yes, well, we needn't tell the innkeeper."

They passed the Earl and Countess of Sommerset then stopped beneath a tree, where a tablecloth of pale green, embroidered with purple flowers, had been laid out. Upon it sat multiple plates of food.

As she lowered herself to sit, Lord Harewood waved over one of the footmen to give him an order for tea and ale before joining her. He sat with his back against the tree, his long legs out and crossed at the ankles. "If you enjoy such stories, then I'm pleased to tell you about the church in town, St. Mary's."

She liked sitting next to him better than standing because they were of more equal height, making her feel as if they had a mutual respect.

As he spoke, he gathered different food onto one plate and handed it to her.

He'd chosen cold roast beef and duck, a piece of pigeon pie, cucumber slices, a scoop of blancmange, and a fruit pastry. She stared in surprise. "This is everything I enjoy. How did you know?"

His grin spoke of confident pride. "I told you. I observe people."

"You observed what I like to eat?" She couldn't quite believe that he had been focused on her and the thought had her heart skipping a beat.

"I did." His smile softened. "You do not like ham or collared calf's head, but you do enjoy your sweets. I had another plate prepared with plum cake, pound cake, and a few macaroons. As we are outside today, transporting strawberry ice cream was not a possibility."

She felt the back of her eyes sting with tears. No one, not even the cook at home, had ever paid attention to what she liked to eat. She swallowed hard. "Thank you. I've never had someone take an interest in my meal before."

He didn't appear surprised. "That is because men today are too busy noticing what women are wearing instead of what they are eating. I suppose it is to their advantage to gift a person with a ribbon to match. But as your dresses, bonnets, and other accoutrements of blues, greens, purples, and maroons are complete, as most women's are, it makes no sense to focus on such frippery."

Though he called it *frippery*, his recognition of what colors she wore had her looking down at her food so he wouldn't see how much his observations touched her. Did he look at all the other women in the same way? How could he focus on everyone and keep their likes and colors organized and to what purpose?

"Is your food not acceptable?"

At his concern, she quickly met his gaze and smiled. "It is perfect. I'm simply dumfounded by how thorough you are."

He gave her a nod before using a fork to bite into his own roast beef.

She followed suit, needing a moment to ruminate on her own feelings. Despite the earl's statements regarding his disinterest in marriage, he seemed to truly enjoy her company. She definitely preferred his to that of any other gentleman present. Maybe if she continued to keep her conversation in line with the others, someone would become interested in her as a prospective wife. Lord Harewood would never be interested in her. He'd loved the Angel. She was nothing like the late Lady Belinda, more was the pity. But she had learned one important trait from the stories of Lady Belinda. The lady had been very kind and wished to aid others for no other reason than in her pleasure in doing so.

Dory reviewed her perfect plate and stabbed her fork into a piece of duck before plopping the moist bite into her mouth. Maybe she could help Lord Harewood find his happiness again. He'd made it very clear he didn't wish to marry anytime soon, and she needed to marry as soon as was respectable, before her mother made that impossible. The only reason she had a chance at accomplishing that now was due to his idea on how to curtail her squiggly conversations. For that kindness, she felt a certain indebtedness to him. She would like to repay him if she could. Helping him find happiness again would not only be kind, it would be a repayment of a debt, so to speak. Yes, that was exactly what she would do.

"Is the duck done to your liking?"

She finished chewing it before answering. "Yes, it's very good."

"Excellent. Then allow me to tell you the story of the church of St. Mary's at the end of this field, since you enjoy the quaintness of the fictional tale over the mundaneness of the facts."

She grinned. "I do. What is special about St. Mary's?"

"If you were to visit this church, you would discover that the bell tower is completely separate from the rest of the building."

"You mean there is no door to it from inside?"

"Not at all. It is a walk away from the main building." He widened his eyes as if that fact were quite shocking, which caused her to giggle.

"So we're to say that if the church bells needed to be rung in a rain storm, the bell ringer would be quite soaked by time he reached the church proper?"

"Exactly." His eyes twinkled with mischief.

Playing along, she asked the obvious question. "Why is the bell tower so far removed from the church?"

"The Devil!"

She laughed at his expression of rounded eyes with his head jerking forward, much like an old man who fully believed in the folklore. She did her part and slapped her hand to her chest, widening her own eyes. "No, it cannot be."

He nodded sagely. "But it is. That devil was so bold and so prideful, he sought to take the bell tower away with him."

She crinkled her brows. "But it's still there."

"Yes." He leaned his head back against the tree and looked at her. "It was far too heavy with the weight of God, and he dropped it."

"He dropped it?"

"Yes. He dropped it. That is why he took that poor man who was playing leapfrog here in this field. He was so embarrassed that he couldn't bring the tower with him that he scooped up that poor soul instead."

She chuckled at the seriousness of his tone. "Oh, yes. Now, *that* story is far better." She held her hand up as if he'd speak. "No, don't tell me the true reason the bell tower sits so far away. I much prefer to know the fiction."

He studied her for a moment before continuing. "I promise not to tell you. But I have a suspicion that were we to stop there, you would scour the ground looking for clues."

At his accurate observation, she laughed again. "You have figured me out, my lord."

"So I have." He appeared quite happy with himself. "As I stated, I observe people."

Remembering the context in which he'd stated that, she lifted a forkful of duck. "And you make predictions. Have you ever attended a village fair and had your own future told?" She popped the savory meat into her mouth and chewed, anxious to hear his answer.

His brows furrowed. "Hardly. Why would I wish to be told

lies? That is just a way to take precious funds from those least able to part with them."

What a curmudgeon he was. "Oh, my, no. You really do not see. Those people are not spending coin they can't afford on lies." She shook her head, surprised he did not see the truth of the matter. "They are spending it for a little enjoyment, something different from their day-to-day lives."

"Are you trying to convince me that they spend money to enjoy being told about a false future?"

"Yes. I know because I've been to a few. Once, I went with Lady Eleanor. We dressed like villagers and had our fortunes told. The old woman told me I would marry the dark one day." She chuckled. "You can just imagine what I was thinking. For an entire day, that cryptic prediction kept my mind occupied. Did that mean I'd be spirited away to Gretna Green? Did it mean I wouldn't know whom I was to marry? Did it mean I would marry an evil man?" She shivered for effect. "So of course, we had to go back, but this time, we dressed in our usual clothes. The old lady didn't even look twice. She simply had me hold out my hand and read the lines on my palm." She paused.

He immediately spoke, his interest in her experience obvious. "What did she say the second time?"

Pleased to have his undivided attention, she continued. "She told me I would have my choice of husbands, but to choose wisely and look beneath appearances, as only one was the right one. So once again, I went home thinking about the old woman's message. Her second prediction was difficult to believe since I have had no men interested in me, never mind many. Still, I couldn't help wondering if I would one day marry a man with a scar or a particularly large nose since she said to look beneath appearances."

He chuckled, his green gaze alight with good humor. "So what you mean to say is that the fortune is a form of entertainment, but to what purpose? It is neither a comedy nor a tragedy. Nor is it a sport on which to bet on the best man."

"It's for fun. It's to make people happy."

His brows furrowed once again, obviously confused.

How could she explain? "It's like you enjoying when your predictions come true. In fact, many people will make the future fit what was told them. Just imagine all the ways I could interpret marrying the dark one day. Why, if it was cloudy on my wedding day, I could say it came true." She grinned, pleased to see him smiling again.

"I see your point and appreciate your understanding of others. I cannot say I ever gave it that much thought. I made a quick judgement when I didn't have nearly enough information."

His gaze was far too admiring, making her feel warm, though the day was quite perfect. She needed to distract him before she did something like kiss him in front of the entire group. "Let me have your hand."

CHAPTER THIRTEEN

"WHAT?" LORD HAREWOOD stiffened. "Why?"

Dory almost laughed as he'd pulled his hand back as if she'd offered him a snake. "I'm going to tell your fortune."

"But you are not a fortuneteller."

No wonder the man didn't participate in charades. It was as if he shied away from having fun for the simple sake of it. "I've studied up on it."

His shoulders relaxed, but he remained doubtful. "They allow you to study fortunetelling at your school?"

She refused to answer. Instead, she held her gloved hand out and waited.

He finally seemed to understand how determined she was and set his bare hand in hers.

She bit back a grin at the fact that he placed it palm down. Turning his hand over, she focused on the deep lines in his palm. His hands were smooth, as were those of most men of her class, and it was easy to see every crease. The heat of his hand penetrated her thin summer glove, making it difficult to concentrate. "This is your heart line." She ran her index finger along it. "See here?" She pointed to a place where a crease intersected it. "This is your first love." Even as she said it, she wished she hadn't. She hadn't meant to mention past sorrow.

His hand stiffened, but he didn't pull away.

Trying to keep her words as vague as a fortuneteller's, she moved her finger to another crease farther along his heart line, the movement sending a small thrill through her. "Someone else will come into your life and stir your heart." At least she thought that was the meaning. It could mean he would travel across the ocean and enjoy adventure, but her first interpretation sounded so much better and might even give him a bit of hope.

She quickly moved her finger to another long line in his palm. "This is your head line. It is very strong. It leads you, but here, it grows confused where this crease between the heart and head intersects."

She moved her finger to the long line that outlined the part of his palm where his thumb was anchored. Slowly, she traced the line, not a little excited by the feelings the movement evoked. She wished she could remove her glove. "This is your life line. You will live a long life." At least she that's what one book stated, though the other said it had to do with experiences. She stopped, a chill racing across her shoulders. "Your children are not clear." It was actually as if he were to have children and then they disappeared, only to reappear. "I cannot tell how many."

She heard the step behind her, but before she could drop Lord Harewood's hand, he wrapped his fingers around her own.

"What is it that goes on here?"

Lady Sommerset's amused tone had Dory turning. She smiled guiltily. "Please don't tell anyone I was telling fortunes. Mother would be very upset." She tried to release her hand, but Lord Harewood held firm.

"Fortunes. I did not know you had such a skill. I promise not to tell if you grant me a session." The lady's secret smile appeared.

"There is no need for blackmail, Lady Sommerset. I have no doubt that Lady Dorothea will be happy to"—he released her hand gently—"allow you the same *entertainment* she gave me."

From his tone, it was clear he still questioned the enjoyment of being told a fortune, but at least he didn't frown as he said it.

"Wonderful. I look forward to it. I have been sent by Lady Enderly to request you gather the gentlemen who are interested in the races and begin setting them up."

Lord Harewood stood then held his hand out to help Dory rise. Once again, as their hands connected, a strong heat coursed through her, but it was far more than the thrill of before. She gazed up at him. "Thank you."

"Of course." No humor shone in his eyes, only studious focus. "I hope our coming race will be entertaining for you."

She couldn't quite make her voice work, so she nodded. Then he let go and strode off.

"Telling fortunes?" Lady Sommerset's doubt was obvious.

Not wishing to make Lord Harewood uncomfortable with the countess's continued speculation, Dory immediately smiled. "Yes. I studied it. Your sister has two books on it at school."

Lady Sommerset rolled her eyes. "I should have guessed. Of course she would. Between her and her husband, they have two books on everything." She chuckled. "Then maybe this evening you can be the entertainment and give fortunes."

"Me?" The thought of giving fortunes to everyone was a bit intimidating.

"Well, at least for those who wish them."

She was a bit relieved by that, but couldn't imagine holding other men's palms in her hand. "I can if the ladies want, but it must be at a side table, where no one else can hear. That makes it more mysterious." She wiggled her brows.

Lady Sommerset laughed. "We shall make all the arrangements to give you the right atmosphere. Now we should join the other ladies gathering to watch the races."

She glanced to the right and noticed not only ladies, but a few gentlemen as well. "I see not all the men are racing?"

They walked toward the standing stone, where everyone had gathered. "Yes. Lady Enderly limited it to only eight so they wouldn't go on and on. There will be two races of four and then the first- and second-place winners of those races will race for the prize."

She had no idea what the prize was, but she planned to ask Rose.

As they approached the gathering, Lady Sommerset began a conversation with another chaperone, so Dory took the opportunity to find her friend. It wasn't difficult, as Rose wore a pretty, rose-colored dress and bonnet while most of the other women wore white, pale yellow, and green. When close enough, she clasped her friend's hand.

"Oh, there you are." Rose turned and pulled her to the front. "I have much to tell you."

"You do?" They'd just spoken a couple of hours ago. "Has so much come to pass, then?"

Rose leaned in and whispered. "My time spent with Lord Manning was all about you."

"What?" More than a bit surprised, she checked those nearby to make sure no one heard, then leaned back in. "Why me?"

Rose's eyes twinkled. "As you know, I didn't want him to be interested in me, so I happened to mention that this outing was your idea and that was all I needed to do. He asked me oh-so-many questions about you. So many that I feel we need to spend hours together for me to be able to answer them all."

"Lord Manning?" She should be ecstatic that the marquess was interested in her, but she wasn't.

"I was as surprised as you are. If it had been Lord Dearling, I would have expected it, as everyone can see he is quite smitten with you."

She had surmised as much. That meant two men were interested in her. If either was serious, she could be wed before the next season. Relief ran through her at that possibility. Her mother was less likely to cause a scandal before the next season started.

Rose squeezed her hand even as she whispered excitedly. "So which would you choose?"

"I don't know. I must think about it, though we can't be certain I will have a choice."

Rose grinned. "Oh, you will. We must talk tonight. I'll come to your room."

"I would like that." Having Rose not only welcome her, but support her was a boon she hadn't expected, and she was far more than grateful. Could she truly have a choice of husband? She tried to imagine herself sitting at the end of a long table of guests with Lord Dearling at the other end. It wasn't as difficult as she thought. She changed the scene in her mind to Lord Manning entertaining their guests in a parlor. That was fairly easy to do as well.

But what would it be like when they were alone? She imagined getting ready to sleep, her maid brushing her long hair before braiding it then leaving. As she sat at her dressing table a man's hands rested on her shoulders and bent to kiss the side of her neck. A tiny trill of excitement filled her as she let her eyelids close and tipped her head to allow him easier access. He eased her shift off her shoulder to kiss that very spot before his hand moved lower to cup her breast. Her breath caught in her chest and her eyes flew open to stare at him in the mirror.

Lord Harewood smiled seductively back at her.

Her heart raced with anticipation when a gunshot startled her. She blinked to see four horses racing across the field, the thunder of their hooves vibrating beneath her own feet.

Confused by her imagination, she squeezed Rose's hand in hers.

"Isn't it exciting?" Rose turned to her and smiled. "Watch. I'm sure my brother on Nyx will place. That black devil will do anything to show he's the best. After talking to Lord Manning today, I'm going to guess he will place as well. He did mention his horse and its speed."

Dory forced herself to focus across the field where the horses ran. The black horse called Nyx was nearest them, but she couldn't bring herself to look at the rider. The horse remained with two others, another pulling ahead slightly. As they reached the halfway marker, or rather Lord Sommerset, the black horse began to move ahead of the others. When they raced to the end of the course, which was watched closely by Lord and Lady Enderly and Lady Sommerset, it was obvious who had won. Rose was correct. Lord Harewood and Lord Manning claimed first and second places respectively.

As the next group of men mounted and trotted their horses to the starting line, she forced herself to take deep breaths. Her imagination was far too strong. She needed to focus on what was real, which could very well be two good men interested in her. To that end, she looked for Lord Dearling in the next set to race. Though she was grateful to Lord Harewood for helping her, he'd made it very clear that he was not ready for a wife yet. She wished she truly knew how to read palms. What if the line that intersected his head and his heart was indicative of this very moment in time? What if she actually had three men to choose from?

Her body heated at such a wonderful predicament when her words not an hour past came back to her. *She told me I would have my choice of husbands, but to choose wisely and look beneath appearances, as only one was the right one.* She shivered. Was the fortuneteller's look into the future true?

"Dory, are you cold?" Rose's lips pressed together in her concern.

"No. I'm just excited to see who will win this next race." It wasn't exactly a lie, but if given the opportunity, she'd have been happy to crawl into a coach and hide to be alone with her thoughts until the festivities were done.

"I know. This is more exciting than the puzzles the men will have to solve tonight. I prefer to see their physical prowess." Rose giggled, a slight blush heating her cheek.

It hadn't occurred to her that Rose had knowledge of men's physiques. She wanted to tease her, but her thoughts were a muddle at the moment. Instead, she asked the first question that came to mind, but in a whisper. "Do you know what men do with women then?"

Rose looked around before wiggling her eyebrows. "I do."

A gunshot went off, and Rose immediately turned back to watch the race.

The younger Ambroses seemed intent on confusing her. They weren't what she'd expected. In fact, she liked them because of that. Now she worried that Rose would talk of nothing but the men's physical prowess tonight, which would hardly help her current dilemma.

"Look." Rose pointed.

She forced herself to watch the second race. Lord Dearling was a full horse length ahead of the others, but Mr. Retfield gained ground. The two men finished first and second. As everyone clapped, she determined to enjoy the moment. "This is far more exciting than I imagined."

Though she spoke to Rose, someone else answered.

"Have you never been to a horse race, then, Lady Dorothea?" At the sound of Lord Leighhall behind her, she stepped forward.

"Lord Leighhall, I didn't see you there." Had the man heard any of her and Rose's conversation? He seemed the sort to eavesdrop and not let on.

"I am here. Since I didn't bring my favorite mount, I declined to join the race. But if I had, I assure you that Caesar would easily win."

She bit back what she wished to say. "I would have enjoyed seeing that. I'm sure your horse would make these races even more exciting than they are."

He didn't say anything at first, as if he expected her to continue. Obviously, he didn't understand that she'd prefer to speak to anyone else.

His forehead furrowed, making it look a bit like an angry owl. "You don't go on and on anymore in conversation. Did you learn to curb your poor habit at that school you attend? If so, I may have misjudged its uselessness."

She was not only insulted on her own behalf but on the school's as well, and her words wedged in her throat like a log jam.

Rose must have sensed her upset and answered. "I'm so pleased you think the Belinda School for Curious Ladies is of high quality. I, myself, will begin attending next month. I've already learned so much from Lady Dorothea. I cannot wait to start my studies."

The man's brows rose. "You?"

Rose gave him an elegant nod. "Yes. My brother and father fully support me in my endeavor to cultivate my mind a bit more."

"But you are perfectly refined. Why would *you* go?"

His emphasis on the word *you* made it clear that he thought Rose much better quality than those who attended the school.

Dory was done being insulted by the man. "Perhaps Rose wishes to attend the school for the same reason you attended Cambridge or Oxford."

The man snapped his head around to look at her as if he'd forgotten she were there. "I attended Cambridge because my father told me to attend. I assure you, I did as little as I could in classes and as much as possible in the physical activities." His gaze roamed over her as if he found her lacking in feminine attributes.

Beyond caring after such an insulting look, she narrowed her gaze. "That is rather sad. The Duke of Northwick, who owns the school I attend, believes a man who does not cultivate his mind is doomed to failure." Though it was the truth, by the intense look in Lord Leighhall's eyes, he was highly affronted.

"I imagine he also expects his students to behave in a proper manner to those of higher intellect."

"Oh, my, yes, and I do." She smiled sweetly, making it clear she did not consider him more intelligent than herself.

The man opened his mouth, no doubt to set her down, but the gun went off and the horses galloped across the field once more. She took the opportunity to turn her back on the odious man and watch.

All four horses were well matched and they kept pace with

each other. She wasn't sure why her heart was beating so fast, but she dug her fingers into her palms as she watched. Eventually, Lord Manning's horse began to pull ahead, but just by a nose. As they sped past Lord Sommerset at the halfway mark, Lord Harewood had joined him in the lead. The two men lengthened the gap between them and the others. As the two drew close to the finish line, Lord Harewood's horse shot out ahead and won by half a length.

Rose turned toward her and hugged her. "I told you! That proud stallion of his refuses to lose."

The four men in the race slowed and turned back toward the finish line. Lord Harewood was the first to dismount, preferring to walk his horse toward the cheering crowd.

Lord Leighhall grumbled. "That's not very sporting of him. This is his party. He should have allowed someone else to win."

Dory didn't turn, pretending she hadn't heard, as it was quite loud.

"My lord." Rose looked behind her. "Do tell me you didn't bet against my brother based on such an assumption."

"Bet? Why would you think I bet? Men do more than that, my lady." The man walked between them and out to meet those coming in from the race.

Dory couldn't help a satisfied smile. "He bet and lost. I do believe he bet on Mr. Retfield."

Rose chuckled and linked her arm with hers. "Let us go congratulate my brother. His horse may be an ass, but it was still well done."

She laughed at that, even as her belly tingled at the idea of congratulating Lord Harewood. They were not the first to meet him halfway across the field, and he was surrounded by the other guests. She took the opportunity to observe him. His smile seemed genuine and he accepted congratulations with humility, consistently patting his horse and giving Nyx credit.

As people moved on to console the other riders, she and Rose finally had his attention, or rather Rose, who threw herself into his arms. "I knew you'd win." She laughed before he set her back and she straightened her bonnet. "That damn horse of yours."

He grinned, not a little proud of *that* horse. "I can count on Nyx for speed when it's needed. He's dependable in that."

"If nothing else." Rose's comment got a neigh from the horse.

Dory's heart pounded at his happiness. "You feel true joy in winning." She hadn't meant to blurt it out, but fortunately, only Rose was near enough to overhear.

He finally turned his attention to her. "Yes, I do." He paused for just a moment before understanding dawned. "It is another activity that brings me happiness." His grin changed into a soft smile. "Thank you for making me aware of this."

She nodded, her throat closing at the look in his eyes. She wanted to say the common theme was winning, but she didn't wish him to stop looking at her in that way.

"Lord Leighhall is not happy." Rose broke the moment, nodding to where the man stood with Mr. Retfield. "Which is as it should be. He was incredibly rude to Dory."

Lord Harewood, who had looked in the direction his sister had motioned, turned back quickly. "Rude? How? What did he say?"

She wanted to tug on Rose to remain silent, but she was beyond arm's length. "It was nothing. He's been rude to me before." She waved her hand, wishing he would go back to smiling. "It was nothing."

"Oh, but you should have heard Dory insult him right back." Rose laughed. "It was wonderful." She linked her arm through her brother's. "Now we will escort you back to save you from Mother's scolding."

Lord Harewood continued to look at her with brows lowered, making her search for a way to make him smile again.

Instead, she addressed Rose. "Why would your mother scold Lord Harewood?"

At that, his brows relaxed, and though he didn't smile, he didn't seem as concerned. "Because my mother would have wanted me to allow one of her guests to win. But too many people here know Nyx and his abilities. It would have been too obvious." He looked at his sister. "I will be happy for your escort."

"Come, Dory. You must come too. Mother won't bother us if you are with us."

Happy to be of assistance, she linked her arm with Rose's free one. As they made their way back to the shade of the trees, she was able to untangle some of her jumbled thoughts. The first thread to come loose was the fact that she wished she were arm in arm with the earl. The second piece of twine to unravel itself made it clear that she had too many feelings for the man. The rest of the jumble tangled around how he felt about her. She had to know.

CHAPTER FOURTEEN

STEPPING OUT ONTO the balcony of his room in his dressing gown, Felton inhaled the cool, night air. There was no moon, which was why his mother had chosen earlier to reveal her lit garden. Many of the guests had not experienced his mother's faerie garden, as she titled it, and they raved about it until well after midnight. No doubt she would be in a pleasant mood on the morrow.

He studied the open field, trees, and the once-lit gardens. Though Lady Dorothea had been through some of the courts before, she had seemed to enjoy them on the arm of Lord Dearling. He wasn't ignorant that three men were becoming far more interested in her. Lord Dearling made it ridiculously obvious. Lord Manning was more subtle about it but no less persistent. Mr. Retfield also appeared interested but didn't jockey for position with the other two, simply stepping in when they were absent.

This should please him. It did please him. It also infuriated him, which was baffling. This was what he wanted, for a student of the school to be sought after. She had taken his advice and had become popular among the bachelors. He should be feeling victorious, not frustrated.

It must be that he didn't know which man she preferred. If he could have a private conversation with her, she would assuredly tell him. He didn't doubt that at all. But having a private conversation with her was becoming more difficult by the day. He could enlist the aid of Lady Sommerset, but then he'd have to explain why he needed to talk with Lady Dorothea. He wasn't yet ready to reveal his part in her success. She had done the work of curtailing her conversation. He had simply guided her in the right direction.

He sincerely hoped she didn't choose Retfield. The man's reticence to show his interest made him far too weak for her. Dearling would do anything for her, at least until his mother asked him to do something else. They all knew the man's mother would have the final say. Would she approve of Lady Dorothea? Manning was the most fitted to her. The man had strong character, was a marquess, and he wasn't afraid to fight for time with her. But could he appreciate the honest Dorothea?

And there was his concern. That must be why he kept replaying scenes of her with the other men. That was the question that wouldn't let him sleep. Could any of the men appreciate her as she truly was, and not the lady she was succeeding at presenting herself to be because she changed how she spoke? The answer was obvious. They couldn't. Very few men could. He'd known that before he'd started this challenge. But did she know it? If she did, would she accept that?

His irritation melted into defeat. She would. She had no choice. It wasn't as if her mother would curtail her amorous activities. If the countess had cared a wit about her daughter's prospects, she would have been at the least more circumspect, but she was whispered about at White's. Her dissatisfaction with her husband seemed to be growing as she'd been spotted leaving two events with a gentleman not her husband in the final week of the season. She either grew careless or purposefully wished to damage her husband. Neither of which aided in making a match for Dory. It was as if the woman had sent her daughter away to forget about her.

The sound of a latch moving broke the quiet night. He turned to see if Sommerset also couldn't sleep. Instead, a shadowy figure appeared on the balcony just beyond his. Dorothea.

She stepped to the edge, laid her hands on the balustrade, and peered into the darkness. Her white shift moved slightly from the gentle breeze, which also brought the scent of lemon drops to his nose. Something in her stance told him she was troubled. He must have observed her more than he'd realized to understand such a subtle posture.

Her hair lay long against her back, slightly tangled while the breeze gently lifted the strands against her cheek. Her profile in the limited light accentuated her high cheekbones and turned-up nose.

Suddenly, as if she sensed his gaze, she turned her head and looked directly at him. He couldn't see her eyes, but her hand came to her chest. "You." Though the word was whispered, it broke the silence of the night.

"Yes. Could you not sleep?" He kept his voice low as a balcony lay between them.

She cocked her head as if she couldn't hear, which made sense since the light breeze carried her words to him, but not so his to hers.

Without a second thought, he jumped up onto the balustrade closest to Sommerset's balcony and stepped across the two-foot space to the balustrade neighboring before quietly stepping down. He continued across the empty balcony to the balustrade closest to her and jumped up once again. When he stepped across the abyss between the two balconies, her intake of breath registered before he stepped down.

She had backed up to allow him room and stood frozen, her hand over her mouth.

"I thought it best we talk quietly," he whispered.

Her eyes widened before she dropped her hand and her brows lowered. "By the beard of Zeus, you scared away two years of my life. You could have fallen. Have you no brains?" The last word ended in what could only be called a hiss.

It took him a moment to answer before understanding set in. She had been afraid for him. "There was no need to worry. I've been walking these balconies since I was half a score. It's always been the easiest way for causing mischief for my sister."

She eyed him doubtfully, her hand swinging back and forth. "You crossed these balconies to cause mischief? You must understand that is difficult to imagine."

He smirked as memories flooded his mind. "I was quite good at it, actually. Ask Rose about the time she found a frog in her bed or when her favorite dress had a mysterious, purple stain in the middle."

"You did that by jumping balconies to slip into her room? Why not use the inside corridor?"

He loved that she pictured and analyzed his story so quickly. "I did it at night, while she slept."

Once more, her eyes widened. "Do you mean to say that she *woke up* with the frog in her bed?"

He grinned. "At least it wasn't a dead frog."

She squealed but quickly covered her mouth, still giggling behind her hands.

"Mother was sorely disappointed in me, but I think my father was rather proud."

She dropped her hand and gave him a stern look, or tried to. "What a terrible brother you were."

"Yes, I was. But to be fair, Rose was just as terrible as I…and still is. Though no one would ever know." The sudden thought that she might have to lose her mischievous nature once married sobered him, leaving behind a sadness he didn't quite understand.

"It sounds like you much enjoyed playing pranks on each other. Do you not anymore?"

"No. We must become proper adults."

She wriggled her nose as a smile lifted her lips. "Rose hasn't, at least not in private."

That was true. He didn't have to think long on when he'd stopped. It was when Belinda had passed. There just hadn't seemed a point to it, or anything else, for that matter.

"Does she not call you anything besides *brother*? I never hear her call you by your name."

The question brought his good humor back. "Ah, yes, as for that, she does not like my name, especially my title. She says it sounds like I'm in charge of a forest filled with rabbits. When she was just a child, she named me 'the King of Bunnies.'"

"Oh, I do like that. Would you mind terribly if I—"

"Absolutely not." He made his quiet voice as stern as he could.

She sighed. "Alas, if not that, then I must find another name to call you, at least when talking to Rose. I will now never be able to say *Lord Harewood* without thinking of all those cute bunnies."

Her comment reminded him of her penchant for creating images in her head, and he groaned. "Then I must insist on approving said name."

"That is acceptable. I shall endeavor to create a number from which you can choose."

That she would go to the trouble, not only of giving him a nickname, but also of allowing him to decide with her, filled a small void in his heart he hadn't realized had been there. "I would enjoy that."

Even in the darkness, it was easy to see at such close proximity that her eyes lit with pleasure as she spoke. "This then is something else that will make you happy. I do believe we are finding quite a number of things, and this one is the first that is not about winning."

Her observation struck him. Was winning truly his only happiness? If he succeeded in helping Belinda's school gain a good reputation, it wouldn't be winning, would it? No, it would be succeeding in keeping her name on a pedestal, where it belonged. That very thought brought him back to the reason he had jumped the balconies. "There is something else that makes me happy, and that is your success here at Sunnydale. You have done very well to curb your conversation, yet here you are on your balcony in the middle of the night when you should be abed."

She glanced behind him as if someone would overhear. "I'm troubled. My thoughts are a muddle."

It was smart to be cautious. Anyone could step out onto their balcony and find them together and then all their efforts would have been in vain. If he remembered correctly, her muddle was a tangle of yarn dropped into a puddle, which did sound serious. "If you would like me to assist you in untangling your thoughts, I suggest we move into your room to discuss what is causing such a ruckus in your head."

"That would hardly be proper." Her more formal tone change reminded him of his sister's regular switches in character.

Dory may not be able to see him well, but he raised his brows. "Do you think someone is more likely to see us in your room or out here on the balcony? Or if you prefer, we can discuss your quandary on the morrow. Perhaps at dinner?"

She hesitated then moved to her door, motioning for him to follow.

As he stepped over the threshold, misgivings filled his head. Her room was lit by no more than one lantern and the fire in the fireplace. An embroidery loop lay on a chair and a book sat on the end table next to the bed. The atmosphere was intimate and comfortable. Being here could prove his mother right about him and society right about Dorothea. This was not the best place to converse. He needed to leave.

"It's about Lord Dearling."

At her words, all thoughts of leaving vanished. "You are troubled by Lord Dearling?"

She stood next to the post at the end of her bed. The lantern provided enough light to see that she was confused about the man. "I believe he holds me in high esteem."

High esteem? The man had almost made a fool of himself over her that very evening by jumping up to escort her in to dinner, even though they would not be sitting near each other. "I would agree." He held back listing the man's faults. For all he knew, she found every one of them endearing.

"Oh, good. Then it makes sense that he kissed me in the gardens tonight." She nodded in understanding.

"He *kissed* you?" His voice rose as fury ignited inside him, almost obliterating all thought but retaliation.

"Shhhh." She held her finger to her lips and stood absolutely still.

His hands clenched into fists of their own accord. How dare the man take such liberties while at Sunnydale? One word to his mother and the earl would find himself halfway home by the time they broke their fast. Or would she assume that Dorothea had enticed him? He squeezed his hands harder, frustrated as well as angry.

She removed her finger from her lips and whispered. "Yes, he kissed me. But I didn't feel anything. He's such a nice man and very accommodating. But it wasn't like when you kissed me."

He swallowed hard to stay in control of his voice when he wanted nothing more than to roar. "What do you mean? What was it like when I kissed you?"

She leaned against the post and wrapped her arm around it. "It was terrifying and exciting, like falling from this very balcony while naked onto a large pile of thistledown feathers covered in soft furs that touch every inch of my sensitive skin."

Her description struck him like a thunderbolt, his body reacting as he envisioned it all. This time, he couldn't even swallow.

"When you kiss me, my thoughts fly and all that occupies me is physical feeling." Her brows furrowed. "It's not just my skin, but inside of me too. It's as if fire is dancing in my veins, but it feels wonderful. It's all so…so freeing."

Even as she spoke, her face flushed and her gaze softened.

He should leave. He must go. But his feet refused to move.

Then she looked toward the fireplace, her brow furrowed in confusion. "But when Lord Dearling kissed me, I felt nothing. My thoughts kept moving about. His lips were not nearly as commanding."

Rage filled him. A need to wipe the man's kiss from her mind sent lightning racing through his body. It was barely three strides before he had her in his arms, his mouth demanding she open to him.

She complied at once, leaning into him, her plump breasts through her shift pressing against his thinly clad stomach. Her body instinctually molded to his, stoking his desire for her. He could barely think as her innocent tongue delved and dipped in his mouth, exciting him more than any experienced courtesan. Warmth radiated from her that was far more than heat. Her honest reaction to him sparked something inside he'd long thought dead. He moved his hand down her back to the curve of her backside and, unable to resist, squeezed.

Her breath caught, but she didn't pull away. Instead, her arms, which held him about the waist, moved and her hands grasped him in the same way.

He would have laughed if she hadn't just sent desire racing through his groin. Grasping her waist to set her back, he found himself instead kissing her neck, inhaling the distinct scent of lemon and something else, something purely feminine. He tried to gain control of his actions, but a burning need pushed him on until he'd lowered the neckline of the modest shift down off her shoulder and his mouth found her hardened nipple. Without a thought, he latched on and sucked gently.

A small moan escaped her before she grabbed his head and pressed closer.

Obeying her silent command, he sucked harder and her hands left his head to grab on to his shoulders as she arched, giving herself to him.

She let out another moan that changed into a word. "Fen."

He drew back, confusion allowing his brain to function on more than a basic level. What was he about? He carefully set her limp body on the bed and stepped back.

She lay there, eyes closed, her breast still exposed to his view, causing his body to harden. She finally opened her eyes and gazed at him beneath hooded eyelids. "That is wonderful."

His groin tightened, but he shook his head silently, unable to find the will to speak, too confused by the need to take her. His mind told him he couldn't, but the craving wouldn't leave.

She sat up, her bare legs dangling over the side of the bed, her hair now partially covering her nakedness. "You make me feel…" She cocked her head. "I feel exponentially alive. Please. Don't stop."

His conscience told him to walk out the door, yet his body hungered for her and would not let him leave. Her plea was too hard to resist, but she knew not what she asked. He tried to form the words, but it took all his control to remain where he stood.

She frowned. "I already know what happens. I just didn't know it could feel like this. My body feels like it's on fire from the inside." She scooted off the bed and stood.

If she touched him, he'd be lost. He had to turn and leave, somehow. He forced himself to take another step back but froze.

She lifted her shift up and over her head, tossing it on the bed behind her.

Her curves were far more than he'd expected. Well-rounded breasts led to a respectable waist, only to curve over wider hips and healthy thighs that begged a man to explore. Her pear-like shape enticed him beyond his control, but he managed not to move, his arms stiff at his sides.

She walked two paces to stop before him, and without asking, she untied the belt at his waist, revealing exactly how much he wanted her.

"Oh." She stepped back.

Her reaction finally snapped his immobility, and he quickly strode toward the door to the balcony.

"Fen?"

He halted at the word but didn't turn around. "What is that word?"

"It's my nickname for you. Is it acceptable?"

His heart pounded, forcing him to suck in deep breaths. Fen.

Understanding how her mind worked, it was easy to see that she'd devised it from compacting his name, crushing the letters together as it were. Not Felton. Just Fen. That was what he was to her. He'd never been that for anyone.

Her hands wrapped around his waist. "Do you like it?"

Cursing his own weakness for being merely a man, he turned in her arms and held her close. "I do…Dory."

She lifted her face from his shoulder, smiling shyly. "Will you suck me again?"

Swallowing down a groan, he nodded. He was a fool, but he couldn't deny her. He just had to deny himself…somehow.

Taking his hand, she led him back to the bed. "Do I sit again?"

"Lie back." His voice came out so gravelly that her brow puckered, but she did as he instructed.

He climbed on the bed and lay next to her. As he did so, she lifted her arms over her head, no doubt to make it easier for him, but the supplication was innocently seductive. Unable to resist what she offered, he leaned over and stroked her hardened nipple with his tongue.

She lay completely still, as if she feared he would leave her. How little she knew and should remain ignorant of, but failure that he was, he couldn't stop. Her soft, white skin begged for his touch. He moved his mouth over her tautened peak and sucked gently, taking in more.

Arching into him, she kept her hands above her as a small moan sounded deep in her throat.

Continuing his homage to her breast, he took her other between his fingers and gently squeezed.

"Yesss," she hissed softly, bending one knee before letting it fall to the side.

The scent of her excitement was too much an invitation to ignore.

DORY MOANED AGAIN as Fen switched and sucked her other breast, his hand replacing his mouth on the opposite one. She'd never imagined she could feel this way, so alive to every touch, with fluid flames filling her inside. An ache started between her thighs, which must mean she was ready for completion, but he seemed bent only on her breasts. Surely, there was something at the end of all her feelings.

His mouth started to lightly nibble at her nipple and new shocks of excitement shot through her. She grasped the pillow with both hands to keep her hands out of the way, but the heat between her thighs was so intense that she spread her legs.

Then his hand left her breast and moved over her belly. She opened her eyes to watch as he smoothed his way down to the patch of hair that hid her very core. His fingers slid through her auburn curls, and she held her breath.

With his hand resting on her mons, he angled himself up with his other arm and looked down at her. "I will not ruin you for your future husband. Do you understand?"

She felt her cheeks heat. It meant he would not take her for his own. Though disappointment wafted over her at his intense stare, she could only nod. Her body didn't care what he did as long as he continued. She raised her hips with his hand, silently asking for his touch.

As if he knew exactly what she wanted, his fingers moved into her wet folds. She widened her eyes at the intense sensation, unable to do anything but press her hips upward.

His nostrils flared at her reaction. "Kiss me."

At his command, she realized it was what she wanted. She wrapped her arms around him and did as he commanded.

His tongue swept into her mouth, demanding she surrender as he played with one spot between her legs, the feelings growing stronger there. She found herself holding on to him, his lips, his body, as she spiraled out of control, his touch taking her beyond mere reality to another realm of existence. Just when the sensations seemed as good as they could possibly be, she exploded into ecstasy, finding a bliss she'd never known existed. He held her there, her pleasure unimaginable, exciting and satisfying at the same time. Finally, the feelings slowly subsided like leaves falling from a tree in autumn, leaving her limp and tired as she had never been before.

His lips left hers, and she opened her eyes to gaze at him with pure gratefulness, but she couldn't seem to muster the energy to speak.

As if he knew how she felt, he rolled away, pulling the covers over her from the side as he did so, leaving her in a warm cocoon. He stood gazing at her with no expression, as if contemplating something of great importance. Then he turned and strode out of view, the belt of his dressing gown dangling from his waist.

She closed her eyes and smiled. She no longer felt she was in a muddle. No, everything was crystal clear. She loved the Earl of Harewood, and though he may think her fit for another man, he would see that he loved her back. All would be well.

CHAPTER FIFTEEN

RUSHING THROUGH HER toilette, Dory quickly dressed, no doubt giving the maid much trouble, but in short order, she was at Rose's door and being bid enter. Walking in, she found Rose still abed. "Oh, you must hurry. We need to go down before the men leave for the hunt."

"The hunt? There is no hunt today. Remember, we are preparing for the play."

She'd forgotten. "But I saw the groom bring a horse around out my window. I thought it was for a hunt." She shrugged. "Then I guess there is no rush." Though she wished to see Fen as soon as possible. Had he awoken this morning realizing how much he wanted her for a wife? She couldn't wait to talk to him.

"But I do know Cook was planning brioche buns for this morning. Shall we sneak down before anyone breaks their fast and steal some?" At the mischief in Rose's pretty, blue eyes, Dory knew there would be more to this stealthy expedition than it appeared, but if that meant she could see Fen sooner, she was ready. "Yes, let's."

Rose jumped from her bed and called her maid. Still, it was a good thirty minutes before they were quietly rushing down the stairs. No one was about except the servants, so they needn't have been stealthy, but Rose insisted on peeking around every corner before moving down a corridor and opening the door to the kitchen.

Once inside, Rose ducked to hide behind a table and put her finger to her lips. Then she pointed toward the fireplace and a long table piled high with brioche buns. Staying low, she skittered over and without looking, put her hand up and pulled a bun from the pile. Unfortunately, the rest tumbled down after it, some falling to the floor, but a few she caught and handed off.

Dory dropped the hot bun into her skirt folds, just before a voice sounded above the bustle of the kitchen.

"Lady Rose Ambrose, don't you think I don't know you're stealing me buns."

They both giggled at being caught. Rose stood. "How did you know?"

"I know everything that goes on in me kitchen. Who you got there with you? I know it isn't your brother, as he already came in and took a basket for his trip."

Hearing that Fen had gone on a trip, Dory stood, losing the buns in her skirts. "A trip?"

Rose stood as well at that. "Lady Dorothea, this is Mrs. Mac-Manus. Mrs. MacManus, this is Lady Dorothea Ansley. She's my good friend."

The older lady was as wide as she was tall, with a head full of white hair, a large nose, and a lopsided frown that she was desperately trying to hold. "Thick as thieves you be. Now come over here and eat those properly."

Rose led her to a small table, where Mrs. MacManus set a plate piled high with brioche buns along with jam, butter, and a pot of tea. Rose immediately poured. "One day, I am going to sneak in and out of here and you will be none the wiser."

Mrs. MacManus clucked her tongue. "Not likely, lass. But I admire your persistence."

Rose bit off a large bite of warm bun.

Dory took a sip of tea and turned to Mrs. MacManus. "Did you say Lord Harewood went on a trip? That is odd in the middle of a house party, is it not?"

Mrs. MacManus yelled to a young boy to take out the slop before answering. "That boy always did what he wanted."

Rose, having finished her first bun, started spreading jam on her second. "Where did he go? Did Mother send him on another errand?" She wiggled her brows as she took a large bite.

"I dinna know nothing about her ladyship, but he did say he was off to Denton Hall. Took a good dozen of my buns with him, he did."

As Mrs. MacManus strode off to instruct a maid in tending a large pot that hung over the open fire, Dory looked to Rose. "Where is Denton Hall and why would your brother go there in the middle of the party?"

Rose stopped buttering her third bun. "I don't know. That's his own estate. I can't think of a reason why Mother would send him there, unless he received word that he was needed?" Her brows lowered. "Though why, I wouldn't know. He has a rather apt steward and the place is always perfect when I visit." She leaned forward and lowered her voice. "Maybe he just wanted to check to make sure everyone was doing what they were supposed to while he's gone. That's something he would do."

Dory swallowed another sip of tea, her bun still sitting on her plate untouched. "But why would he do so during your mother's party?" Something didn't make sense and her thoughts were running into each other. Had he indeed woken up and realized he loved her and then left on pretense to ride to her father and ask for her hand? Had he gone to his estate to tell his people to redesign a room for a new lady of the house? Or had he left because he was ashamed of what he had done with her last night? Or worse, he never wished to see her again because he was disappointed in the way she'd acted?

"That's a good question." Rose took a sip of tea. "I suggest after we finish here, we follow the clues. First, we'll find out if Mother and he had yet another fight. If not, then we will subtly look for a letter, maybe in his room. We just can't tell him we were in there. He would be sure to take revenge on me." Though

Rose appeared scared, her eyes twinkled with mischief.

Dory wished she could be as excited by the prospect of solving the mystery as her friend suggested, but a deep disappointment had settled in her belly. Why wouldn't he have at least left a note?

"Now you'd best eat, as it looks like we have more to do today beyond practicing for the play."

At Rose's suggestion, Dory forced herself to take a bite of the brioche bun, but no flavor registered. All she kept seeing in her mind was the long look he'd given her before leaving. Had she misread it?

After Rose had eaten no fewer than five buns, and Dory had managed to finish one, Rose led the way on their hunt for clues. Since no one was yet about, Rose suggested her brother's room was a good place to start. They waited until his valet left then sprinted across the hall.

Rose turned and locked the door once they were inside. "Just a precaution."

Dory stood stock-still. Being in a gentleman's bedroom was simply not done. Her reputation would be in ruins if she were caught. Even with those worrisome thoughts, she found herself drawn to the bed, not yet made. The room smelled of him and his subtle pine scent that made her miss him all the more and yet he was not gone but a few hours.

"I don't see a note anywhere. Look by the fireplace, maybe on the mantel. I'll check his dressing room."

Dory walked to where a black, leather wingback chair sat before the fireplace and ran her fingers along the top of it. Of course, it would be black. Had he sat here last night and contemplated his future? She wished so, but she shouldn't. He hadn't said anything when he'd left. Hearing the dressing room door creak, she quickly moved to the mantel before examining the small, empty table next to the chair.

"Did you find anything?" Rose walked over studying the area, even looking under the chair.

"No. I don't even see a book here."

"In his dressing room, his valet has him half-packed, so he left in a hurry." Rose sighed. "He's rarely here anymore. He has his estate to tend to and his friends."

Her friend's wistfulness registered and Dory pushed away her own wishes. "You miss him."

Rose sat in the chair. "I do. I know it's silly, but he's been a wonderful brother. I try to help him remember what it was like before Lady Belinda passed, but sometimes I feel it's not enough. I worry about him, which is of no matter to him."

"Oh, but I think it does matter. He speaks of you fondly."

Rose smiled. "I know. I—"

The doorknob turned and they froze.

Grumbling on the other side made it clear the valet was back.

Rose's eyes widened. "We have to leave. I'm sure he will get the housekeeper to open it."

They both walked toward the door, the sound of voices in the hall making it clear they couldn't escape yet, when Rose grabbed her hand and yanked her back. "That's the housekeeper's voice," she whispered frantically. "We can't let them know we're in here." She glanced at the room, as if there were somewhere they could hide, when Lady Enderly's voice asking what was the problem came clearly through the door.

Dory's heart stopped. She had to escape. She snapped her head to the door of the balcony and without a second thought strode to it.

Rose followed. "What are you doing?" Her voice, though soft, contained true fear.

Dory walked onto the balcony and looked toward her own. If Fen could make the trek in the night, she could do it in the daylight. "You can be caught in his bedroom. I can't. I have to go." She pointed past Lord and Lady Sommerset's balcony to her own.

Rose's eyes widened. "My brother used to do that, but it's too dangerous. I can simply explain."

Dory shook her head. "No. What you can do is go back in there and keep them occupied so I have time."

Rose worried her bottom lip but finally nodded and went back in the room.

Convincing Rose to go inside was easier than convincing herself she could walk from balcony to balcony. She was far shorter than Fen and the space farther for her, but at the sound of the key in the door inside, she stepped onto the balustrade, her hand against the wall for balance. She just needed to focus on the next balustrade and not on the open space between them that was far too high to survive. That was all.

Voices inside the room told her she had to move. Lifting her skirts, she took the wide step onto the next balustrade but just as her other foot found purchase, she lost her balance and teetered for a moment, her breath leaving her before she fell forward onto the floor of the balcony.

Her heart pounded with relief. Sitting up, she brushed herself off and rose on shaky legs. She looked at her own balcony with yearning but was not sure she could bring herself to attempt another jump.

Rose's voice rose near the earl's balcony doors. "Really, Mother. You are making more of this than need be. I simply searched for the reason my brother left. I promise, I did not loosen the seams in his pantaloons. I'm not a child anymore."

Surely, Lady Enderly wouldn't venture out onto her son's balcony for any reason.

Yet something hitting that very door had Dory freezing in place.

"Of course not, Mother. Why would I wish to search the balcony? I doubt very much that my brother left any note he may have received out there to be swept away on the wind."

Lady Enderly's tone of voice came through, though her words did not, but they didn't need to. She obviously expected Rose to open the doors.

Panicked, Dory turned toward the balustrade and swallowed

hard.

The latch on the door next to her sounded and she jumped, stepping back.

Lady Sommerset's eyebrows rose at seeing her there, but before Dory could say anything, Lady Enderly stepped out on Fen's balcony.

Lady Sommerset waved. "Lady Enderly, what a surprise to see you out here."

The marchioness turned and looked at them in surprise. "You are up early, Lady Sommerset, Lady Dorothea."

Rose stepped out next to her mother, her eyes widening. "Lady Sommerset. Isn't it a beautiful morning?" She gestured toward the lawns. "Mother chose the perfect day for breaking our fast on the terrace. You will be there?"

Lady Sommerset gave a nod. "Oh, yes. Lady Dorothea and I are looking forward to it. We shall be down shortly."

Without another word, Lady Sommerset linked her arm with Dory's and pulled her into the room. She let go and closed the doors before turning, her hands on her hips. "What are you about? I saw you *jump* onto my balcony. Tell me you did not spend the night with Lord Harewood. Tell me." It was a demand, not a question.

She shook her head. "No, I didn't." Though what they *had* done made her cheeks heat.

Lady Sommerset stalked past her. "I'm your chaperone. As a student of my sister's school, I insist you conduct yourself in an appropriate manner. Since you say you did not spend the night in the next room, you need to tell me why you jumped onto my balcony. It was not from your room."

Before turning, she glanced at the curtained door to see that the drapes were sheer and it was quite easy to see all that had occurred. Finally, she faced Lady Sommerset. "Rose and I discovered while in the kitchen that Lord Harewood has left for his estate. She wished to have some fun by finding out why. Her first place to search for clues was Lord Harewood's room. She was looking for a missive that would explain why he'd left. When her mother arrived to unlock the door for the valet, we knew that if I were caught there, it would do damage to my reputation, so I stepped out onto the balcony, hoping to get to my own."

She shivered at her remembered fright. "But I almost fell backward between them and couldn't bring myself to attempt another try. I'm truly sorry. I did not mean to conduct myself in so poor a fashion." She looked down at her hands, quite sure she would be locked in her room for the rest of the week for such unladylike behavior.

"Well, thank the heavens you didn't fall. I truly don't know how I would explain *that* to my sister."

Startled by the thought, she looked up to find the countess smiling. "You aren't angry."

"How can I be? It's obvious Rose was the instigator. She always was as a child, but I thought she'd left that in her childhood. I'm just pleased that you didn't fall and Lady Enderly did not catch you in her son's room. It looks as if all is well and we can move on with our day. I would suggest you return to your room by the corridor and wait for me there. We will go down for the morning meal together."

"Of course." Still feeling very guilty, she quickly left the room and walked the short distance to her door. Just as she'd reached for the knob, she caught movement at the top of the stairs. The man's face was in shadow and rather than be caught in the corridor unchaperoned, she turned the knob.

"Lady Dorothea."

At the sound of Lord Leighhall's voice, she quickly stepped into her room and closed the door, leaning her back against it. He was the last man she wished to talk to now or ever.

"You can't hide from me. I saw you from the terrace below. You are obviously no different than your mother, as I suspected."

Her belly squirmed as if filled with the frogs Fen had spoken of. She wanted to argue she was nothing like her mother. Instead, she clamped her jaw tight. She would not have a conversation through her door. But what if he told everyone what he'd seen?

He laughed. "No wish to defend your actions or is it that you admit them?" He paused, obviously trying to goad her into speaking. "Very well. I will keep your little secret for the moment, but only as long as I receive the same attention Lord Harewood receives. Otherwise, I will be happy to inform everyone here."

She curled her hands into fists, too angry to be frightened but worried nonetheless. She'd never liked the man. Why did it have to be him who'd seen her?

Finally, she heard his footsteps walking away.

Moving into her room, she slumped into the chair at the dressing table. Now what was she to do? If only Fen were present, then they could discuss the best option. Her mind was a whir with calamities that could occur, the tangled mess starting to give her head pains.

What did Leighhall mean, give him the attention she gave Lord Harewood? The earl was gone.

She sat up in the chair. Of course! That meant she didn't need to give Leighhall any attention, either, and he would keep her secret. Then when Fen came back, they could discuss what to do with the arrogant Leighhall. Feeling better, she tucked in a strand of loose hair and smiled at herself in the mirror. She hoped whatever had taken Fen to his estate wasn't too serious and he could return in a day or two. Though she should probably find out from Rose where, exactly, was Denton Hall. If it were a three-days' journey, that would mean she'd be on her way back to Silver Meadows by time he returned, *if* he returned. Did Lady Enderly know that her son—

A knock on the door halted her thoughts before Lady Sommerset stepped in. "Shall we?"

She rose. "Yes." The idea to tell Lady Sommerset about Lord Leighhall flitted through her mind, but not now. She would wait until they were in private. She wouldn't let Lord Leighhall ruin the final week at her first house party. Especially now that she'd found the man to marry.

CHAPTER SIXTEEN

FELTON RACED ACROSS the field, one final rock wall the only obstacle between Nyx and his morning meal. They cleared the wall easily and bore down on the stables of Denton Hall. Slowing his horse the last part of the way, he noticed a coach parked beside the stables. It didn't take long to recognize his parents' crest. If it were his mother, the day would go from poor to hell. She should be tending her guests.

Bringing Nyx to a halt, he jumped down and handed the reins to a groom. "Be sure to walk him and rub him down before allowing him his oats."

As the man walked his horse away, he strode into the house, his anger already building. His mother's house party be damned. That she couldn't understand Rose would not marry before attending Belinda's school didn't mean he had to be an accomplice in her efforts. He'd been gone four days. She could muddle her way through the last three. Striding through the rarely used dining room into the parlor, he found it empty.

His butler approached. "The Marquess of Enderly is in the library, my lord."

He gave the man a nod, then strode across the entry to the library, where he found his father sipping tea and reading the newspaper. He halted in the doorway. "She sent you."

His father set the paper on the small table before him. "Of

course she did. You expected no less."

Some of his anger dissipated. "Was it because she couldn't leave her guests or because she thought you would do better at convincing me to return?"

"Both." His father gestured to the chair across from him.

The table, usually for chess, held a tray of tea and his favorite breakfast food. Taking the chair his father indicated, he ignored the tea and grabbed up a cake. "I see she even sent Cook's rout cakes."

"She wants you to return."

He waved off the request. "I know that, but why? Why is my presence so important?" He held his hand up. "No, I know. Her numbers are off now." As if numbers were the most important part of a gathering. It wasn't the numbers—it was the people. People like Dory who made a house party successful.

His father grinned. "I always said you were intelligent." He took another sip of tea.

"You can tell her I won't be returning. We all know, even she knows, that Rose isn't going to garner a proposal in the next three days. The entire party has been for naught."

"Yes, but she still hopes." His father lowered his brows. "You didn't place a bet at White's on Rose not receiving a proposal, did you?"

"No, but I believe Sommerset did, not that many bet against him, which is disappointing. That is why I agree with you. I think Rose should have at least a year at the Belinda School for Curious Ladies."

His father eyed him shrewdly. "You do? I thought you were skeptical of the school."

He shrugged, not willing to admit his change of opinion had a lot to do with a student from there. "I was, but I've made further inquiries and discussed it with Rose. I believe it would be good for her chances to marry."

"That could well be the case. One of the students, Lady Dorothea, has a number of men partnering her in the games your mother devised. Just last night, Lord Leighhall insisted on—"

"Leighhall?" The man was an arrogant dandy who thought all women should be his playthings. "The man is a horse's ass."

His father chuckled. "Yes, it appears Lady Dorothea feels the same, yet he's one of four men vying for her attentions and your mother says she needs you to make the other ladies feel special too."

There was only one lady he wished to make feel special, but he was not the man for her. Dory deserved someone who didn't have to search for the small pieces of his life that made him happy.

"Why did you leave so abruptly? Did something happen? Because I know there was nothing here that required your attention."

His father's question caught him by surprise. Yes, something had happened. He'd lost control of his baser instincts and had almost sabotaged his own goal. If he had stayed, he wouldn't have been able to remain detached and in control. "I grew bored."

"Felton, you're always bored. There was something else that sent you running like a rabbit set upon by the hounds."

He didn't like the analogy. "That's an apt image since Mother is constantly sending women after me."

His father picked up his cup and took a sip before letting out a sigh. "I know it's difficult for you to understand. She so wished you to marry a Mabry, but when they all found husbands, she despaired. She just wants you to be happy."

There was that word again—happy. He rose, unable to sit still any longer, and walked to the tall window to stare out at the sloping lawn that ended in forest. "I *was* happy. With Lady Belinda, I found happiness. She was perfect in every way."

"Son, I do not know how it feels to lose the one you love, but I do know you cannot go through life looking for another Lady Belinda."

When his father paused, he turned to see his parent contemplating the teacup. "I'm well aware of that, which is why I'm not.

"Are you sure?" His father studied him. "There is no other Lady Belinda. She was unique. Just like your mother is unique, though she is far from perfect."

Felton snorted but didn't respond. How his father lived with the woman was beyond his comprehension.

"If you search for perfection, you will go to your grave alone. You would do better to seek out someone who is different from Lady Belinda. Someone whose own uniqueness can make you happy. That, my son, is why I married your mother."

He tried and failed to picture his father courting his mother. First, his father rarely expended effort on anything unless it was very important and then it was a slow process. Second, his mother never stopped moving, jumping from one project, one event, one guest to the next without stopping. But judging by the soft smile that played about his father's lips, he spoke the truth. It was a revelation he planned to cogitate on at some later date.

His father rose and brushed the crumbs from his waistcoat. "I will expect you to return to Sunnydale for the ball this evening. It is the culmination of your mother's efforts, and you will be there out of respect for her. If you wish to arrive earlier, that is your decision." The tone, so different from a moment ago, brooked no argument.

With no choice in the matter, he gave a curt nod. "Yes, sir."

"Good." His father strolled toward the entryway but stopped short and turned. "It will make my wife very *happy*." Then, without another word, he strode out.

He shook his head at his father's retreating form. The man's expectations were far simpler than his own. But he was right about Belinda. There would never be another woman as perfect as she. His gaze moved to his desk, knowing the miniature portrait of her lay safely in the top drawer. As much as he would like to spend time reminiscing about her, he had a ball to prepare for and an overnight at least.

Striding out of his library, he forced himself to ascend the grand stair and give instructions to his valet to pack once more. Then he returned downstairs to walk the path through his own wild garden. There was no order to the array of flowers and shrubs, his gardeners having strict orders to allow the plants to ramble as they would, trimming them to keep them healthy. He had sworn long ago that he would never light them at night, as he enjoyed them perfectly well during the day. Their lack of order made him think of Dory's thoughts and his step slowed.

He needed a plan to navigate the evening. Obviously, avoiding Dory was paramount. He could spend very little time with his mother, but there was no hope for it but that he must dance attendance on the other ladies. That would allow the men interested in Dory to keep her entertained. It was just a ball, after all.

Except Leighhall. Dearling may be weak, Manning arrogant, and Retfield too patient, but Leighhall was dangerous. He would keep his eye on the man. That Dory did not seem happy with the man's attentions showed her intelligence, but she had much to occupy her. He would make sure the man did nothing untoward. That was one gentleman he wouldn't mind laying flat out with his fist.

Coming to the end of his garden, he turned and strode back through. He would find out from Sommerset how the week had progressed and if there were any other men to dissuade from pursuing Dory. While his opinion of all of them was not particularly high, each was a good match socially for her in the eyes of her parents. Hopefully, her mother would continue to be careful until next season was underway. There had to be better men to choose from with the new season. Though he could not be near, he would stand as her protector until she was safely married, not only for the school's reputation, but for Dory. She deserved to find the happiness she sought.

Walking into the house, he called his butler and had his coach brought. The sooner he arrived at Sunnydale, the sooner he could talk to Sommerset in private.

Within a few hours, he arrived at his parents' home once again. Preferring his mother, who was resting, not know of his presence, he had a servant bring Sommerset to him in the library. He poured himself a whisky and brought the glass through the open doors on to the terrace and examined the liquid. His father always had the best scotch whisky. A light afternoon breeze caressed his face, reminding him of the softness of Dory's skin. Just being back at Sunnydale, he could almost smell her lemon scent.

Taking a gulp of the copper-colored liquid, he focused on the smooth burn as it traveled down his throat.

"You're back."

He turned as Sommerset closed the door to the library and strode forward. "Do we have something to celebrate?" He nodded to the drink.

"Perhaps."

Sommerset moved to the sideboard and poured himself a glass before joining him on the terrace. "I'm glad you've returned. It has been delightfully entertaining without you. I needed your dark thoughts upon our daily activities to dampen the festivities."

Sometimes Sommerset took their penchant for dressing in opposite colors, Sommerset in light and himself in dark, a bit too far.

"My thoughts are not dark. They are simply observant."

"Call it what you will, but your company was greatly missed. I'm also a few pounds lighter in my pockets without your counsel."

"There was betting?" Disappointed he hadn't had the chance to join, he frowned.

"Yes, there was. Much of it our hostess did not know about." Sommerset smirked. "Most was on cards and billiards, but there were a few odd ones too. We actually bet on the theme Lady Enderly would choose for the ball." The man shook his head. "I bet on butterflies, but it's night faeries."

"Yes, I could have saved you that loss. Are there any bets still on the table? Perhaps I can make up for my absence."

"As it would happen, there are still two bets waiting to be settled. The first is whether our hostess will serve trifle or syllabub for dessert tonight. There seems to be differing views on what would be fitting."

"Now that is one I cannot bet upon, as I already know the menu. My mother shares far too much with Rose and me when she has these damned parties." There were many a detail he'd prefer to forget.

"In other words, you won't help me win back some of my money, after all." Lord Sommerset didn't sound disappointed in the least, so he didn't stand to lose much. The man had inherited financial problems, which, though since solved, had made him financially cautious.

"I didn't say that. If you guess, I could perhaps indicate if you are correct." He took another sip of the whisky, happy with both the company and the conversation. "What is the second bet?"

"The last bet is who will win Lady Dorothea's hand. The competition has been most interesting to watch. My wife and I have had to spend all our time with her except when she is in her room."

"I will not bet on that." He couldn't help the cold turn his voice had taken.

"Why not? You always tell me you make your bets based upon observation. Have you not observed Lord Deerling, Lord Manning, and Mr. Retfield enough to choose one as the triumphant suitor?" Sommerset raised his glass as if toasting.

"None of the suitors here are a good fit and until I see her interaction with others during the season, I won't have enough information."

Sommerset swallowed his whisky. "That is a fair point. The lady has been surprisingly popular. I don't remember men flocking to her." He raised his glass. "I even thought *you* might have an interest."

"Me? You know my heart is already taken, though I am the reason Lady Dorothea is here at all."

"You?" Sommerset grinned, obviously assuming the wrong reason. "I thought your mother had chosen the guest list. After all, I'm on it." He chuckled.

His mother adored Sommerset, which had been convenient more than once for getting them out of trouble. "True, but she allowed me to suggest additional guests. I knew Rose wished to attend the Belinda School for Curious Ladies, so I thought having one of them here would give her a chance to learn more about it before she made a decision."

"That does make sense. You have always been protective of your sister. If I remember correctly, your words to me when we came home from Oxford that first year were something to the tune of *'Do not even consider the thought.'* And I do believe all I did was comment on how much she'd grown."

He smiled at the memory as he took another sip. "Yes, well, it was *how* you said it. Remember, at the time you were hardly a saint."

"And as I remember it, neither were you."

No, he hadn't been. He'd taken his pleasure where he pleased with whomever he pleased since his heart had died. Filling his physical needs had given him some relief. He smirked. Mayhap that constituted a bit of happiness, but he'd never tell Dory about that. "True. But discovering that Rose sincerely wished to attend Belinda's school gave me additional motivation. You see, I had already decided to make those students more popular among the *ton* so Belinda's name could be honored, and I set about determining how to do so."

"Ah, that does put this into perspective. And what did you decide upon? As I'm quite sure you crafted a plan of some sort."

"Of course. I realized that each woman had something unique that made her less palatable to society. Since Lady Dorothea accepted the invitation, I set out to discover what the problem might be and fix it."

"'Fix it'? I'm not sure I understand. Are you saying you *fixed* Lady Dorothea?"

"I did. She is already quite beautiful and well trained as a lady, but she had a habit of rambling in her conversation without input. I researched what could be done to shorten or eliminate the many soliloquies she falls into. There was no clear answer, but I found enough information and suggested a solution, an experiment if you will. She put it into practice and has become, as I had hoped, a success." Dory's success did make him happy, but he couldn't tell her, for to talk to her would bring them too close for him to not touch her. They'd already been far more intimate than he'd ever expected. Better to keep his distance.

"We should celebrate that, but I need more. Shall we replenish our glasses?"

"Yes." He followed Sommerset in and poured them both more scotch.

Sommerset moved to stand near the cold fireplace. "I will say both Amelia and I had secretly hoped that your attentions to the lady were of a personal nature."

Unfortunately, they had become far too personal. Felton walked over and rested his forearms on the back of a winged back chair set there. "Since I don't want her success ruined, tell me about Lord Leighhall. My father seems to believe the man is also interested in Dory."

"'Dory'?" Sommerset lowered his brow.

Berating himself for his slip, he shrugged. "It is what my sister calls Lady Dorothea."

"Hmm, well I can tell you Leighhall is not interested in the lady for any noble purpose. He's blatantly accused her of being like her mother."

He choked on his whisky, coughing to get it out of his throat. "Why would the man say that?" He well knew she had been innocent before he'd touched her.

Sommerset didn't look at him. "Let's just say your sister might have instigated something that would not have reflected well upon Lady Dorothea if anyone discovered it. Unfortunately, Leighhall did, according to Lady Dorothea. Amelia and I couldn't have your parents ask him to leave without divulging what happened, so instead, we have stayed with her constantly. Except, of course, when she's in her room." He motioned toward the ceiling.

He couldn't help looking up. He'd have to get the truth out of his sister, but no matter what they'd done, it wasn't good that Leighhall knew. "I don't like this situation. You and your wife have protected her here, but about when she's home or at the school? I've learned that Leighhall becomes obsessed with whatever he focuses on and doesn't give up easily."

Sommerset put his drink down on the mantel. "That was my sense, though I don't know him and have heard only rumors. Since he's older than we are, I never paid him much attention."

Felton threw back the rest of his whisky, not happy with this turn of events. "All the rumors you heard are true. Even the ones you find difficult to believe. I once saw him stalk a young lord just out of Cambridge because a woman preferred him over Leighhall. Leighhall bided his time. When the young man's mother died and he came to the club to drown his sorrows, Leighhall was there to take every penny from him. His father paid his debts, but the young man never set foot in White's again. I believe he married a rich, American woman after the first woman spurned him for being imprudent."

"So how do we protect Lady Dorothea?" Sommerset crossed his arms. "I know I'm only her chaperone for this party, but from what Amelia tells me, her parents are so at odds with each other, they barely notice their daughter."

He'd sensed that as well. "Didn't you have a man you used to track down an art dealer who had sold you a forgery? I believe you said he'd been a Bow Street Runner at one time."

Sommerset uncrossed his arms and lifted his glass. "Yes. Mr. Taylour. He also served with Lord Blackmore in the war. He's a smart man and well versed in, shall we say, disguise and persuasion. Why?"

"I would like to hire him. I can't keep an eye on Leighhall, but he could."

Sommerset grinned. "Yes, he can. He's quite good at blending in and he's done similar work for the Duke of Northwick. I will write him and have him meet with you."

"Excellent."

"We have accomplished much since you returned." Sommerset lifted his glass. "I suggest we have another drink and enjoy the solitude."

"In other words, we stay in here until it's absolutely necessary to change for the ball."

Sommerset nodded, a wide grin on his face.

Felton lifted his glass in a toast. "I'm amenable to that." Then he would do his duty as a good son and leave first thing in the morning, hopefully without saying more than a few words to Dory. As he poured more whisky, he could feel an odd ache in his chest. As strange as the idea was, he would miss her company.

CHAPTER SEVENTEEN

ORY GRIPPED THE balustrade so hard, she wasn't sure if she could let go. She was an experiment? To better the school's reputation? For the dead woman Fen—Lord Harewood still loved?

Her heart pounded as tears sprang to her eyes. He hadn't done it to help *her*. He didn't care about *her*.

She'd been so excited, so happy when Rose told her Harewood would be at the ball. The idea that he might ask for her hand in marriage had made it impossible to rest, as Lady Enderly had demanded. But that had never been his intention.

With her hopes and dreams shattered like the leftover crumbs from a pound cake, she felt a piercing pain fill her chest. She released the balustrade as she covered her mouth to stifle the sob. Turning, she stepped back into her room and closed the door on the men's now-muffled voices.

She was no more than an experiment. An experiment. A successful experiment. As the truth of his attentions to her settled in, it erased every tangled thought in her head, leaving her with one. He didn't care about her.

A new pain in her belly grew so strong that she ran for the chamber pot. Tears streamed down her face as she emptied her stomach. That he could be so cruel as to make her think he cared was unpardonable. She grasped on to her anger as she wiped her mouth and moved to her bed. She fanned the flames, trying to burn out the heartache seizing her chest.

She grabbed on to the post at the foot of the bed to hold herself up. Memories of their time together flooded her in neat order. No wonder she'd been confused when he'd drawn her into conversation and wasn't sure if he sought to help or simply liked to see her ramble and play the fool. Then there was his assurance that he'd known exactly what to do for her and why it would work, when it had been no more than a guess.

She pushed away from the post, pressing her nails into her palms. How could she have not realized it when she read his palm? That crease in his heart line must mean his heart was dead. And their night together? Had that been more preparation for her successful marriage? *"I will not ruin you for your future husband."* His words returned in a rush. He'd truly meant it.

The pain in her chest just made her angrier. He'd played with her for his own amusement. Oh, yes, and for the precious reputation of the school, not because he valued the school and its intent, but solely because it was named in honor of his lost love, the Angel.

She spun around and grabbed up her favorite cheerful blue dress that had been laid out for the ball, a choice made by her own naïveté. Stalking to the armoire, she shoved it back in and pulled out her maroon dress. It fit her mood better. She was far from naïve now. She brought it back to the bed and laid it out. She didn't care if it had wrinkles, though there didn't appear to be any. She hoped it made her appear like an avenging fury of ancient Greece.

A vision filled her head of her as an angry goddess flying down to grab up Harewood by her claws, high into the sky on her way to a giant falcon nest where three babies awaited their meal.

"My lady?"

Hearing the voice, she shook her head as knocking on her door brought her back to her angry present. "Yes." Walking to the door, she unlocked it and allowed Lady Sommerset's maid to come in. "I've chosen a different dress."

As the maid helped her change and decorate her hair, she forced herself to focus on her appearance. She wished to look her best when she revealed what she knew to Lord Harewood. Now she was anxious to attend the ball for a completely different reason.

No sooner was the maid finished than Lady Sommerset came for her and they made their way into the ballroom, which had been transformed into a celestial night with stars, with a bright, full moon and faeries upon night-blooming mythical flowers. The light, instead of casting a golden glow, had been transformed into white, making the entire room unearthly.

"The marchioness prides herself on creating atmosphere." Lady Sommerset kept her voice low as others milled about the room, commenting on the decorations. "I understand there are dryads and even a mechanical owl that hoots."

"Are there any bats?"

Lady Sommerset looked askance at her. "I don't believe so."

Dory wanted to see bats hanging from the high ceiling, but of course that wouldn't do. Obviously, her mood had darkened with the room. "Oh, good. They would eat the faeries."

"Perhaps my sister can better appreciate your observations."

At the mention of her teacher, she brightened. Lady Northwick, who, with her husband, the duke, ran the school and always had wisdom to spare. The pair were guests of Lord and Lady Enderly and Dory would be leaving with them the next day for Silver Meadows, her father having made the arrangements. She was pleased she would be traveling directly to the school and not going home.

As she and Lady Sommerset approached the duchess, the lady in question held out both her hands. "Lady Dorothea, have you enjoyed your stay? I have heard that you have been quite popular."

She took Lady Northwick's hands and shrugged, not particularly pleased that Harewood had succeeded in making her so. "It has been very educational. Now, I am anxious to begin my second-year studies. Thank you for allowing me to return with you."

Lady Northwick smiled warmly, her hazel eyes sparkling with delight as the single curl of dark hair brushed her shoulder. "We are very pleased to have you. Perhaps you can tell us all about your stay during our travels. I wouldn't want to keep you from your final fete."

As Lady Sommerset asked about their older sister, the Viscountess of Blackmore, who was with child, Lady Northwick relayed what was in her last letter. The two women chatted about all that had occurred since they last saw each other during the season. They appeared like the sun on a lake, Lady Sommerset in a pretty yellow dress and Lady Northwick in a bright blue, very close in shade to one Dory had planned to wear earlier instead of the deep maroon she wore now. The reddish color matched her somber mood much better.

Studying the room, she found Harewood talking to his father. He appeared bored, which she quite relished. Now that his experiment had succeeded, whatever would he do next? Suddenly, she remembered what he'd said about making all the ladies at school a success. She glanced at Lady Northwick. She was fiercely protective of her school. What would she think of that?

A small pleasure rippled through her mind at the prospect of thwarting Harewood's plans. Now, if only the night would end quickly so she could leave for Silver Meadows and tell Lady Northwick about everything. Then she could leave the problem in her capable hands and be among her friends again, in a place where she wouldn't have to count her sentences. Not that she'd said much to anyone over the past half hour.

She moved her gaze over the room. Lady Rose grimaced at her as she danced side by side with Mr. Retfield, no doubt to please her mother. Lady Arabella was partnered with Lord

Manning in the same dance. Lady Matilda conversed with Lady Enderly, who appeared a bit distracted. Interestingly, Lord Leighhall had not approached her. She'd expected some untoward action to separate her from her chaperone. It was the final night, after all. Either that or he planned to make an announcement to everyone that he'd seen her leaving Harewood's room.

She barely held back a snort. What would Harewood think about that? Part of her wished Leighhall *would* tell everyone, so Harewood's *experiment* would be a failure. Waiting for Leighhall to say something or for her mother to do something had worn on her nerves and now she was tired with all of it. It was as if she were dead inside and all that kept her breathing was her fury at Harewood.

"Lady Dorothea, you look lovely this evening."

At Lord Dearling's words, she turned toward him, not having seen him approach. He wore the usual black trousers and tailcoat, which didn't complement him. He was best suited to grays and tans.

"Thank you, Lord Dearling. You are quite skilled at the quadrille, I see."

His neck turned slightly red at her compliment, though to be fair, she thought him no better than anyone else, but that was what she was supposed to say. Maybe he'd ask her to dance and she wouldn't have to speak any more. She was sure she could continue to be polite even when she wanted to yell.

"That is kind of you to say so, but as you taught me by example, there is nothing wrong with admitting I'm only adequate."

She smiled kindly, hoping that would be enough, her mind blank, no yarn, no twine, no lines of any kind, just empty. No, not empty. Her mind was like a great medieval hall with a fire burning at the center, one slowly growing.

"I had hoped you would be willing to take some air on the terrace?"

She stiffened. He would want to converse, maybe find out what event she would be at next. She didn't want to attend anything. What if she said something completely out of character?

"With Lady Sommerset as well." He smiled crookedly, as if he wished it could be otherwise.

"Did I hear my name?" Lady Sommerset turned her head and smiled at Lord Dearling.

"Yes, I wish to speak to Lady Dorothea on the terrace, where it is a bit quieter, and was hoping you could accompany us."

Dory crossed her fingers behind her back in hopes that Lady Sommerset would demure.

"I would be very pleased to. Allow me to wave down my husband, as he very much enjoys the terrace at night."

As Lord Dearling's face lit, Dory pasted on a smile, gritting her teeth. Mayhap she could simply listen. The conversation would be short if she didn't respond. She looked about the room as if searching for Lord Sommerset as well, but her gaze caught upon Harewood, who conversed with the Duke of Northwick.

As Lord Sommerset strode over at his wife's wave, Lord Dearling offered her his arm. Seeing no way to avoid it, she laid her gloved hand upon it and allowed him to lead her. They traversed the edge of the ballroom, since the dance floor was quite filled. Not only were the house guests attending, but also a number of neighboring families.

"Are you enjoying the evening so far? I noticed you haven't danced as yet." Lord Dearling's question held deeper meaning that she was far too distracted to contemplate.

"I have been enjoying conversation with my instructor, the Duchess of Northwick." It was hardly the truth since she'd not added a single comment between the sisters, but truthfully, she heard the entire conversation and actually caught a few points that seemed to leave her head as soon as they'd entered.

They strolled through the doors behind Lord and Lady Sommerset, the slightly cooler temperature the only recognition that they were outside, as the terrace was lit brighter than the ballroom. Maybe Lady Enderly had wanted it to appear as if sunrise were approaching.

"I do hope I can make your evening far more enjoyable." Lord Dearling leaned in, and his breath tickled her ear.

She forced herself not to raise her shoulder in defense. Did he mean to infer that the duchess was not thoroughly interesting? He well knew that she was a student at the school, as they had discussed it many times. Did he think it a chore to attend? It was the only home she—

He stopped, releasing her before taking her hand and facing her. "May I?" He held out his other hand.

For a moment, she didn't understand what he wanted but finally, comprehension dawned and she put her other gloved hand in his.

He swallowed hard, his Adam's apple bobbing in his neck. How odd it was that men had one and women didn't. She hadn't read the reason for the difference. But then again, there were many differences between the genders.

"Lady Dorothea, surely, you have remarked on what high esteem I hold you in. I mean that I hold you in the highest esteem." His right eye twitched. "Your grace and your beauty have won me over, and I find my heart is full when with you."

"My lord, I am honored." Honored, but also uncomfortable, as she could not reciprocate his feelings. Her heart had died and to feel was to be in pain. Could he not tell? It was much better to be angry.

"No, I am honored that you would grant me your attentions on so many occasions. I have become quite dependent upon them. So much so that the thought of leaving this lovely place and not seeing you again until in Town once more fills me with such sorrow that I cannot bear it."

Surely, he did not wish to visit her at school? If he asked, she would say it was not allowed, though she wasn't sure if that were the truth. She tried to remember if any of her classmates had been visited by anyone not of their family. The squeezing of both her hands brought her back to Lord Dearling, who gazed at her as if she were the most beautiful woman in all of England.

"Lady Dorothea, I fear I cannot live without seeing you daily. So to that end, I would ask you to consider becoming my betrothed. I have already written my dear mother and told her of my feelings toward you, so I know she will approve. I will, of course, travel to request your father's permission as soon as the morrow, but I wish to know you would be amenable to it. We could be married in your parish church, as I would travel far and wide to have you as my wife. I find my heart beats only for you and this strong emotion I have inside me can only be labeled love. I believe you may hold some small affection for me, and I'm sure that in time, it would grow. Would you consider such an arrangement?"

She stared at him in shock. He was asking her to marry him? She forced the fire in her mind to be covered and studied him, knowing he was kind and would no doubt treat her well. This had been her hope in coming to Sunnydale, that she find a man who would consider her for marriage before her mother embroiled the family in a scandal. She blinked, trying to find some emotion for the man, but she could not. Another had shown her what it was to be in love and had killed that feeling. "My lord, you have truly surprised me."

His neck turned red. "I did not mean to. I thought my feelings were quite clear."

As she looked back upon it, they were. It was her own focus on Harewood and her feelings for that man that had led her to ignore what was before her. Even as she thought of Harewood and the fact that she was an experiment, the fire threw flames out from beneath its cover. She wanted to turn away from Lord Dearling's offer simply to prove Harewood wrong. But as she looked into Dearling's hopeful eyes, she could not in good conscience do him such an injustice. She needed to sort out her own situation. She would probably never love a man again, and now that she knew what it was to be led astray, she couldn't be so cruel.

She managed a small smile. "Yes, you have made your feelings very clear. I simply did not expect such a proposal this evening. Your enthusiasm is very flattering."

His stiffened body relaxed and he grinned. "I am pleased. It was only this morning that I decided I must ask you. Do you find my proposition favorable, then?"

It was all she had hoped for before the end of the season, before she'd fallen in love with the wrong man. Though two other men had danced attendance on her, she could not be sure either Lord Manning or Mr. Retfield would ask for her hand in time. Despite the panic that started in her chest, she took a deep breath and nodded. This was what she must do. She had no alternative. "I do."

Chapter Eighteen

N O SOONER HAD she said the words than Dory wished them back.

Lord Dearling's smile grew wide, but before he could say anything, Lord and Lady Sommerset's voices caught their attention. They seemed to be arguing in hushed tones that were growing louder. Thankful for any excuse to escape from what she'd just done, she looked to Lord Dearling and shrugged.

Rather than be alarmed, he appeared pleased and started to lean toward her.

She released his hands. "I do believe we should wait to announce our betrothal until you have permission from my father."

He pulled back at her statement. "Yes, of course. That would be appropriate. Good news such as ours flies on the wind, and it would not do to have your parent surprised. I wish to present my best self to him."

She almost told him to wear gray and not black but held her tongue. What did it matter what he wore? He would be her husband. He loved her. That should have been important, but she could find no enthusiasm at the prospect of marrying anyone.

He held his arm out to her. "Would you like to return to the ball? I'm sure there are a few friends of yours you wish to tell."

Besides Rose, there were many friends she wished to tell back at school. Hopefully, she could hold off the wedding until at least the first term. She'd promised both Rose and Lissette that she would be there, after all. She looked toward the earl and countess, not willing to go in without them. "Just one moment."

She walked slowly toward the couple, catching phrases here and there as she drew closer. There was little doubt in her mind it had to be about the proposal she'd just accepted. But who was pleased by it and who was not was unclear. "Lady Sommerset, would it be acceptable to rejoin the ball?"

The countess turned, obviously surprised by her presence. "So soon?" Her usual secret smile was missing from her face.

Did that mean she wasn't happy and her husband was? Why would she not be pleased? "Yes, we had a lovely conversation, but it would be rude to remain when Lady Enderly has put so much thought and creativity into this Night Faerie ball."

"You are correct." Lady Sommerset walked forward and hooked her arm in hers. "Let us return post-haste. I believe Joanna will be anxious to talk to us."

Not a little surprised, Dory could do nothing as the countess escorted her past Lord Dearling. She gave him a crooked smile. No doubt he'd expected to ask her to dance once they reentered so they could celebrate. She wasn't disappointed said dance would have to wait. She would prefer to cry than to dance. How her life had changed so much in just a matter of hours.

Lady Northwick welcomed them back in with a smile. "I am pleased to see that you have caught the eye of Lord Dearling."

Before she could answer, Lady Sommerset rolled her eyes. "Not just Lord Dearling, but Lords Manning, Mr. Redfield, and Harewood."

Dory couldn't stay quiet at such an absurd statement. "Not Lord Harewood. He is not interested in me for a wife."

Lady Sommerset's brows lowered. "I'm surprised by that. He has spent a significant time with you."

"That may be true, but not at my request." She wished to elaborate, but as Harewood was a good friend of Lady Sommerset's, she forced herself to say no more on the subject.

Lady Sommerset turned back to her sister, no expression on her face. "Actually, it is Lord Dearling who has clearly won Dory's heart. She just accepted his proposal of marriage, once he receives permission from her father."

Lady Northwick did not immediately rejoice. "Dory, is this true?"

She nodded, surprised that her teacher would not be more pleased.

Lady Sommerset, who still held her arm, answered. "It is true. I just heard the proposal. I would like to discuss this with Dory further. If anyone asks after us, we will be in the library where we can have some privacy. Joanna, would you like to join us?"

"No. You are Dory's chaperone and know more about what has occurred than I. However, if you need my counsel, I am always available."

The last was directed at Dory, and she appreciated the offer. The duchess was respected by all of them.

"Now, I need to search out my husband, as I'm sure a waltz will soon be played, and we do not dance together nearly enough." Lady Northwick chuckled before moving away through the crowd.

Dory didn't have time to aid in her instructor's search as Lady Sommerset pulled her forward, heading for the ballroom doors to the main corridor.

Her chaperone's lack of smiles had her instinct telling her this may not be a pleasant conversation. Nervous, she walked with Lady Sommerset, but as they approached the wide opening to the corridor, she felt a chill. Looking to her right, she found Lord Leighhall scowling at her, his fury not only clear in his blue eyes, but in his curled fists. She glanced past him to see Lord Dearling talking animatedly to Lord Manning and another man she didn't know.

She quickened her steps to match up to Lady Sommerset's, not at all sure what Leighhall would do now that he knew she was to marry, but confident he would do something.

As they entered the library, Lady Sommerset closed the doors, then walked past her to two chairs set at a large, rectangle table. "Join me." The countess sat in one of the chairs and arranged her dress. "I'm anxious to hear how this proposal came about."

With no help for it, Dory walked over and pulled out the chair next to her chaperone. Lowering herself into it, she slumped back. "To be truthful, I did not expect it, but I should have. And to think I bragged one night about being observant."

"Now, that was not what I expected to hear. Were you not hoping for a suitor by the end of this house party?" Lady Sommerset cocked her head, a kind smile lifting her lips.

"I did." Even as the question as to what she should reveal materialized in her mind, her trust in Lady Sommerset, built over the last fortnight, especially the last six days, gave her the answer. She would tell her everything, or rather almost everything. Sitting up, she folded her arms on the table before her and narrated all that had happened concerning Lord Dearling and Lord Harewood, except the personal moments she and Fen had in her room. She would treasure those as if he'd been a different person from the arrogant earl who played with her affections.

She wasn't sure how long she spoke, but by the time she finished with the unexpected proposal, she felt as if she'd relived every moment and wanted to simply sleep and forget. The fire of her anger seemed to have been snuffed out by a lack of will. That Lady Sommerset did not interrupt once had her wondering if she'd conducted herself poorly.

The countess rose, stepping behind her own chair, one hand resting lightly on the back. "I don't think I can truly express how proud I am at your conduct here." She held up her hand. "No, going into Lord Harewood's room with Rose was not admirable. However, from what you have told me, you have conducted yourself beautifully."

"I did?" It was the last statement she'd expected to hear. She was sure she had made many missteps or she wouldn't be in such an awkward position of having a broken heart over one man and accepting the care of another man's heart for life.

Lady Sommerset rolled her eyes. "Yes, you did. Tell me. Why did you accept Lord Dearling's proposal?"

"My mother."

"Your mother? Oh, I see. Is it that you fear your mother will…"

"Yes, cause a scandal by being caught with a man who is not my father."

Lady Sommerset clasped her hands over the back of the chair. "That, I understand. But you do not love Lord Dearling."

"No. But he loves me and is very solicitous, if a bit awkward at times." She forced a weak smile. Compared to Harewood, Dearling was like a lamb to a wolf. But unlike Harewood, he *wanted* her in his life.

Lady Sommerset straightened, her brows lowering. "I am not pleased with Harewood. He did not treat you well. Not only did he make you think he cared for you, he made me think so too. I wonder if that is why my husband didn't think you should accept Lord Dearling's proposal. But if he already knew you were an *experiment*"—she shook her head, obviously not pleased—"it doesn't make sense. And I can tell you that when my sister discovers Harewood felt the need to make her school appear worthwhile, when it is already, she *will* confront him."

She relished the idea of the duchess giving Harewood a set down far more than she should. While his motivation was understandable, his execution had lacked forethought. That was what hurt. She wished he'd only damaged her ego and not her heart, but he had the opposite effect.

"If it were anyone but Harewood, I would confront him for his arrogance myself." Lady Sommerset sighed as she resumed her seat. "My sister's death changed him, so over the years, we've all made allowances, but that he chose you as an experiment is far beyond the pale."

Dory set her hand on the table, as if she could somehow explain her riotous emotions now that her anger only simmered. "He is suffering enough that he still loves your sister, and if I had been more observant, as the duchess taught us, I would not have expected more than the truth."

Lady Sommerset patted her hand. "I understand your feelings and will respect them. I'm more concerned with you. I can have my husband send a message to your father immediately telling him Lord Dearling is not a good match."

Now this was a topic she felt particularly well versed in and could keep her heart out of it. "Lord Dearling is a perfect match. He is an earl in his own right and as the oldest will inherit his father's title of marquess. The man is also not a gambler, a rake, or of mean disposition. He is fit and his breath does not smell. To be honest, if I hadn't been distracted by Lord Harewood, I would have looked very kindly upon this proposal."

"But if you hadn't been distracted by Lord Harewood, would you have *received* this proposal?"

The truth of Lady Sommerset's statement did not sit well with her. "If you mean for me to be grateful to him, I cannot."

"No, I do not mean for you be grateful." Lady Sommerset gave her a sad smile. "I hope you will be angry. But I also want you to be happy. Which man would you be happier with if given the choice?"

She wanted to cry as the truth emerged from deep in her heart.

"All I ask is that you understand that begging off on a proposal can be weathered, but a life with the wrong man can be debilitating. I know of what I speak. My own biases almost cost me Andrew. I could not imagine my life if I had done what I'd thought was correct instead of following my heart."

Surprised, a small hope fluttered in her chest before she squashed it like a boulder on a daisy. "But your husband loved you, correct?"

Lady Sommerset nodded. "I understand what you're thinking, but there are other men who may be interested in you and you them after your heart has healed. Are you sure you wish to rush into this marriage?"

No, she didn't want to. Could she risk another season of her mother's behavior? As much as she wanted to, her instinct told her that her mother was becoming far less careful, not more. "It's not that I wish to, but I must. If I don't, I could well be a spinster and living at the will of my brother…or worse. At least by marrying, I will have my own home and a comfortable life."

Lady Sommerset rose, walked over to her, and embraced her. "You are a far braver woman than I could ever be." She let go and stepped back. "Did you want to forgo the rest of the ball?"

She stood and nodded. "I do, but I won't. I don't believe that making an enemy of Lady Enderly would be wise."

"True. I truly wish Harewood could see what a wonderful woman you are." She opened her arm to indicate they should leave the library. "Now to remind my husband that I'm always right."

Dory tried to smile, but couldn't manage it. Perhaps if she hadn't had such high hopes as to marry Harewood, she'd be truly happy now. But she had, and now she was to be married to Lord Dearling instead. Surely, there were far worse fates than that.

As they reentered the ballroom, Lady Enderly greeted them at the opening. "Ah, there you are. I was just telling my son he needs to dance with Lady Dorothea. You will accept, won't you? He's danced with all the ladies of my house party except you. I wouldn't want them to think he held any ill will."

Before Dory could respond to the surprising request, though to be sure, from Lady Enderly's perspective, it made perfect sense, Lord Harewood stepped forward.

"I think, Mother, that we have depended too much upon Lady Dorothea's goodwill to help make your party a success."

He didn't look at her as he spoke, which fanned the flames of her resentment. "I'd be pleased to dance with Lord Harewood, as it is you, my lady, who requested I do so."

"My dear, I cannot begin to express my gratefulness for all you have done to assist us in our endeavor to provide happy entertainment to so many." Lady Enderly's voice was sincere, proving her kind intentions.

"It is I who am grateful to *you* to have been invited to such a wonderful fete." She glanced at Harewood, who appeared distracted. Maybe because the musicians wound down into silence after a waltz.

Lady Enderly placed her hand on her son's arm. "I believe another quadrille is next. Do take Lady Dorothea onto the dance floor. Now where did your sister disappear to?"

Dory sensed more than heard Lady Sommerset step closer. As Lady Enderly bustled off, Harewood finally met her gaze. "My lady, if you do not wish to dance, you need not on my mother's account. I noticed you have yet to dance this evening."

Clearly, he did not wish to dance with her, which irritated her further. She certainly didn't wish to love him. Sometimes they didn't receive what they wished. "I would much enjoy a dance, Lord Harewood."

He swallowed hard, his Adam's apple moving as if he were uncomfortable, just like Dearling. But there was no reason for him to feel that way…yet. Finally, he offered his arm and she set her hand atop it, a strange anticipation growing in her belly that had nothing to do with dancing and everything to do with speaking her mind.

"Lady Dorothea, are you sure. You were just saying you were feeling particularly fatigued." Lady Sommerset's ready excuse for her, had her turning.

Though grateful for her kindness, Dory, nodded. "Yes. I very much wish to be in the company of Lord Harewood before I leave for school. This is the perfect opportunity."

The countess didn't smile. Instead, she gave a short nod. "Very well. Return to me immediately following."

"I will."

Harewood walked her into place opposite of Mr. Retfield and

Lady Arabella. As the dance began, she met Mr. Retfield and then returned to her place to wait as Harewood met Lady Arabella. Then Dory and the earl linked hands and turned. "You should be very pleased, Lord Harewood. Your experiment is a success."

He dropped her hand before fully stopping beside her.

She smiled as she met Lady Arabella in the center and stepped back. When Harewood returned to take her hand, his voice was low. "Did Lord Sommerset say so?"

"No, you did, to him this afternoon."

They joined hands with the other couple, completing the steps.

When they returned, they faced each other before stepping forward to meet. He was obviously shocked. "My motivation has only been to help you."

They stepped back and the pattern restarted. At the next opportunity, she made her position clear. "No, your motivation was for the school, which I'm sure the duchess will appreciate when I tell her."

She watched him as he stepped away, his movements far stiffer than usual. Was he angry? He truly had no cause. *She* was the one who was angry, but she smiled, actually pleased he was not happy. She'd never thought of herself as vengeful, but perhaps he'd struck something deep inside her. Socrates said that all humans had a beast within and it was those who did not rein it in who became tyrants. She'd never understood that particular philosophy, as she couldn't imagine not having control over one's desires, but now she did, as she wanted Lord Harewood to feel guilty. Even as the thought arrived, it tangled with her sympathy of his plight. Because now, she knew what it was to love and have no hope it could ever be returned.

Harewood returned to stand beside her once again. "Are you not pleased with your own success? You made it happen. I only made a suggestion."

As they stepped away again, she could not respond immediately. Finally, they came back together. "I didn't know I *needed* success. I only thought to attract a husband. To think, I had no idea I must first be 'fixed.'" Her resentment colored her tone and she received an odd look from Lady Arabella as they came together. Dory forced a smile as she nodded and stepped back.

"You did not need to be fixed." His brows lowered. "I only wished to help you in your goal of finding a suitable man. You still may."

Oh, she had, but he couldn't see that. A sudden thought sent a cold chill through her. When they linked hands again, she kept her voice low. "Did you place a bet at your club that I would marry this year?"

His hand jerked as if slapped, but they separated once again before he could reply.

As the dance ended, he bowed and took her arm immediately as he leaned in. "I did not place a bet on you. I would not be so callous."

A slight relief helped her keep from squeezing his arm as they made their way back toward Lady Sommerset, but the vengeful beast inside her couldn't allow him to feel good about what he'd done. "That is too bad, as I have accepted Lord Dearling's proposal. You could have been very happy having placed such a bet."

He stopped in midstride, causing her to catch her balance. His head turned and he stared at her. "Why? The man cannot appreciate you. You will be bored within the year."

That she agreed didn't help the sting of tears in the back of her eyes. "Yes, but he at least loves me, and I will have a home of my own before my mother can ruin my prospects."

Harewood's arm beneath her hand seemed made of granite and a tick started beneath his right ear. "I do not think this is a wise decision."

She lifted her chin and glared at him, despite his face starting to blur. "And I do not care what you think." Nor did she care about standing there with him. Ignoring protocols, she let go of his arm and made her way to Lady Sommerset on her own, not caring if he followed for appearances' sake or not.

She had just reached Lady Sommerset, who watched her with her husband, when Lord Dearling stepped up. "Lady Dorothea, may I have the honor of this dance?"

Taking a deep breath, she forced a smile, swallowing down her tears. "I would most appreciate a dance with you, Lord Dearling."

As her future husband led her to the dance floor, the musicians began, and the strains of a waltz filled the room. She stifled groan. Surely, the evening could become no worse.

She took her position opposite Lord Dearling, glancing behind him to see Harewood heading for the terrace. Just then Lord Leighhall stepped into his place on the dance floor and into her view. The viscount looked past his partner, and studied her. A shiver raced through her just before she took her first stumbling step.

CHAPTER NINETEEN

August, 1817
One month later

"WELL, SHOW HIM in, man!" Felton barked at his butler then regretted it immediately. "I apologize. Please bring him in."

The man simply nodded and turned on his heel.

Not sure why he was so irritated with everything, he strode to the window and tried to focus on the rolling lawns and forest beyond, but the lawns were no longer green and the leaves had turned a dead yellow.

"Lord Harewood. I'm Anthony Taylour."

He turned back toward the room, determined to hold in his temper. It wasn't as if he were angry, just frustrated. Frustrated that Dory was to wed Dearling, who would have no idea how to protect her, even if he were smart enough to recognize a threat. That the man had no understanding or appreciation for who she was made the arrangement even less palatable.

He still didn't understand why she'd accepted, or why a low, burning rage simmered in his gut at the thought of her being Lady Dearling. Since being correct made him happy, as she'd pointed out, it must be because he'd been wrong that she would wait until the next season to choose a husband. He was rarely wrong.

In addition, it had been a fortnight since he'd corresponded with Mr. Taylour, and there had been nothing unusual reported about Leighhall. Of course, he hadn't explained *why* he wanted the man followed, just that he be followed. So the letters about the viscount's visits to brothels and the homes of a couple of married ladies were of little use.

He strode across the room to greet Mr. Taylour. The former Bow Street Runner didn't appear to be as deadly as Sommerset had suggested. In fact, his broad frame, wavy, blond hair, blue eyes, and full smile made him appear quite jovial. His clothes were impeccable and well-tailored. If he'd met Mr. Taylour on St. James Street, he'd think him of the peerage, which did not inspire confidence in the man's abilities. Peers were not suited to this type of work. "Mr. Taylour, thank you for journeying out here to Denton Hall. I wished to speak to you with the utmost privacy."

The man immediately sobered, looking far more like what a detective should have looked like. "Of course."

"Please, have a seat." He gestured toward a wingback chair before his desk, then strode toward the door and closed it. Returning to his desk, he found Mr. Taylour reading one of the open books. He reached over to close the book and added it to a pile.

"I see you are a philosopher." Mr. Taylour ignored the rudeness of the action and perched on the arm of the chair, a rather odd way to take a seat.

Felton leaned against his desk. "Not I, but a friend of mine. I thought to study up to better converse. Now what is the latest on Lord Leighhall?"

Mr. Taylour's brows lowered in confusion. "I believe I outlined it all in my last letter."

"Yes, yes, but what about since then?" He needed to know if the man had traveled anywhere near Northampton, where the school was located and where Dory even now prepared for her marriage in between her studies.

"Lord Harewood, if you told me what you were looking for particularly, then I could delve into the details of the man's life with more success. But with no instructions beyond following Leighhall and reporting on his activities, which I have done, that is all I can help you with."

Which was why he'd brought Mr. Taylour to Denton Hall, only after corresponding with the Viscount of Blackmore himself on the man's ability to keep his mission to himself. Still, Felton tapped his fingers on the desk, hesitant to make his true motivations known.

"If you are concerned about my trustworthiness, I assure you that I hold many secrets that have never been divulged nor will be. I also first investigate those who would hire me to be sure they will not use my specific talents for nefarious purposes before accepting an assignment."

Affronted, his irritation raced through him. "You investigated me?"

"I did. And in the course of those investigations, you received high recommendations from not only Lord Sommerset, but also the Duke of Northwick."

Appeased somewhat by the duke's favorable opinion, he forced himself to remain civil. "Then it appears I have no choice but to take you into my confidence."

Mr. Taylour remained relaxed on the arm of the chair. "I understand." The man nodded sagely as if he'd been among other peers with similar needs.

That was highly doubtful, but he could not ignore his own need to protect Dory. "Very well. My interest in Lord Leighhall is in regards to his threat to a young woman whom I have taken under my protection, though neither she nor her betrothed are aware."

The man didn't move a muscle in his face to indicate any level of surprise. Still, Felton felt the need to justify his actions. "Lady Dorothea Ansley is a student at the Belinda School for Curious Ladies. Lady Belinda Mabry and I were planning marriage, but she passed. I have a vested interest in the school's success, so to that end, I aided Lady Dorothea in making a match." That was a bit of exaggeration, but the easiest way to explain his stake in Dory. "Fortunately, she accepted a proposal, but not before catching Leighhall's eye. The man is convinced that Lady Dorothea is like her mother, Lady Preston. The Countess Preston is rumored, though no proof has been produced, to be enjoying the company of a variety of men."

"Ah, if Leighhall believes the future bride like her mother, I imagine he will wish to have access to her at some point."

Somewhat relieved that the man understood the delicacy of the situation, Felton found his tension abating. "Precisely. You see, her betrothed is Lord Dearling and though the man worships Lady Dorothea, he is not aware of his surroundings. He's much like a hound's puppy in his excitement, ignorant of the danger lurking in the bushes. This is why I hired you. I need to be sure Leighhall does nothing to Lady Dorothea."

"When is the lady to wed?"

He moved off his desk and strolled toward the window before facing the man again. "Within a fortnight. The banns have been read and the license procured." He had contemplated lodging an objection to the marriage, but Dory would never forgive him, and a future husband being weak was generally not considered a strong enough reason to halt a wedding.

Mr. Taylour nodded, clearly contemplating the new information. "And you believe once married, Leighhall won't be a problem?" The man's doubt was clear in his voice. "As I have watched Lord Leighhall, I have discovered that marriage does not hinder the man's actions in the least. Is your goal to preserve the woman's reputation only before the marriage?"

"Devil it!" Of course. Once Leighhall's mind was made up, he became obsessive. If Leighhall destroyed her reputation after her marriage, she would be shunned. He felt the tick beneath his ear start as his tension spiked. "That means I'll need something to keep Leighhall in line for the rest of his life. Pity he could not meet an untimely death."

Mr. Taylour jumped to his feet. "I'm an honorable man and will not commit murder."

Belatedly, Felton realized what his words sounded like. "No, of course not. Nor will I be a party to one. I was simply hoping, perhaps wishing that the man would die of the pox. Lord Sommerset's father did, so it is possible."

Mr. Taylour relaxed but did not sit. Instead, he leaned his elbow on the top of the chair. "This kind of investigation could take years. Is this lady worth it?"

"Yes." At his quick answer, the man's brows raised. "I mean, she is a rare woman among the peerage with a unique mind and a kindness of heart not often encountered. She is the epitome of what Lady Belinda wished for in all women. Not that Dory is perfect." He grinned as he remembered her foibles. "Her conversations are tangled at best, her game of pall-mall truly lacking, and her waltz rather deplorable. But she is unique and stunning both in mind and body."

Mr. Taylour studied him. "Wouldn't it be easier to simply marry her yourself? A broken betrothal won't ruin her reputation like Lord Leighhall would."

He sighed, having given that much thought long before he'd known of the Leighhall threat and his reasons were still sound. "It would not be a good match. I couldn't make her happy. And unfortunately, she discovered my motivation for helping her, so I am hardly in her good graces."

"And this Lord Dearling *would* make her happy? From what you've told me, he doesn't sound as if he has many good qualities beyond loving her."

And was that enough? He certainly didn't want it to be. There were so many eligible men who were far more protective, but having thought about that as well over the last weeks, he found they also came up short. "I have to believe he will make her happy, as he was her choice." That is what he'd told himself, but as he voiced that very idea, it felt shallow.

Mr. Taylour shook his head. "That is your concern. I am simply here to help how I can. Now that I know what you want, I will not only look into Leighhall's activities in more detail, but I will also be sure to alert you if he moves in the direction of Silver Meadows. I'm very familiar with the area, as I stay with Lord Blackmore, a neighbor, when not on an assignment."

Having heard that the two had served together in the war, Felton was not surprised by that fact. "I greatly appreciate your aid in this matter. If there is anything I need to do in order for you to access places or items as you dig into Leighhall's activities, do not hesitate to contact me. I want any possible weakness recorded."

Mr. Taylour's brows rose. "Do you suspect something beyond his sexual activities?"

"I do. I'm not sure exactly why, but I'm convinced there is something beyond his supposed prowess with women. I would like to know what it is to use it as leverage, if you will."

"Those very activities could well be a distraction from what he's actually into." The man grinned. "There is nothing I like better than a puzzle to figure out." Mr. Taylour straightened and gave a nod. "I shall be sure to report to you as soon as I discover his secrets."

"Thank you." Felton strode forward, opened the door, and called his butler. "My first priority is Lady Dorothea's safety. My second is that no one know what you are about."

"I understand." Mr. Taylour gave a solemn nod then followed the butler out.

He wandered to the sideboard and poured a short glass of whisky, his mind filled with the conversation. Surprisingly, he felt more confident in Mr. Taylour's abilities after meeting him. No doubt it was because the man's mind worked much like his own, even if he didn't resemble the two Bow Street Runners he'd met. That Mr. Taylour had also concluded Dory could be more easily protected if Felton were to marry her showed how quickly the man had sized up the entire situation.

Returning to the desk with his drink, Felton pulled out his desk chair and sat. He took a sip before opening the top drawer and withdrawing a miniature.

He set the oval frame on its stand upon his desk and sat back. "We haven't spoken in a while, Belinda. But I know that you are aware I never stop thinking of you." He stared at the little portrait, wishing as always that she would actually speak, but well aware that would never occur. The portrait had been one of many Lady Amelia, now Lady Sommerset, had painted and discarded as not good enough. Belinda had her signature poignant smile, her head slightly cocked, but a strand of hair had come loose and fallen across her eyebrow.

He'd never forget the afternoon Belinda had shyly handed it to him, explaining it wasn't the best, but it was the one she liked most because it wasn't perfect. She liked that it showed her hair having a mind of its own, as often happened. She said the picture captured the living, breathing Belinda, and not the perfect one whom her sister had sought to paint. But in his eyes, Belinda had been perfect. Or rather, she'd been perfect for him.

"I imagine you have been perplexed by my actions over the last month or so. To be honest, so have I." He waited, always having that hope that he would hear her in his mind, giving him the counsel he needed.

"My father thinks I keep looking for the perfect woman. I'm not. I already have you, and I know no one can be you. I don't want them to be you." He paused, not sure what he wanted to say, but talking to her always helped him find solace, if not solutions.

"As you know, I'm determined to protect Lady Dorothea. She's interesting. Like you, she is unique, but in a far different manner, and she is far from perfect. I know if you met her, you would be very kind to her, but probably puzzled by her. I befriended her to help her be successful with finding a husband, and she has. But I am not happy with my success. I thought by helping her, I could make the school named for you as revered as you are. But I fear my priorities have become entangled, as she might say."

He tapped his fingers on the desk even as Belinda's soft, blue gaze never wavered. "I still want the school to be a success. You deserve to have your name on everyone's lips. Lady Dorothea took my advice, changed how she conversed, and is now betrothed." According to Dory, he should be happy because he'd succeeded, yet he felt unsettled.

"But I actually prefer her as she was. I should be pleased she managed to change, but I wish she hadn't. Why? That's the question. Maybe I don't want her to be successful because I like that I'm the only one to understand her and appreciate her for who she is, flaws and all. That's what you always told me. You said to love others for their flaws, not despite them. I don't think I ever understood that until now."

He stopped tapping the desk as his heart started to pound in his chest. "Am I in love with her?"

Even as he said the words to the empty room, a shiver raced over him. He shot to his feet. He couldn't be. He looked at the portrait, the gaze now focused on his groin. Quickly, he lifted the image. "This can't be. I love you." He shook his head, then set the portrait down and quickly strode around the desk to the window again. He stared unseeing. How could he be in love with Dory? She was an experiment to help the school. His heart was dead.

Or was it?

He thought back to their first encounter, to their first kiss, to when she'd told his fortune, sensuously running her finger over his bare palm. Then the night he'd given her pleasure. As much as he'd wanted to bury himself inside her, he couldn't defile her because…because he loved her.

He spun around, his gaze going to the stack of books on his desk. He strode to them and opened the top one. Even in his frustration, he'd been reading the philosophers Dory had mentioned, unconsciously prepping for their next conversation despite the fact that he hadn't planned to have another with her…ever.

Rifling through the pages of Immanuel Kant's writings, he found what he sought. "'Love is a matter of feeling, not of willing…so a duty to love is an absurdity.'"

It was not a matter of will.

An odd relief filled him at the thought that loving was not of his choosing. Of course, he hadn't chosen to love Belinda, he simply did.

And he hadn't chosen to love Dory. "But I do." His spirits lifted as if a shroud had been pulled from over his heart and allowed it to beat freely. "I love her."

His gaze returned to the portrait. Did Belinda know? Did she approve? Even as he asked the question in his mind, he heard her voice in his head. *Yes.*

He closed the book as new possibilities stretched before him. If he loved her, she could be his wife. He lifted the portrait. "Thank you." Reverently, he returned it to the drawer.

For the first time in over ten years, he could see beyond his past to a future. He would make it perfect. No, not perfect. According to Dory, perfect was boring. According to Belinda, perfect was not a human possibility. According to his father, perfect was loneliness. No, his life would be perfectly unique with Dory by his side.

Would she accept him? His enthusiasm dimmed. She was betrothed, but she could break the betrothal. She was also angry with him. Could he convince her he regretted his actions? After all, he was her Fen. It would be no easy task. He'd hurt her.

His heart began to pound, fear of rejection seeping into every vein. Maybe he could simply tell her it would be safer if she married him. Even as the thought materialized, he discarded it. Dory wouldn't care about that. She would demand his heart.

If only he knew how she felt about him, besides angry. Had he truly lost her before he had her?

CHAPTER TWENTY

DORY SAT IN the parlor of Silver Meadows with her two very good friends, her back to the portrait of Lady Belinda, not wishing to look upon the perfect lady. She sewed lace onto the neckline of her sky-blue gown. It was to be her wedding gown, and she'd put off the task for weeks. With only days left before her marriage to Lord Dearling, she'd forced herself to work on it. Having Lissette and Rose with her helped. She sighed, not looking forward to the rest of her life, but still confident she'd made the right decision.

"Dory, I'm confused." Lissette's dark-brown gaze seemed to look into her soul. "You are not excited to be marrying. Is it not what you wished for over the last two years and the reason for attending the season?"

Lissette's blunt questions were one of the traits she liked most about her. Being from France, and the country, no less, she was often confused by the complicated ways of society in England. But as soon as she was ready to come out, she was bound to be sought after. Not only was she a dark beauty with the slightest of accents, but she was very skilled at being a lady. She just didn't understand the intricacies yet that she needed to know to debut.

Dory shrugged, not sure she could clearly explain. "It is and it isn't." At Lissette's raised brows, she tried. "Yes, the season is for finding a husband, and I had greatly hoped for that to happen. We have to find a titled lord whom we can care about. I was fortunate in finding someone at Rose's house party."

Rose grinned, quite happy to explain. "Yes, she found Lord Dearling."

"But then why is she not happy?" Lissette lifted her hand in question.

Rose put down her needle and studied Dory as well. "*Are* you not happy?"

Dory shook her head, no longer able to hide it from her two good friends. The Duchess of Northwick and the Countess of Sommerset were well aware of why she was marrying, and that Lord Dearling was not her choice, but Lissette and Rose had been so happy for her, she'd not gone into the particulars. Yet now, she found herself crying every night, and she could no longer keep her sadness from them.

"Wait, I thought you were very happy." Rose looked about to cry herself. "You seemed a bit unsettled the day of the ball but then you accepted Lord Dearling's proposal. I thought you were pleased, but you're not. Is this why you've been focusing on your studies and not on your wedding?"

Dory gave Rose a sad smile. "Yes."

Dory looked to Lissette, who nodded knowingly. Not for the first time, Dory wondered how old the woman was. They had been told nineteen, but Lissette was worldly wise beyond that. "I am happy I am marrying, as I need to. However, I'm not happy because Lord Dearling is not the man I wish to marry."

Rose inhaled loudly, but Lissette shook her head. "This is not good." Again, the woman's dark stare focused on Dory. Then, much like the fortuneteller from the fair, Lissette spoke as if she knew more than was possible. "You are in love with a different man."

She froze. Lissette's ability to assess a situation was a bit unsettling at times. It was one reason why they had nicknamed her *Dague*, which was French for "dagger." She was particularly good at accurately focusing in on the issue at hand, which is when they would use the nickname. The woman also happened to be an expert with weapons.

"What?" Rose's exclamation gave Dory a moment to decide how to answer.

She would be leaving Silver Meadows forever in a few days' time. She owed her good friends the truth. Perhaps they could learn from her mistake. "Dague is correct. I fell in love with someone else at your house party, but he did not reciprocate those feelings."

"Oh, Dory, that is awful. But then why marry Lord Dear-ling?"

While Lady Elsbeth had been well aware, Dory had never told her other classmates about her mother's activities. She took a deep breath, hoping they wouldn't think less of her. "I must marry before my mother causes a scandal. She is miserable in her marriage to my father, and I'm not sure when that happened, as I remember them happy when I was young. But because of her misery, she finds solace in the arms of other men."

"No." Rose's eyes rounded and her hand flew to her mouth.

Lissette shook her head. "I have seen such before. So you accepted Lord Dearling."

"I did. He does love me. He's also kind and anxious to please me."

Rose grasped her arm tightly. "I am so disheartened for you. Who is the man who could not see what a wonderful woman you are? Was it Manning? Retfield? Tell me, and I will happily snub him the next chance I get."

Dory shook her head, not willing to put a rift between dear Rose and her hard-hearted brother.

"I say, do not wed. Wait for a man who loves you and whom you love in return." Lissette's gaze took on a dreamy look. "Life is about love. We French know this."

Dory had spent so much of her time teaching Lissette about the life of an English lady, she'd never considered what her friend's life had been like in France, except that it had been hard with the war. "Have you been in love before?"

"*Oui*, I have. It is glorious. Étienne and I were much in love."

At Lissette happy visage, Dory found herself feeling jealous. "If you were in love, why did you not marry?"

The woman's face changed, her full lips thinning. "The war. It kill my Étienne."

Immediately, Dory laid her hand on Lissette's arm, her heart aching at such sadness. "How awful."

"The war does not care about people. It cares only for land." Lissette hard gaze bored into the rug as if she could somehow exact revenge with her stare.

"You are now here, where it is safe." Dory squeezed her friend's arm before releasing her. "We have many men here. I hope that you can love again."

Lissette shrugged. "I do not know. But I do know that I will not marry unless I am in love, no matter what Grandmaman say."

Dory wanted to give her comfort, but Lissette was not one to accept it. It was clear she was truly upset. She only spoke French or switched her words about when her feelings took over her thoughts. Maybe when she learned about the relationship of reason and emotion when she studied Aristotle, it would help her. Both ladies were enjoying their studies, Rose excited to have more subjects to discuss and Lissette simply hungry for all knowledge.

Dory remembered feeling the same but now felt as if it mattered little in the end for in a only a couple of days, she'd be married and running her own household. She would ask Lord Dearling for pin money so she might purchase books. Hopefully, he would continue to love her. She did not wish her marriage to be like her parents'. She would never seek the arms of another while married. Would Lord Dearling? Would he keep a mistress? Did he have one now? She'd heard men had needs that had to be met. Would it matter to her? With so many unknowns, she felt like a man thrown overboard with no more than a piece of flotsam to keep—

"Lady Dorothea. Lady Northwick requests your presence in her study."

She jumped at Harrison's voice. "Oh, of course. Is something amiss?" She set her dress aside and rose.

"I believe you have a visitor. Lord Dearling."

Dory ignored Rose's gasp and quickly walked into the corridor to follow the butler. What could it mean that he was here so few days before the wedding? When he visited last week, he said he couldn't wait for Sunday.

"Your Grace. Lady Dorothea." Harrison announced her, then backed out, closing the door behind him.

While Lady Northwick appeared calm, Lord Dearling did not. In fact, he pulled at his cravat and his neck was red. Had he embarrassed himself before Lady Northwick? Immediately, she felt sympathy for him. "Lord Dearling. What a wonderful surprise." She strode forward, a reassuring smile on her face, or what she hoped was reassuring.

"My lady, I wish to speak with you." He held his hand out toward the settee placed in the bay window of the duchess's study. It was not far from her, but it did allow some privacy for their conversation while she observed.

She looked toward her teacher, who gave her a nod. Since Dearling didn't offer his arm, she walked to the settee and sat.

He stood. "My lady, I'm sure you have heard of the unfortunate circumstances of your mother."

Her mother? A chill raced through her. "I'm afraid I have not. I have been preparing for our wedding." Did he wish to move it to today? She wasn't ready. She still needed two more days to accept her fate.

Lord Dearling's face crumbled, his brows lowering, his upper lip lifting and his eyes squinting. "Oh, this is not well done at all."

He pulled at his cravat before looking behind her, no doubt at Lady Northwick. "I'm afraid that your mother was caught in a most unseemly circumstance."

Unseemly? Then it had finally happened? Still, she needed to know exactly what her mother had done. "I'm not sure I understand you."

"You wish me to explain?" His voice had risen with his brows.

Blast the man. They were to be husband and wife. Surely, he could tell her. "Yes, I need you to explain." She wouldn't look away, willing him to be candid.

"Ahem. Well, it is hardly fit for a young lady's sensibilities."

"I understand that you mean to protect me, and I'm grateful that as my future husband, you care about me so much. However, this is *my* mother, and if there is any way in which I can help her, I must know what has happened."

The man's red color rose from his neck to cover his entire face. "If you so insist, then you should know that there is nothing you can do. Lady Preston was discovered in a box at Haymarket Theatre unclothed with Lord Leighhall, also unclothed, atop her."

"Oh, Mother. How awful." She had little doubt that Lord Leighhall had orchestrated the entire scene so as to publicly reveal her mother's adultery. But how incredibly crude, even for her mother. Was her mother heartbroken? No doubt embarrassed. Sympathy for how unhappy her mother truly was rose within her. Perhaps that was because she knew what it was to not have love returned.

"Yes, well, in light of this disgrace, *my* mother feels it would not do for me to marry you this Sunday as planned."

Her belly tensed as if filled with metal armor. "I understand that you wish to wait. When, then, do you propose we marry?"

His eyes widened. "You misunderstand me, my lady. I mean to say that I cannot wed you at all."

She rose, her anger rising with her. "But you said you felt love for me."

"I did. But please understand the situation I am in now. With this scandal, I cannot in good conscience marry you. People would snicker behind my back and question your whereabouts.

Not to mention how it would reflect upon my family. No, my mother is correct. This makes it impossible for me to love you or marry you."

Furious that exactly what she'd feared was happening, she lashed out at him. "Then, sir, you obviously have no idea what love is to allow this to dissuade you. If I had loved you in return, and your mother caused a scandal, I wouldn't have let anything keep us apart. Fortunately, I do not, so I do not have to nurse a broken heart simply because you are too weak to ignore a few snickers."

His head snapped back. "My mother? My mother would never comport herself in such a way."

She curled her hands into fists at her sides, her frustration mounting. "No, of course she wouldn't as I'm sure she controls what your father thinks and feels as well as you. I must say with the utmost sincerity, that I owe a debt of gratitude to my mother. If this had not occurred, I would have never known what a poor husband you would make." She pointed to the door. "Now, if you would be so kind as to leave."

The man's face had reddened so much during her tirade, she wasn't sure if he'd have apoplexy.

His mouth opened and closed a few times before he finally made words come out. "You, my lady, are no lady." Without another word, he strode for the doors as if the Calydonian boar of Artemis were upon his heels. Yet even as he stalked out, he closed the door softy behind him.

She collapsed upon the settee, her head falling back upon its top as a profound relief filled her. It was all over. Everything.

"Dory?" Lady Northwick sat down next to her. "How are you feeling?"

She turned her head as it lay back to look at her teacher and mentor. As she tried to put into words the array of emotions filling her, she giggled. "I believe I'm happy." At the look the duchess gave her, she began to chuckle until she laughed out loud, finally sitting up. She held up her hand as she tried to control her laughter. "Do not think me bound for Bedlam until I explain."

Lady Northwick gave her an understanding smile. "To be truthful, if you were hurt by that man, then I would think you needed to be there."

That caused another laugh. She found herself drying her eyes with the handkerchief Lady Northwick produced. "I know it may seem odd, but I am relieved that I no longer need worry. I didn't realize how much I had worried. How many years I had worried, until this very moment."

"Do you mean about marrying?"

"Yes, and much more. I worried about marrying, my mother, and finally about Lord Leighhall. But now it's over. I will never marry. My mother has done the unthinkable, and Lord Leighhall, who had sworn to ruin me, has done so in the most creative of ways. Now, I no longer have any choices or need to make them. I am at fate's whim, if you will. I simply await what my father determines for me." The relief was profound after years of torment, fighting to somehow make it all right, and controlling what could not be controlled. Now, she found herself feeling sleepy. Unfortunately, the happiness that came with her relief floated by like a leaf on a stream, leaving behind only the cold, clear, and lonely water. With the worry gone, she was left with only the pain of her tortured heart.

"You know you are welcome to remain at the school as long as you wish."

She leaned over and gave her teacher a hug. Releasing the duchess, she stood. "I appreciate that very much. I have always felt more at home here than anywhere. I imagine my father will not remember me for months as he handles my mother's actions, so I am pleased to stay at school. Now, I think I will lie down. Would you let Rose and Lissette know?"

Lady Northwick stood as well and took her hands. "Of course I will. I'm very proud of you, Dory."

Warmth filled her chest, dispelling a bit of the cold. "I wish I could do more to deserve your judgement."

"No, you could not do more. You are a rare gem that is truly precious. I will have Cook make strawberry ice cream for you to celebrate your freedom from such a man. Now, go rest."

At least her love of strawberry ice cream was well-known. Nodding, she released the duchess's hands and left the study. The lightness in her belly was a strange feeling that she doubted would last, but she would be content while she could. For now, she was in a safe place and need not worry about anything but healing her heart.

CHAPTER TWENTY-ONE

FELTON RACED UP the grand drive of Silver Meadows, barely waiting for his horse to come to a stop before jumping off. Handing the reins of Nyx to the boy who'd run up, he took the ridiculously wide stairs two at a time. The door opened just before he reached the top. "I'm here to see my sister, Lady Rose Ambrose."

The butler showed him to a parlor, and Felton immediately went to the front window to be sure his horse behaved. He'd had plenty of time to plan his strategy on the long ride from Denton Hall. He'd been halfway to Shefford to ask Lord Preston's permission to marry Dory instead of Dearling when Mr. Taylour had met him on the road and told him what Leighhall had done. Even as he remembered the conversation, his hands curled into fists, his anger as much at Leighhall as himself for not anticipating the man's cunning. Turning about on the road, he'd returned home before heading to Silver Meadows. He would marry Dory with or without her father's permission, *if* she'd have him.

That gave him pause and had his heart skipping in his chest. Her wedding was on the morrow, so he only had today to convince her he was the best choice. And if she didn't agree?

He wasn't sure he could survive losing another woman he loved, especially because this time he wouldn't be able to rail at fate. It would be purely his own fault.

With his horse having been walked out of view, he turned toward the room, only to have his breath taken away by a full-length painting of Belinda. She stood beneath a tree, one hand resting on the trunk as she looked out into the room. At her feet were three books, one open with a rabbit sitting on it as it stared adoringly up at her. She wore a pale-pink dress but no bonnet. Her dark-brown hair flowed down her back and about one shoulder, tied back by a matching ribbon.

He breathed in as he noticed a few strands of hair had come loose of the ribbon and fell about her eyebrow. This was the real Belinda. He walked closer, unable to resist staring into her lifelike gaze. It was as if the artist captured her very soul. Glancing at the signature at the bottom, the painting made sense. Belinda's own sister had painted it, and with the wisdom of years, Lady Sommerset had captured Belinda as she truly had been.

He moved his gaze up again to the books, the image triggering a memory. Yes, she had been forever leaving books about, much to her sister Joanna's consternation. Belinda had also allowed many an animal into the house, which had caused one of her maids to quit. As he studied the painting further, he noticed dirt on the hand that lay against the tree. He'd forgotten how much she'd enjoyed working in the soil with her wildflowers, the Mabry gardener allowing her a space, despite the fact he had to consistently weed out those same flowers from the formal garden.

How had he forgotten such endearing quirks? Had his loss created a saint from the woman he'd loved, erasing all her humanity, which was what had called to him from the start?

"It's a wonderful painting, isn't it?" Rose's voice had him turning to face her.

"It is. It captures who she truly was."

Rose sat on a chair, still looking at the painting behind him. "I was so young, I don't remember her like this. Instead, I remember feelings like warm, kind, caring, and comforting." She moved her gaze to his and smiled.

He forced himself to sit on the settee opposite her, not sure he could focus on their conversation if he could see Belinda. He was here for another warm, kind, caring, and comforting woman. One it had taken him too damn long to realize he loved. "I've come to talk to Dory, but I wished to hear from you if she has heard about her mother."

"Is the word truly making it to every village?"

He grimaced, knowing how harsh the repercussions could be, but determined to stifle them as soon as possible. "Yes. Does she know?"

His sister narrowed her eyes at him. "Is that what you wish to talk to 'Dory' about? When did you start using her nickname? I do hope it is only between us."

He ignored her second question. "Yes. No." He tapped his fingers on the arm of the chair, not comfortable explaining his true reason for the visit. It would involve admitting he'd been oblivious of his own feelings.

Rose's eyes suddenly rounded. "It's you!"

He jerked back. "What do you mean?"

Rose cleared her throat. "Nothing. I was just telling Dory that people had different habits when they were uncomfortable. I simply couldn't remember who it was who…tapped their fingers." She waved off her comment. "You do not need to be uncomfortable about talking to Dory about her mother. She's always expected it."

That was true, but she always worried about it. Unless Dearling had already come and reassured her of his intentions. He had to know. "Has Lord Dearling visited her?"

"As a matter of fact, he was just here yesterday. Dory was very much relieved after his visit. So unless you had something else you need to discuss with her—"

"I do."

Rose eyed him shrewdly. "Will she want to talk to you?"

Again, he tapped his fingers, his concern growing. "I would like to. If she will see me. She was not pleased with me at

Mother's final ball." His sudden unsureness felt awkward on his shoulders. Did Rose know what he'd done? She seemed very protective of Dory.

"No, I have heard she wasn't." His sister studied him a moment before she rose. "I suggest we see what she says. Mademoiselle Lissette and Dory are practicing how to throw a knife."

"What?"

Rose's eyes sparkled. "It's part of our lessons. Lady Northwick has us all learn some self-defense techniques. From what I understand, the duchess was in need of them once when with the duke and Lord Mabry. Come, they're in the back."

He stood and followed his sister from the room, glancing one last time at Belinda.

Rose brought him down a corridor that ended in a large arch into what could only have once been a ballroom, but now was filled with bookcases upon bookcases of books, not just along the walls, but dividing the space into rooms. Two young women noticed them and followed. They looked to be Lady Georgina and Lady Eleanor, if he wasn't mistaken.

He lengthened his stride to walk next to his sister. "Where are the duke and duchess?"

"Oh, they are about. I believe the duke is instructing the gardener on where to place birdhouses. The duchess said she needed to finish a book so she could meet with Sophie to discuss it this afternoon. Later, I will have a class on philosophy with Dory and tomorrow is my first science class with the duke." Rose halted as they stepped out onto the terrace. "Brother, I cannot tell you how happy it makes me to be here."

His sister's smile was as bright as the sun. He also noticed her skin had darkened from being out in said sun and there was a liveliness in her step he hadn't noticed before. "You really enjoy this school?"

"I do. I wish I could stay forever, or at least through my second year." She winked, something he'd never seen her do.

"Maybe you could help me persuade Mother if I don't have an offer next year?"

His heart filled that she had found something exciting to focus upon. "I give you my word I will do whatever I can."

She grabbed on to his arm and squeezed. "I always thought you the best sibling a lady could have."

At that, he chuckled. "I don't recall that exact phrase the morning you woke with a frog in your bed."

She laughed, a full, hearty laugh, not the gentle ladylike laugh she used at home. It was as if in just a month's time, she had accepted who she was, and he couldn't be more pleased for her.

"There they are." She pointed to the lawn with a pair of targets set up. "Lissette is very patient with Dory."

Two women stood facing the targets, one with midnight-black hair and Dory, with the sun catching the red strands in her mahogany hair. Neither woman wore a bonnet, no doubt their skin darkening like his sister's.

He and Rose strode toward them.

The Frenchwoman explained something then eyed the target and let her knife fly. It hit dead center. Despite the warmth of the day, he felt a chill at such precision. Dory lifted her knife, eyed the target, and let it fly, its handle hitting the top of the target and bouncing into the grass. Both ladies celebrated as if it were well done.

Rose grabbed his arm. "Come. It's time. Choose your words carefully." At such a serious tone coming from his sister, he glanced down at her to see her scowling at him. Her statement sounded like a threat.

"Dory, look who came to visit." Rose's face changed in an instant, but he knew her false smile.

Dory turned, her eyes widening.

She appeared more beautiful than he remembered, and in that moment, he knew himself to be an idiot to think he could ever allow her to marry another. "Dory."

Mademoiselle Lissette came forward. "Rose, let us retrieve

the knives so we can use them again."

As his sister and the Frenchwoman walked toward the targets, he tried to find the words he wanted to say, but they were a tangled pile of twine. That thought had him smiling. "I had much I wished to say to you, but I find my thoughts are a muddle."

Dory's brows lowered. "If you came to tell me about Lord Leighhall, you're too late. I know." She stood straighter, as if expecting an argument.

"That is not why I came."

Uncertainty flashed in her multi-colored gaze, though at the moment, green seemed to be dominating. "Then do not let me take time away from your visit to your sister." She turned away and took a few steps before he found his voice.

"Wait." Where were his words?

She stopped but didn't look at him. "Lord Harewood, I don't believe we have anything further to discuss."

A spike of fear ripped through his chest. He needed to remain calm. She was not married yet. He had today to convince her. "But we do. We need to discuss your pending marriage to Lord Dearling. I understand from my sister that he visited yesterday."

She looked at him then. "He did." Her voice sounded wary.

"I don't believe that Dearling can protect you from the *ton*, or even his own mother, to be completely honest. Whatever he may have said to convince you of his loyalty, I promise it will not last long. He may even fail to arrive at the church."

She glanced back toward his sister before walking over to face him. "Lord Dearling would never be so uncouth. He told me quite clearly that he could not marry me because of my mother. So if you think to find another man for me to marry, you do not truly understand the damage my mother has done."

He wanted to shout with joy but kept his own counsel. "But I do understand, which is why I am proposing that *I* marry you." That didn't sound like he'd meant it to. Why couldn't he think? Was this how she felt most of the time? If so, her concerted efforts on conversation were quite admirable.

She lifted her chin and placed one hand on her hip. "If you think to come here to play the martyr and marry me to save the reputation of this school, then you are as ignorant as a baby in a lumbermill. Why would I marry you when I have a perfectly lovely place here, where I can learn all I wish? I will no doubt be left here since neither my mother nor my father have thought about me in months. In fact, I may stay here until I'm expert enough to teach future students, thereby enjoying my life to the fullest whilst doing what I wish. I understand that spinsters do have a bit of independence, though certainly not as much as widows. Now, being a widow would be the perfect situation for me, as a widow has no need to be a companion or to have a chaperone. Widows truly have the best of society, as they can enjoy the events they choose with no one judging their actions or expecting them to marry. Of course, paradoxically, to become a widow, first one must secure a husband, which we've already established is beyond my means and unnecessary. And why are you smiling at me?"

As if the stars had aligned in her single soliloquy, his mind cleared. "I have missed your squiggly lines."

"My squiggly...? Oh. I did not know you enjoyed my ramblings. In fact, it was you who helped me to stop them." She frowned at him, clearly not pleased with his experiment.

"Yes, I did, but only to help you with others. I have always enjoyed them." He smiled at her, unable to stop. Everything about her he loved. Her rambles, her humor, even her pique.

"Yes, well, I'm glad I have been able to entertain you, but I still don't see any reason why I would marry you." She lifted her hand as if to dismiss him.

Once more, panic set in. "Because I love you." He waited, his breath stuck in his lungs.

"You love me?" Her words came out in a whisper, as if she couldn't believe it.

He took her bare hand. "I do. I love you, Dory. I don't wish to go another day without you as my wife. I would marry you tomorrow if I could, but I still wouldn't because I would want all of England to know that I am marrying you, and they are invited to attend."

She continued to stare at him in disbelief. "But I can't be Belinda."

He squeezed her hand in his. "I loved Belinda with all my heart. When she died, I thought she took my heart with her. But then I met you. You made my heart beat again. You showed me what happiness could be. You brought me love. At first, I was blind, so busy observing others, I failed to observe myself. But I finally understood my feelings. I had Belinda. Now I want Dory. I believe you love me. Tell me I'm right, Dory. Please." He took another deep breath to steady his heart. "Do you love me?"

Her eyes almost glowed green now as water filled them. "I do."

Relief, joy, and happiness washed over him like the sun's first rays warmed the Earth, his heart finally able to beat without a heavy rock holding it down. "Since I love you, and you love me, I ask you now, Lady Dorothea Ansley of Preston. Will you be my wife?"

She sniffed, but her smile had returned. "I will, Fen."

At the use of her nickname for him, he couldn't resist her another moment and pulled her closer to kiss her.

"What are you all about?" The duchess's voice rang out from behind him.

Rose ran past him before he could turn around. "Lady Northwick, my brother just proposed to Dory and she said yes!"

Devil it. He leaned down and kissed his love.

Her mouth opened to his, but he refused the invitation, suddenly aware from the chatter of voices that there were many as their witnesses. Just as he pulled away, Dory licked at his lips, sending a shock through his body.

She smiled up at him before walking forward, forcing him to turn and face their audience. As he counted the faces, he swore he'd been to plays with fewer people. The duchess stood above on the terrace studying Dory. His sister stood a step below. On the ground at the bottom of the terrace were Lady Georgina and Lady Eleanor. Mademoiselle Lissette stood off to the side with Lady Sophie, and striding toward them all was the Duke of Northwick.

He tensed. Whatever the man had to say, nothing would dissuade him from his current path. The duke stepped in front of them.

Dory spoke at once. "Lord Northwick, I can explain."

"No." Felton squeezed Dory's hand. "*I* can explain. I am marrying Dory as soon as the banns can be read."

The duke's gaze remained steady as it moved from Dory to himself. "Then I expect an invitation to the wedding."

Relieved the man wouldn't try to stop him, he nodded. "We would be honored."

Within seconds, they were surrounded by everyone, or rather the ladies surrounded Dory, clearly happy for her. Lady Northwick took the opportunity to pull him aside. "Felton, I'm so pleased you have found another love."

"I think Belinda would approve."

"I agree." She gave him a kind smile. "For me, it still feels like you are marrying into my family. This school and these students have become my family. Maybe both you and Dory can be guest lecturers sometime. It would be a shame to only see you at Christmastide and in Town."

"Joanna, we would be honored."

"Good, but I do have one concession I must insist upon."

He stiffened, immediately wary. "And that is?"

"That you never, for any reason, interfere with my school or my students again. The duke and I are well equipped to handle its reputation. Understand?"

He swallowed hard, his own efforts in light of the duke's influence seeming suddenly childish. "Yes. I had only Belinda's name in mind." He didn't add that his marriage to Dory might help, though the damage her mother had done kept him silent.

The duchess raised her brow. "Your intentions may have been honorable, but my sister is long gone. It is time you joined the living."

He nodded, in full agreement. As the duchess turned away, he felt a hand take his, and he immediately turned to see what his sister wanted. "Yes?"

"I'm so happy for you." She rested her hand over her heart. "Dory is perfect for you."

"You knew Dearling had broken the betrothal and didn't tell me. Why?"

Her gaze turned wise beyond her years. "I had to know you truly cared for Dory. If you did, then you would hurt like you had hurt her. It also meant you were feeling again. Truly feeling. I wanted to be sure my brother had returned from living in the shadows."

He pulled her forward and hugged her so she wouldn't realize there were tears in his eyes. "You are far more intelligent than you accept."

She pulled away and grinned. "Imagine how much more so I'll be after this year at Belinda's school."

He had no doubt she would absorb ever piece of knowledge she could and become a far better person than he could ever hope to be. "When you are ready to find the man you want to marry, I will help you in any way I can."

Rose wiggled her brows. "I'll be sure to remember that."

He squeezed her hand and she let go, off to talk to her new friends. He searched for Dory and found her speaking with the duchess. He headed that way, breaking into their conversation. "I do not mean to interrupt, but I request a walk with my betrothed, if that would be acceptable?"

The duchess nodded. "As long as you stay within sight, I will allow it."

"My lady?" He offered his arm to Dory and they strolled down the grass. Her lemony scent filled his lungs, and he breathed deeply.

"Must we wait three weeks?" She looked up at him, her love shining in her eyes.

His brain, for once, was in sync with his heart as he gazed at her. "I would prefer to. I do not want our wedding to appear hurried in any way. I'm proud to make you my wife."

Her shoulders sagged. "Then I guess we will simply have to hide our kisses from prying eyes."

Hide their kisses? "No, we need not hide them because there will be no more until after we wed."

She smirked. "Not even to stop me from rambling?"

He chuckled. "No, not even then."

A devilish light came into her eyes. "We'll see."

He groaned silently, quite sure this would be the longest three weeks of his life.

CHAPTER TWENTY-TWO

DORY STROLLED INTO her husband's library anxious to see how many books he might have in it while he gave instructions to the butler. After three long weeks, she was finally Lady Harewood. She grinned as she imagined a forest filled with bunnies. Turning in a circle, she studied the room and smiled, thrilled at the number of volumes on the shelves. Since her husband had a well-stocked library, she would spend her pin money on statues and pictures of rabbits and set them about the house until the King of Bunnies noticed and told her to stop. After all, he did say he was observant. She had quite a clever husband after all.

Husband. She was well and truly married. And Fen had made sure everyone was there, well everyone but her mother. Father had forbidden it. Still, all the Mabrys and Curious Ladies had come, and of course Lord and Lady Enderly. Surprisingly, even the countess shed a few tears at seeing her son wed, and had welcome her warmly, which was a relief.

Dory sighed happily as she wandered past the fireplace, the windows, the desk, until she came upon a table with four books on it. She reviewed the titles and her heart filled with love. They were some of the philosophers she'd mentioned to him over the last few weeks. Had he been reading them to converse with her? While their conversations had been quite satisfying, there had been but a few, as he'd come back to Denton House to have it prepared for her, as she had once hoped. She greatly appreciated his thoughtfulness, but she'd missed him. Missed their conversations and his kisses the most.

Fen strode in, his gaze immediately searching her out. He took her in his arms, exactly where she wished to be.

She wrapped her arms around his neck. "You have a preponderance of books."

He smiled. "I do. Would you like to see them?"

"Not particularly." She looked up at him from beneath her lashes.

He laughed, a sound that had been so rare when she'd first met him and now was common. "Then what would you like to do, Lady Harewood? This is your home now. You've already met the servants. Would you like to see your room?"

"Not especially." She licked her lips.

His smile disappeared. "Then I admit that I am at a loss as to what you would like see."

She played with the dark hair at the back of his neck, twining the silky strands around her fingers. "I believe I wish to see *you*."

His chest filled as he took a deep breath. "You *are* seeing me."

"No, I wish to see you *sans vêtements*."

His nostrils flared, causing a ripple of excitement to flow through her. "Without clothes? What has Mademoiselle Lissette been teaching you?"

"She says the French are well educated in the art of love. I thought it best to learn all I could while waiting for our wedding." She moved one hand down between them to unbutton his tailcoat.

He pulled her tightly against him, effectively stopping her efforts to disrobe him. "Dory." His voice had lowered and a shiver of excitement raced to her core.

She had learned much in the last few weeks from a book Lissette had found in the library at Silver Meadows and thought she should read. Lissette was very good at discovering things, her mind working in ways foreign. Lissette had seen Lady Blackmore give it to the duchess and had searched it out. It had been tucked away on a high shelf, and Dory was quite sure they hadn't been meant to find it. It had a false cover claiming it discussed feminine education, but inside it was *The Illustrated Pleasures of Seduction*.

Since she still had one hand around his neck, and he'd pressed her so close, she raised herself on her toes, liking the feel of his hard chest against her breasts. "Will you not kiss your bride?"

Immediately, his head lowered and he took her lips with his.

She opened her mouth and nudged his open, delving in to taste him. The scent of pine filled her nostrils even as she tasted the faint hints of brandy on his tongue from the wedding breakfast.

His mouth became demanding as if he were starved for her. She understood and tangled her tongue with his until she could barely breathe, her thoughts shooting into the sky. His arms pressed her closer, one hand pushing her pelvis tight against him, where she could feel his desire for her. His other hand moved against her back where her purple gown was tied.

She broke the kiss and his hold, shaking her head. "You are still clothed."

"As are you, and we are in my library. Perhaps we should move upstairs."

She shook her head and backed up two more steps. Looking around, she finally brought her gaze back to his. "No, I like it in here." She bit her lip to keep from laughing at his surprise.

"Did you wish to read, then?"

His confusion made her laugh. "No, I have already read much." She moved to the opposite side of the table with the books. Lifting the first from the pile, she held it up. "I've read this." She lifted the next. "And this." She added the other two to the pile in her arms. "And all of these." She set them on the bookcase nearby next to a small statue of a horse. Trailing her fingers over the table, she walked halfway around it. "I like the table bare. The same way I like you."

His brows lifted before his gaze turned shrewd. "I like you bare as well."

Her heart skipped a beat at the predatory gleam in his darkened green gaze.

He slowly unbuttoned his black tailcoat and, shrugging it off, pulled a chair from the table and laid the coat over the back. Then he untied his white cravat and laid that atop the coat. Next, he unbuttoned his white waistcoat and dropped that on the chair as well. "Now let us see about your dress."

She'd thought to entice him, but she was caught in a dream of her own making. Walking alongside the rest of the table, she stopped in front of him and laid her hand where the V of his shirt opened wide, revealing his skin. His chest was warm, with small, soft hairs and beneath, she could feel the beat of his heart. Its strength must be due to his fitness, which she had only seen in candlelight. Now, in the afternoon sun, she wished to see him again. She used both hands to push his shirt from his shoulders, but before it could fall, he pulled her against him once more.

He lowered his head and whispered into her ear. "Will you be my wife in all ways?"

Her heart filled with love even as her excitement rose at what was to come. "Yes. I want to be your wife in all ways." She lay her face against his chest, enjoying the feel of his hard body against her cheek.

His hands moved once more to the strings holding her wedding dress together. Then the neckline of her shift loosened and cool air caressed her back.

She lifted her head and looked at him. "I understand there are many ways to be a wife." She expected him to be shocked, but instead, he gave her a sly smile.

"Indeed, there are. I promise to show you them all, but it will take many months if I show you one each day."

"Months?" She'd seen dozens in the book. There must be more. Her curiosity had her anticipation rising. "I look forward to learning every way possible. I believe I'm going to be very happy as your wife."

His eyes widened at first and then he broke into laughter. "And I will be quite pleased as well. Now, shall we start with your dress?"

She nodded and lifted her arms as he pulled her favorite dress over her head to join his clothes on the chair. Her shift fell off her shoulders and down on top of her stays, exposing half her breasts and barely covering her nipples.

He turned and moved toward her, but she stepped back again. "Your shirt."

He looked down, as if he'd forgotten it, and quickly pulled it over his head, throwing it on the table. Covering the space between them in a single stride, he cupped her face in his hands. "I'm going to make you feel pure bliss. I'm going to show you with my body how much I love you."

Confident she'd never been so filled with joy in her entire life, her breath caught and her eyes itched with tears. "I want to show you with my body too."

His lips came down on hers in a kiss of promise and love. Then he moved behind her and untied her stays, dropping them over the chair.

She smirked. "I do believe we are going to need another chair."

He didn't agree or disagree. He simply started unbuttoning his black trousers.

Standing in her shift, she watched his every movement. She felt a strong, feminine need to see him rise up from the depths of her belly. Never had she wished to see a man as she craved to look at him once more.

Kicking off his shoes, he pulled down his socks and set them aside. Straightening, he stepped out of his trousers and turned his back as he folded them and placed them on the chair seat.

She sucked in her breath at the strength of his thighs and buttocks, no doubt built from years of riding. She may have fallen in love with him in candlelight, but in daylight, she discovered a sexual need for him that would not be denied.

When he finally faced her, he did not move, allowing her to look her fill, and she did. He was all lean strength, coated in a smattering of dark hairs that tried to soften the hardness but did little to hide his need for her.

Tired of waiting, she pulled her shift over her head and threw it on the table before walking to him. "Fen, love me."

He pulled her against him, holding her as he lowered his head and spoke into her ear. "I will." His mouth traveled down her neck then, kissing her sensitive skin, causing excitement to skitter down her arms and chest. He walked her backward until her bare behind touched the table. With nowhere to go, she bent backward to allow his lips full access to her body, but instead, he left her skin to capture her mouth in a kiss that left her dizzy with wanting.

Breaking their connection, he stared into her eyes. "Are you sure you don't wish to see your new room, your new bed?"

It took a moment for thought to return to her head, but as it did, she recognized the smirk on his face. He expected her to want a bed, but she'd experienced a bed with him. "No, I want this table." It was her turn to smirk as his green eyes darkened and his smile disappeared.

"Then that is what you shall have. Up you go."

Before she knew what he was about, he sat her on the table. She shivered as her hot bottom made contact with the cold, hard surface, more from anticipation than from the temperature.

"Now, I must take your boots off." Kneeling down, he untied each one and lifted it from her foot.

He made her feel delicate and wanted, causing her eyes to water. Blinking rapidly, she dispelled the tears, not wishing to miss anything he might do. She didn't have long to wait as he spread her legs and stared at her very core.

Heat seemed to start at the juncture of her thighs as her belly tightened. She remembered how good he could make her feel. Would he stand now and make her his?

He did stand, but he did not move closer. Instead, he bent his head to kiss her once more. She wrapped her arms around his neck and sighed into his mouth as he teased her with his tongue.

Before she realized what he was about, he was kissing the corner of her lips, her cheek, her jaw. She tilted her head and his mouth traveled lower, to her neck, her collarbone, her chest. As his mouth moved lower, his hand cupped her breast.

She held her breath, anxious for what would come next.

His tongue licked at her nipple before he blew on it.

"Oh." The chill made it harden more, and she leaned back, locking her arms to allow him full access.

He bent forward and sucked her wet nipple into his mouth, tonguing her hard peak at the same time. She let her eyes close and her head fall back, happy to allow him his feast. And feast he did, teasing and sucking both breasts until her body ached with need and a warm wetness permeated her folds. She could barely catch her breath and she didn't care.

His mouth left her.

She opened her eyes to see what he was about, but he no longer looked at her, as he had knelt down once again.

"Fen?" Her voice came out in a breathy whisper. She tried to swallow, but his hands on her thighs, spreading her legs wider, made her mouth go dry.

His fingers reached her folds and gently explored. "Beautiful." His voice floated through her, easing her tension, allowing her to swallow until one finger found the place he'd touched before.

She gasped. This was what she wanted. She grabbed his shoulders, needing him to continue, to bring her to that feeling only he could give her.

His finger swirled the warm wetness of her over her nub, tantalizing her, making her squirm with need. She found her breaths becoming shallow and fast. She dug her fingers into his shoulders, holding him there, wanting more.

He chuckled softly. "Lean back, love. I promise I won't stop."

Since even as he spoke, he continued his play, she did as he asked, though it was hard. But then he leaned in and his mouth found the same spot.

Her body shivered with tension as he laved her, circling her pleasure spot with his tongue, her belly tensing for what was to come. Then his hands smoothed their way up her ribs and cupped her breasts, his thumbs finding her nipples and rubbing them.

She closed her eyes at the intense dual feelings, the air leaving her lungs as soon as she brought it in. Waves of pleasure rippled over her body. They built one on top of the other, the next more intense than the last, until she was lifted so high, she crashed in upon herself, her ecstasy spinning her about in pure bliss

Her elbows buckled and she collapsed on the table, sucking in air to gain her equilibrium again.

THE ABSOLUTE HAPPINESS that ran through him at Dory's release was tempered only by his body demanding its own. As he rose to enjoy the view of his wife fully sated, he became stuck on that word—*wife*.

She was his. He'd almost lost her due to his own blindness and lack of self-reflection. He would learn from that, keep her safe, and keep her close. But first, he needed to make her his forever.

Even as the thought entered his head, it pushed all other thoughts out. His curvy wife lay before him, an offering to the gods, yet he, a mere mortal, could claim her as his. His body tensed and his erection jerked.

Stepping between her thighs, he laid his hands on her hips. "Dory, I'm going to make you mine now."

Her eyelids fluttered open and her full lips parted, but she didn't speak. She was a natural enchantress, her cheeks ruddy from her satisfaction, half her hair loose from her bun, her arms spread out as if offering herself.

Then she spoke, a barely audible sound. "Make me yours."

Her words sent a shiver down his back that tightened his sack. He could not wait any longer. He didn't have to. Gently, he positioned himself at her entrance, the slickness wearing at his control. Leaning over her, he took a luscious breast into his mouth and sucked hard.

Her hips rose, causing him to slip inside her just a little.

"Oh. More." Her legs wrapped around his arse as if she would take him in all at once.

He wanted that too, but he didn't wish to hurt her. Moving his mouth to the other breast, he repeated his action. This time when she raised her hips, he slowly moved forward. Her legs squeezed him, wanting more. Her need for him had him giving in. Lifting his head from her breast, he watched her as he moved carefully all the way to his hilt.

She stilled, her eyes rounding as her body adjusted to him. "Fen?"

Her whisper sent erotic sensations over his entire body. "Yes." His voice was gravelly, his throat dry with need.

"I feel loved, complete."

His heart skittered at her words. "You are. We are one now."

Her nose crinkled. "Is this it? I thought it would be...more exciting."

He laughed, moving inside her, causing a gasp. "It will be. Allow me to show you." He didn't wait for an answer. Instead, he slowly pulled back before pushing in again.

As her eyes closed, a smile formed on her face.

He pulled back again, going slow, making it almost unbearable, but for her first time, her body would need to adjust. Yet before he could move his hips forward, her feet pulled him toward her and he drove into her.

"Yes." Her voice was strong, making it clear what she wanted.

Standing straight again, he pulled back, holding her hips in place to set the pace. He was careful but gave her want she wanted, what they both wanted. She was warm and welcoming, holding him as he pulled out, only to move in again.

His pleasure mounted and he needed her to reach her pinnacle with him. As he pulled out once more, he used his finger to encircle her pleasure spot while he moved forward again. At once, she tightened around him and soft moans came from her open lips. He watched her as her excitement rose, his own matching hers as he slid in and out.

His control began to slip. His need became unbearable, her body pulling him to the edge. Then she constricted around him, her back arching as her feet held him against her and she gave a long, soft cry, sending him spiraling into his own sweet joy with her.

One. The word flitted through his mind as he held her to him, his very soul seeming to heal and rejoice as he filled her. The feelings were so overwhelming, he couldn't move. He could only hold onto her, his anchor to life, his joy.

Finally, he opened his eyes to find his hands still gripping her while her chest rose and fell quickly with her breaths. He loosened his fingers and bent over to pull her up against him, keeping them together yet feeling her heart beat against his. He found himself looking forward to the future instead of ignoring it.

He wanted to know all her thoughts and ideas on life, love, learning, lanterns, everything. A different excitement built in his chest. He looked at each new day now with an anticipation of how she would see it and what they would do together. His breath caught as the image of a baby settled into his mind. For the first time in his life, he could see having children.

"Dory?"

"Hmm?" She remained limp, her arms and legs hanging loosely at her sides.

He took a certain amount of pride in that at the same time a fierce protectiveness filled him. "Would you like to go upstairs and lie down?"

She didn't lift her head. Instead, she spoke to his shoulder. "Won't the servants talk if we walk naked through the house?"

An image of them walking hand in hand naked up the stairs while the servants peeked from behind doorways had him laughing. He squeezed her tighter, not sure how he had been so fortunate as to earn her love. "Yes, I expect they will, even if they just peek around the corners."

He felt her lips lift against his skin before she turned her head and looked at him. "We could be the talk of all downstairs."

"I'm not sure that would be something to brag about." He gazed into her eyes, which appeared a pretty aqua color at the moment. "But I could put your dress on you and carry you up."

She tilted her head and a devilish look came into her eyes. "No, I absolutely forbid any of the maids to see you unclothed. No, we will just have to stay here, in the library. Do you think they would mind bringing our meals in here? Then tonight while everyone is asleep, we could sneak up to our rooms?"

His breath hitched at her suggestion. Stay in the library all day with no clothes on? It was so beyond his thought process that he found himself studying the idea from all angles. He'd never imagined it, but there was no reason not to. He gave her a sly smile. "I can think of no better way to spend the day."

She wrapped her arms around his neck and brushed a kiss across his lip. "I can, but we can do that tomorrow."

He laughed outright, the sound filling the room, reverberating against them. At her widening eyes, he laughed harder, a happy tear escaping. Hugging her close, he felt her giggling in response.

Whatever his future held, he was convinced it would be filled with the unexpected and laughter. Much laughter and happiness. Lowering his lips to hers, he whispered, "My joy," before losing himself in her once again.

EPILOGUE

September 1817
Denton Hall

DORY FLOPPED DOWN into the chair at the table in the garden. "I'm so tired, I may just sleep here."

Lissette chuckled. "We didn't walk *that* far."

"Not far? We were in the woods for two hours!" How could Lissette appear ready for the next ball? She still hadn't taken a chair yet. "Are you not tired?"

Lissette shook her head as she walked to a blackberry bush and plucked a berry off. "This is the most beautiful garden I've seen since arriving in England. The natural chaos of the plants and flowers makes it feel welcoming. It reminds me of walking in the woods, but with fewer trees."

Dory studied the wild garden, quite happy it was hers now. There was surely none other like it among those of any of her peers. "I like to think that the plants are happy to do as they wish."

"I would be happy if I could do as I wish as well." Lissette turned around and finally took a seat. "But Grandmaman has expectations." She popped the blackberry into her mouth.

"I understand. I do hope you like being at the school." She noticed the butler coming out with lemonade, no doubt sent by

Fen. "I know there is much to learn, but you are very quick to understand."

As the butler set down the tray with the glasses, Lissette waited. After he'd left, she waited still longer before answering, always intentional in her comments and actions. "It is not as exciting as when I lived in France, but it is very safe. I had forgotten what it was like to be safe."

Dory took a large swallow of lemonade, thankful for its coolness as it went down. "If wearing men's clothes and learning to throw knives and to track animals like we did today was all part of your days, I'm not surprised the school here is a bit boring for you. What we read about in books, you've actually done."

Lissette twirled the glass, not yet taking a sip. "It may seem romantic, but it was not. It was war, and those of us who lived there were caught in the middle. We did what we had to, as would you have."

As much as she'd like to think that she would have adapted, she was far less sure after learning more about Lissette's life, something her friend had just begun to share with her. Little did the other Curious Ladies know how fitting their nickname of Dague was for Lissette. Not only did she have skills they would never have, but she was precise, sharp, and to the point in her actions.

"Did you try on the pantaloons?"

She grinned at Lissette's question. "I did. I fear my behind is much larger than yours, making them indecently tight, but since my husband is sure to enjoy them that way, I'm very pleased with them."

"Ah, you mean he will enjoy *you*." Lissette's dark eyes held knowledge far beyond her years.

Dory refused comment on that, taking another gulp of lemonade instead. Her husband was most inventive in ways and places for them to enjoy each other's bodies. She quite enjoyed the challenges of inventing her own. She studied the area where she and Lissette sat. It was in view of the house, but only the second floor. It definitely had possibilities.

"I am pleased that you found the earl and that he finally recognized what a wonderful person you are."

Dory shook her head. "I never imagined how enjoyable it would be confounding the earl or that it would lead to love. I can only surmise that I was able to keep him wondering about my ideas long enough for him to appreciate my many charms."

Lissette looked askance at her. "As to that, you may enjoy those pantaloons. I still have another pair that Grandmaman doesn't know of. The rest, she made me burn."

It took her a moment to remember what they had been speaking about. "The rest?"

"*Oui*, I did not wear dresses once the war started. It was far too dangerous." Lissette finally lifted her glass and took a delicate sip before continuing. "I enjoy these pretty dresses, but they are not so good for tracking, *non*?"

"No, they are not." Dory grinned sheepishly. She'd barely kept up with Lissette, but the woman knew so much, Dory had been anxious to learn it all, especially that there were indeed many bunnies in the forest.

She definitely missed the school, though. She'd asked both Rose and Lissette to visit, but Rose didn't want to leave her studies. She understood that feeling. "I so enjoyed our trek through the woods, and as promised, I will return the favor this evening. Which philosopher are you most interested in learning about?"

"Jean-Jacques Rousseau."

Lissette's quick answer didn't surprise her. The woman never meandered in her thoughts, like Dory did. "This French philosopher writes much on equality and the state of man. I believe there are two of his works in our library here, though the school has a good dozen. He was quite interested in man's natural state and how he was the same in two ways yet different in his perfectibility from animals. He believes that a man can improve himself. I believe that by attending our school, we all seek to improve upon ourselves—otherwise, why attend? I wonder, though, if there are different motivations for each woman or if at the heart of it, we all attend for a similar reason. I do not believe the latter is the case, as from my talks with fellow students, I have been given different reasons. But if we could look at all these reasons and discover that we all essentially want to improve ourselves, then that is what could be said for the Curious Ladies."

Lissette held her hand out. "As you say it, it does make sense, though I lost where man's nature is involved."

"I apologize. I promise to focus on the philosopher's ideas this evening and not my own."

Lissette raised her brows. "I highly doubt that, but I look forward to our conversation nonetheless."

Dory grinned, pleased that Lissette was her friend as well as classmate. Taking a sip of her lemonade, she caught sight of her husband walking down the path toward them. That he took inordinate amounts of time from his day to spend with her made her feel truly treasured. It was such a change from being at home with her parents. Now, her heart ached for her mother, who had been banished to dowager house in Shefford, while her father lived in London. She'd seen her father at her wedding, but her mother had already been banished. That Felton had agreed on a trip to see her mother made her love him that much more.

"I see you ladies have completed your tour of the east wood." He passed behind her to take the empty seat next to her, his pine scent filling her nose.

"We didn't *tour the wood*—we tracked animals."

His brows raised. "Truly? And what animals did you find?"

Dory laughed, too excited to tell him. "We found bunnies! Many, many bunnies."

His eyes rounded. "Tell me you are only teasing."

She yawned before smiling widely. "No, it's true. I cannot wait to tell Rose."

"I forbid you to tell Rose."

She stared in shock, as he'd never forbidden her anything, but his lips twitched as he obviously held back a smile. Straightening her shoulders, she gave him a single nod. "Very well, I bow to your wishes." She turned her head toward Lissette. "Please tell Rose that there are hundreds of bunnies in the east wood."

"I would be pleased to." Lissette tilted her head before speaking to Felton. "You may also enjoy knowing you have pheasants, martens, and foxes."

Dory hid a smile at Felton's attempt to hide his surprise. "And my wife can now spot these creatures by following their tracks?"

Lissette shook her head as she lifted her glass. "No. We only saw rabbits. The others stayed well hidden."

Dory's husband glanced at her as if for confirmation and she nodded.

"It seems I have underestimated Belinda's school once again."

"Oh, no. We didn't learn that at the school. Lissette has skills from living in France during the war. Tracking is not on the slate of subjects. I just wished to learn about it and tonight, I will help Lissette understand Jean-Jacques Rousseau." She yawned again, the morning's activity taking a toll.

Felton sat back and crossed his legs. "I wish the school had a weapon's expert among its instructors as well as a knife thrower."

Surprised, Dory blinked. "Whyever would you wish that?"

"I received a letter from Mr. Taylour. He—"

Lissette spoke up, suddenly very attentive. "Mr. Taylour? Is that Mr. Anthony Taylour?"

"Yes." Felton turned his attention to Lissette. "Do you know him?"

"I do." She waved her hand. "It has been a long time. My grandmaman saved Lord Blackmore's life and Mr. Taylour, he came and found Lord Blackmore at our home. He also made the arrangements for Mr. Blackmore to help my grandmaman and me to travel to England. Grandmaman has met with him several times, but I have not seen him in a number of years. Is he well?"

"I believe he is. He has been investigating various people for some of the peers. He has a very good reputation."

Lissette seemed to mull over the information Felton had given her. "I would expect as much. He is thorough in all that he does. Please give him my regards."

Lissette's connection to the mysterious man whom Felton had tracking Lord Leighhall gave Dory an idea. "Silver Meadows *does* have a weapons expert."

"Is that who taught you how to throw a knife?"

She nodded. "Yes, though I never finished my training. Tell Mr. Taylour to go to Silver Meadows and request a meeting with Dague."

Lissette's eyes widened in surprise, but she quickly schooled her features.

"Dague." Her husband gave a nod. "I will write to Mr. Taylour this very afternoon."

She would have to remember to tell Fen about "Dague" after Lissette was reacquainted with her old friend. She yawned again before finishing her lemonade.

Felton stood. "My dear, it appears that you need to rest. Allow me to escort you to your room."

She eyed his hand speculatively. Now that he mentioned it, she was tired, but if he were to escort her, she could think of something they could indulge in together first. "You are very kind, but I would not leave Lissette alone."

"If it would be permissible, I would like to find those books by Rousseau you spoke of and begin reading." Lissette stood. "I have no need of companionship for that."

She placed her hand in her husband's and he helped her rise. "Of course. The books are on the second bookshelf on the right. That's where I keep all the philosophical texts." She didn't add that there was a statue of a rabbit on the shelf. Since Felton hadn't mentioned the various new decorations, she didn't care to make a point of them.

"Yes, I had to move my natural science books to another bookcase entirely." Felton grimaced, though he'd been more than willing to move them.

"It was such a sacrifice." She looked to Lissette, who strolled next to her as they headed for the house. "I found one volume where the pages were stuck together with some kind of sticky substance, so he'd hardly missed reading it."

"I'll have you know, wife, that was from a scientific experiment."

She looked askance at her husband. "Then why did it still smell of strawberry jam?"

His lips twitched. "As I said, it was a science experiment, which I might add was quite successful when compared to my attempt to make the school successful."

"Anything is more successful than that."

The trio stepped into the parlor and Dory found the cooler air rather reviving.

"I will go into the library, then." Lissette strode ahead of them then halted at the doorway. "I trust there will be no jam in the Rousseau book?"

Felton chuckled. "No jam. That one is clean, but I wouldn't look into the one by Voltaire. I believe a rather large bug was killed between the pages."

"I have seen far worse." Lissette waved her hand as if it were of no consequence and continued down the corridor.

As Dory and her husband passed the mantle, she gave a nod to the small portrait of Belinda she'd found in the desk in the library. Felton had thought to keep it there, but she'd insisted on having his first love and the Angel she'd come to admire out where they could see her. Next to it was a small, porcelain bunny.

Felton led her to the grand staircase and spoke as they took the first step. "Do you miss the school very much?"

"Sometimes I miss my friends and our lively conversations, but I find the more days I am wed, the more I enjoy my life here. I'm not sure how I would have time to continue my studies if I wished. I'd actually taken out a treatise discussing Hippocrates's seven stages of life for this very reason, but that was a fortnight past. But it does bear upon this topic, as he thought there were seven stages of man. Of course, I would have preferred seven stages of woman, but the premise remains the same. According to this, I am still at the young woman stage, which I believe would constitute still growing and learning and changing. I do believe that my life as a wife is a new stage, which no doubt will change again when I become a mother. Can you imagine all the changes in thought that will need to occur in my head, which does bring to mind the idea of humans as natural beings and what is instinct and what is reason. According to—"

Felton's lips on hers sent her thoughts flying skyward as usual, and she wrapped her arms around his neck to fully enjoy him.

After making her dizzy with desire, he pulled away and opened the door to her bedroom. "Perhaps we should continue this inside."

She kept her hands around his neck, not sure her balance had returned yet. "The discourse or the kiss?"

"Most definitely the kiss. If you mean to talk further about you becoming a mother, then we should dispose of our clothes and continue this in your bed, where the topic is much more relevant."

Oh, she did like that idea. "I agree."

"Good." He kept one arm about her and led her into the room, closing the door behind them. Guiding her to the bed, he allowed her to sit as he began to undress. "Now as to this discourse. I believe we first need to determine if you wish to populate this house with as many children as you have populated it with rabbits."

She laughed, thrilled that he'd noticed. She moved forward and unbuttoned his pantaloons as he undid his cravat. "I'm not sure I'm ready for one and twenty children, but we can start and just see how it feels." She slipped her hand beneath the loosened fall of his pants and pleased at his intake of breath.

He grabbed her wrist. "One and twenty?"

"Of course. I've put one in every place we've enjoyed each other...so far."

"Is there one in your dressing room?"

She frowned, as it was not that large a space. "No."

A sly smile formed on his face. "Then I say that is where we shall go." Taking her hand, he pulled her into the dressing room.

"Why would you want to—" She stopped as he turned her to face the full-length mirror in the corner and cupped her breasts. "Oh."

He dipped his head near her ear and growled. "I hope you desire many children, Lady Harewood, because I intend to have a rabbit in every room in this house."

Her breath caught at his meaning, but he had already let go and begun to loosen the ties on her dress. As it slipped down, exposing her shift and stays, she smiled. "I do hope we can add some rabbits in the garden too."

His head jerked up as he met her gaze in the mirror, his own having darkened to almost forest green. "Now that's a muddle I'll gladly jump into."

His words sent both a thrill and joy rifling through her before his hands dispelled all thoughts except one. "Fen."

The End

About the Author

Lexi Post is a New York Times and USA Today best-selling author of romance inspired by the classics. She spent years in higher education taking and teaching courses about the classical literature she loved. From Edgar Allan Poe's short story "The Masque of the Red Death" to Tolstoy's *War and Peace*, she's read, studied, and taught wonderful classics.

But Lexi's first love is romance novels so she married her two first loves, romance and the classics. Whether it's dashing dukes, hot immortals, sizzling cowboys, or hunks from out of this world, Lexi provides a sensuous experience with a "whole lotta story."

Lexi is living her own happily ever after with her husband and her two cats in Florida. She makes her own ice cream every weekend, loves bright colors, and you'll never see her without a hat.

Website: lexipostbooks.com
Lexi Post Updates: app.mailerlite.com/webforms/landing/c1w1g3
Facebook: facebook.com/lexipostbooks
Twitter: @LexiPost
Instagram: instagram.com/lexipostbooks
Amazon Author Page: http://amzn.to/1IEL2cc
BookBub: bookbub.com/authors/lexi-post
D2D: books2read.com/author/lexi-post/subscribe/1/16171
Goodreads: goodreads.com/goodreadscomLexiPost
Instagram: instagram.com/lexipostbooks
Blog: happilyeverafterthoughts.com
Pinterest: pinterest.com/lexipost77
Email: lexi@lexipostbooks.com